DATE DUE

At
Paradise
Gate

**Center Point
Large Print**

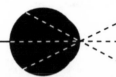

**This Large Print Book carries the
Seal of Approval of N.A.V.H.**

ॐ श्री गणेशाय नमः

At Paradise Gate

A Novel by
Jane Smiley

Center Point Publishing
Thorndike, Maine

This Center Point Large Print edition
is published in the year 2001 by arrangement with
Simon & Schuster, Inc.

"Scrawns" from *In the Teeth of the Evidence* by Dorothy Sayers.
Published by Harper & Row Publishers, Inc.
Excerpt from *Tristes Tropiques* by Claude Levi-Strauss,
translated by John and Doreen Weighton.
Published by Atheneum Publishers.

The text of this Large Print edition is unabridged.
In other aspects, this book may vary from the original
edition. Printed in Thailand. Set in 16-point Plantin type by
Bill Coskrey.

ISBN 1-58547-073-2

Library of Congress Cataloging-in-Publication Data

Smiley, Jane.
  At paradise gate / Jane Smiley.
    p. cm.
  ISBN 1-58547-073-2 (lib. bdg. : alk. paper)
  1. Mothers and daughters--Fiction. 2. Fathers--Death--Fiction. 3. Terminally ill--
Fiction. 4. Women--Iowa--Fiction. 5. Sisters--Fiction. 6. Iowa--Fiction. 7. Large type
books. I. Title.

PS3569.M39 A93 2001
813'.54--dc21

                                                              00-064536

. . . while I complain of being able to glimpse no more than the shadow of the past, I may be insensitive to reality as it is taking shape at this very moment, since I have not reached the stage of development at which I would be capable of perceiving it. A few hundred years hence, in this same place, another traveller, as despairing as myself, will mourn the disappearance of what I might have seen, but failed to see. I am subject to a double infirmity: all that I perceive offends me, and I constantly reproach myself for not seeing as much as I should.

—Claude Levi-Strauss, *Tristes Tropiques, 1955*
(translated by J. and D. Weightman, 1974)

Like their father, Anna Robison's three daughters loved to remember. They were around most of each day now that Ike was sick, and sometimes Anna thought of them as sort of a committee, hammering out an agreed upon version of their common history. Except that they rarely agreed. Their stories varied widely in the most basic details, and none of the three could be convinced of anything. As Anna put down the butter dish and surveyed the table (ivory plates, mats she'd crocheted herself, ice-filled water glasses), the discussion jangled around her.

"It wasn't that way at all," caroled Helen, the eldest, the blondest, the one who had inherited Ike's stature and commanding manner, bringing salad from the kitchen. "I met him at a USO dance, and two weeks later he introduced Claire and Geo. I remember it distinctly!" Cutting across contradiction, she continued, "Are we ready, Mother? It's a shame that Christine. . ."

Christine, Helen's daughter, was due to arrive from Chicago at any minute.

Claire, the second child and Helen's lifelong challenger, seemed by contrast normally brown-haired, conventionally hazel-eyed. She pulled out her chair with an air of immovable conviction.

"He married Vida Deacon. Don't you remember her, Claire?" Helen sat down in her own place, on the other side of the table.

"I knew Geo for three weeks before that USO dance, Helen. I met him through Dennis Somebody, that fellow whose plane got shot down the last day of the war."

"Claire! You're wrong!" Helen lifted her hands and pitched her voice high in the I-won't-say-another-word range. That Geo had been Claire's husband for twenty-five years, which somehow certified her version of the meeting, was not alluded to. To Susanna, the youngest, Anna passed scalloped potatoes. Susanna, who was a little overweight, received them reverently, then said, "Remember Daddy used to say that that guy had the biggest feet and the smallest chin in six counties?"

"Bobby had a perfectly normal chin," said Helen. "You're thinking of Bob Lowe, who had those freckles too. Even on his eyelids." These Anna could recall. In the folds of his ears as well. Bob Lowe was the most freckled person Anna ever knew. Ike had turned so many of the incidents in Anna's life into tales that usually she tried to avoid recollection, but fragments, like the fall of light or the shape of someone's cheek, often occurred to her, as Bob Lowe, freckled into the very caves of his ears, did now.

"Is that Daddy?" said Claire.

7

The women at the table hushed, their forks suspended in air and their eyebrows lifted, but no call came again.

"Mother, you really . . ."

Anna stared doggedly at her plate. Claire and Susanna were at her about this ten times a day—wouldn't she please move Ike into the living room or the dining room. But Anna would not, and dared not mention the idea to Ike. Such an illness, an illness that meant displacement of furniture and attention to the minutiae of her daily routine, was sure to be a final illness. Silence fell around the table again, not a listening silence, but a worried one.

"Do you know that story about Uncle Abel and the bull, Mother? Christine spoke of it over the phone the other night, and I didn't recall it all exactly." Of all her daughters, Anna thought Helen had the only interesting voice, musical but with a hollow quality that made it both strong and fragile. Although her clear, effortless tones were always cheering and alluring, they were never convincing. She sat in an upright, perching posture, and her eyes or hands often strayed after the cigarettes she had given up five years before. Anna wondered if she realized this habit.

"I do," said Susanna. "Daddy told me himself. You were living on the ranch, weren't you, Mother?"

Anna nodded. And the lupines were in bloom. They spread in a great azure triangle behind the house, stiff, cone-shaped, vibrating against the green of the back paddock.

Susanna went on. "Uncle Abel was castrating a bull

8

that he'd tied to the fence post."

"I can't believe he just tied the animal to a fence post, Susanna," said Claire.

A quick snip, Abel always said. He was a huge and terribly impatient man who wouldn't have the vet, or even the neighbors, on the ranch to help. Anna nodded.

"It's true," declared Susanna. "That's how it started to get loose. It was tossing its head and the loop in the rope fell out, and Uncle Abel looked up and saw the bull with its head turned, peering at him."

Anna had sometimes wondered if Abel had been afraid or merely angry. He had such a large head and gruff manner that she could never imagine him afraid, only transported into a higher degree of fury.

"Then it started to bellow."

"Yes," said Anna. Desperate bellowing that the Big Horns to the west threw back at them.

"Daddy was coming out the door. He saw what was happening, grabbed the ax from the chopping block, and flung it across the backyard, and struck the bull exactly between the ears. Dropped it in its tracks."

"Hatchet," said Anna. "It was the hatchet."

"Daddy said ax. Anyway, then he said, 'First and ten.' "

"He did say something funny. I can't remember what it was."

Anna had followed him out of the house, Helen in her arms. June colors in the mountains, especially vivid in the silence that followed the death of the bull. The animal lay in a black heap on the ground, his hide still glistening with health, and Abel stood behind, the shears dangling from one hand, his mouth agape, red blood across the indigo front of his new overalls. And blood covered the head of the bull like a bandanna trailing in the dust. Helen had said her newest word, "Bye? Bye-bye?"

"What's that?"

This time they all heard it—"Mother! Mother!" in a thin, demanding voice. "I'll go," said Claire. She scraped her chair back and threw her napkin on the table. Ike would not be glad to see her, Anna knew. He preferred to keep his illness private between husband and wife. Her calves hurt so, though, and her heels too, that she welcomed a few moments of preparation. If Ike really wanted something, he would want it from her alone. Anna and the others ate without speaking until Claire returned. Sure enough. "He wouldn't tell me," she reported. "He just said, 'Where's Mother?' "

"He generally does." Anna could not suppress a small scowl. In spite of Helen, Claire, and Susanna, she felt tired to death by dinner every evening. The staircase creaked under her weight, and she pulled herself up the last two or three steps with the bannister. He was already calling out, "Mother? Mother?"

"Yes, Ike?" It was only since the onset of these latest problems that she'd begun to feel comfortable with his given name again. For most of their married lives they'd addressed each other as the children did. Sometimes, recently, he too called her Anna. Maybe it was a bad sign. He'd put on a shirt, and was now propped against the wall at the head of the bed, fingering *Winesburg, Ohio.* He loved *Winesburg, Ohio.* He looked at her without speaking, waiting for her to ask him if he needed to go to the bathroom. She did not want to ask, but did anyway. He nodded. It annoyed her that after all these years he couldn't bring himself to speak of going to the bathroom. In the hospital, the nurses had had a terrible time with him, and finally had to give in. He would use a bedpan only when Anna was there to help him. She didn't see how he could tolerate the discomfort, but it was something she could not ask about. He threw off the covers and pivoted his feet to the floor and his slippers. "Is Christine here yet?"

"Not yet."

"It's getting late, don't you think?"

"She'll be all right."

"Is he coming with her?"

Ike was ashamed that he couldn't ever remember Todd's name, though Christine had been married for a year and a half. Anna shook her head. She'd answered this question repeatedly for the last three days. "He's got to work, Ike." This was a good sign. If the boy were to skip work, it would mean that something urgent was bringing him to his grandfather-in-law, but nothing was. The boy was safely at his job. Anna held out her arms, and Ike took them.

As always, she left him standing in the middle of the bathroom, then went out and closed the door. She had, of course, never told him that she could hear his labored steps over to the bowl, and then his grunts and exhalations as he lowered himself upon it. Fortu-

11

nately the sink and the bathtub were within reach, so that once finished, he could stand, wash and dry his hands, then call for her. On his bad days she waited, anxious, for the loud thump of a fall, but it never came. Outside the door, she was breathless herself. Though Ike had grown terribly thin, he topped her by seven inches, and it was not easy to support him, even as far as the bathroom.

Claire met her at the bottom of the stairs. "Does he want any dinner, Mother? I'll be glad to make up a tray."

Anna shook her head. "He's going to read his book for a while. We can take something up to him later."

"Maybe he'd like to come downstairs."

"He said not."

They had finished. Helen was fumbling in her purse. Susanna pressed her finger onto the last crumb on her plate and put it to her tongue. Hardened potatoes, scattered succotash, and the partially eaten pork chop at her place repelled Anna so completely that when Claire, seeing her distaste, offered to warm them, she could not regain her appetite.

"I'll make coffee then," said Helen, swallowing the last of her water. "I wonder where Christine is, I really do. She was supposed to leave by eight this morning, which would have gotten her here hours ago."

"Helen, don't you realize that kids never know when they're going to do anything? You've got to ask them their plans, then give them three days either way, in case something comes up!" Claire's twin sons had been home for Christmas.

Susanna followed Helen into the kitchen with a stack of plates. When Claire shifted into her sister's place beside Anna, Anna knew that a scenario had been planned in her absence.

"Mother, listen!" Claire leaned forward energetically, causing Anna to wince involuntarily for the water glasses, but Claire pushed them out of her way. "Susanna and I have mentioned it, and Helen agrees. You've got to bring Daddy downstairs! What if he were to call you, and you didn't hear him? His voice isn't that strong anymore!"

"I generally hear him fine, Claire."

"Mother, be sensible! Anything could happen! He could fall and be unable to call out, for instance. Please, let us move the dining-room table out back just for a little while, and put him in here."

"But then maybe I wouldn't hear him at night, Claire. This is the best way. It's more important that I be nearby in the night."

Claire took a deep breath. Obviously they had foreseen this argument and discussed it. "You could move into the living room." Her glance at Anna as she said this was nothing so much as furtive. Anna sat back in her chair. The house was very neat now that Ike spent most of his time upstairs. Since his illness she had shampooed the rug and made a slipcover for his old chair. The magazines were stacked and put away, the tabletops were clear of everything except their allotted knickknacks. If she moved Ike down here, and worse, if she moved down here herself, furniture would be pushed to the wall and new furniture introduced;

13

nothing would have a place of its own; she'd always be stepping on things or rummaging for them among a million other things; there would be nowhere to sit down, nowhere to get away. The place would never be clean again. And worst of all, everything about their recent problems would be as open and vulnerable as Ike's white sheets. He would hate that. In a flash she realized that she would, too, although she had always championed candor in the face of his secretiveness. She looked at Claire, who was now peering at her. It was hard to deny logical and self-confident Claire, whose hardships and griefs never seemed to have thrown any doubt upon the efficacy of logic and confidence.

Anna cast around for excuses. At last she said, "Claire, I could never get him upstairs to the bathroom." Claire continued to look at her searchingly. "And you know, or you should know, that your father would never use a bedpan, especially in the dining room." Anna could not help feeling a little triumphant at dredging up this insuperable difficulty, but Claire smiled. Yes, Ike was peculiar. She sat up and arranged some pieces of silver on the placemat before her. At last she brought it out. "Then, Mother, you've got to get Daddy a nurse. He deserves it, and you do, too."

Anna opened her mouth.

"Mother, if Medicare won't pay for it, we three will." Susanna was standing in the doorway to the kitchen, and Helen, craning her neck, came up behind her. Anna glanced at Claire and saw her give the briefest notion of a shrug. The other two sprang to the table as if choreographed. "Mother, it really is best,"

14

exclaimed Susanna. "You've got a third bedroom right across from Daddy's room. It would be just like having somebody for a boarder, except that she'd be helping you instead of you taking care of her. You're seventy-two years old now, and you just can't be running up and down the stairs all day."

"Don't use my age against me."

"She's not using it against you," said Claire. "Nothing is against you. This is for you."

Anna looked at Helen and saw that Helen was looking around the room. After a moment, her eyes met Anna's and her eyebrows lifted. She said, "Mother doesn't want to be invaded, Claire. I understand that." She would go no further, though, and Anna felt as if she were being accused of mere house pride. Her arthritic shoulder began to throb. Telling her to embrace the nurse idea? To show her interfering daughters to the door? She had lived all her married live with relatives—Ike's brother, her children and grandchildren, for ten years her own sister—but all of them had pursued their own lives, and she had never felt observed by them. Now these daughters wanted to introduce a stranger whose whole life would be to observe. She didn't want her marriage to end as a topic of someone else's conversation. End? Well, it wasn't about to end, anyway, but that wasn't the point.

Helen sighed with audible resignation. "I go along with them, Mother. Daddy deserves it. It should be easier for him than it is."

"Nothing will ever be easy for your father."

Helen waved her hand, dismissing the remark.

15

Susanna, always practical, offered to find the nurse herself. "You won't have to budge, Mother, really. You can have any kind you like—small and silent, large and jolly, young, old, any kind."

"How about none at all?"

Each of them, in a gesture supremely characteristic of Ike, pursed her lips. They were thinking how stubborn she was, and Ike, she knew, had taught them to think this way. Her eyes filled with tears.

"Mother, please?" pressed Claire.

"Let's talk about it tomorrow," suggested Helen. The others nodded, and Anna did, too. "We can ask Daddy what he thinks." This they wouldn't do. Ike had only likes and dislikes. Anna, though, with her self-doubts and her wish to do the elusive Right Thing, was the chink in the family armor. "Will you promise you'll talk about it tomorrow, Mother? Really?" Anna sighed and nodded again. Helen got up and went to the front window. "Maybe that's Christine, now," she said.

The Airedale came in first, wiggling and sniffing and trailing his leash. Christine was full of apologies: for bringing the dog ("Todd has to work late twice this week, and I just hate to leave him by himself that much. Sit! Now, stay!"); for being so late ("I dropped Todd at the office, and then I was going to leave, but I had to go back home and pick up something, and then this evening I got so hungry I just had to stop."); for dropping her coat on the floor ("I'm sorry, Grandmother, let me pick that up! How's Grandfather?

Nelson, you must sit, this instant!"). As she kissed each relative, Nelson wagged his tail and pressed himself between their legs, until finally she cried, "Nelson! You're driving me crazy, damn it! Go lie down!" She flopped into Ike's large armchair, and apologized again, this time for cursing in front of them. She was so brisk and rosy from the damp outdoors that Anna wanted to inhale her.

Claire, unimpressed and disapproving of the dog, declared, "He's certainly not well!" but Anna made a point of smiling at her granddaughter. She, too, had always found the dog rather frisky, but now she decided that with his alert, curly head and stiff little tail, he introduced a note of levity she appreciated. She turned on another light. Helen brought out the pot of coffee, the house warmed and quickened. Christine's coat lay over the back of a chair, her hat and scarf hung on the doorknob, Nelson's coiled leash occupied the center of the coffee table. She acted completely welcome, and why not? She was.

Anna said, "You'll be surprised at how your grandfather looks, Chrissy, but his condition's pretty stable. It's not good, but it's stable." Christine nodded, her face sober.

From upstairs came, "Mother! Mother!"

Christine jumped up. "Let me go, Grandma." Nelson followed her to the foot of the stairs. She was elaborately firm with him. "No, Nelson! Stay! You sit! Good dog. Now stay!" Nelson cocked his head as she ran up the stairs. On the landing, she kicked the phone off the hook, replaced it, called, "Grandpa!" At the

17

sound of her voice, Nelson tore up the stairs, slipping, scrabbling for purchase, knocking against the bannister. From upstairs came, "Oh, Nelson! Well, all right. Heel! Now sit! Good dog," then the murmur of voices.

"Mother—" began Claire.

"The dog won't hurt anything," interjected Helen. "Daddy probably appreciates a little life around the place, the way we go around on tiptoe all the time."

"Daddy's not as strong as you think, Helen," continued Claire. "I think we all tend to overestimate what he can do, frankly. In fact, I'll tell you what I think. I think he needs a hospital bed, with a crank, preferably downstairs, and some kind of full-time attendance, as well as a respiratory machine just in case. I think the attendant should be fully trained, including in cardiopulmonary resuscitation. I think that to do less is to take a risk, really." She lifted her chin and finished rather ringingly.

Helen set her own chin and fixed Claire with her steadiest gaze. "Even if he were on his last legs, Claire, Daddy would never need that kind of breathless, alarming treatment. I am at least as worried as you are, and I don't think that I overestimate his strength. In fact, I think it takes more strength to deal with that kind of readjustment than to put up with minor inconveniences that are familiar."

"I think—" began Susanna, but Claire interrupted. "Helen, you'd have to agree that I've had more experience in this area than you have, and I know what I'm talking about. When Geo was ill, we didn't care for the

18

changes any more than Mother and Daddy would, but what you gain in terms of efficiency and safety far outweighs the initial difficulties. I wish you would listen to me, Mother."

Anna opened her mouth, to say she knew not what, but Helen sat forward, cutting off her view. "Claire," she said, "your experience is precisely what is standing in your way. You think that because something was right for Geo, then it is right, period. You know, you've always been this way. Once you make up your mind about something, then that's the right thing, forever and ever. Well, Daddy isn't Geo, and there isn't much similar about the two situations. I wish you'd listen to me, actually. I went along with you about the nurse, but this other stuff has gotten to be an obsession with you. A respirator! My God!"

"Open your eyes, Helen . . ."

Anna stood up. "Don't bicker," she said. A creak on the landing silenced them and drew their gaze. Ike had pulled on trousers and smoothed down his hair, and was now beginning to descend the stairs on Christine's arm. "Grandpa wanted to come down and watch the fight," said Christine.

"You bet!" said Ike. "Claire's pretty tough, but Helen's got a good twenty-pound, four-inch advantage, anyway." He cocked his head and laughed weakly but merrily at his own joke. "Don't let me stop you! Don't let me stop you!" Their descent was painfully slow. On the landing sat Nelson, ears pricked forward, manners somehow attained.

Claire stood up. "Sit here, Daddy." Ike made his

way to the chair and sat heavily, with evident relief.

Christine said, "Grandpa, did you really used to pit Mom and Aunt Claire against one another?"

"You bet!" said Ike. "Best fight on the block. Your Aunt Claire's got quite a temper, you know. I'd sneak up to her and whisper in her ear that Helen was going to jump her if she went into the kitchen."

"Meanwhile, he would have told me that Claire was looking for me, and I'd better get the jump on her when *she* got to the kitchen."

"Then he'd turn out the light at the last minute," added Claire. "Just terrific, let me tell you."

"Who usually won, Grandpa?"

"Depended on who had the strategic advantage."

"And you know who that depended on, Christine," said Claire. "Your grandfather!" Ike laughed again.

"What about Aunt Susanna? No, lie down, Nelson."

"Now, Susanna was different. Best not to get on the wrong side of Susanna. We handled her career with kid gloves."

"Kid gloves! That's the first I've heard of any kid gloves, Daddy. It felt more like an iron fist!"

"What else?" cried Christine.

"Well," said Claire, "after we were in school, there was the Breakfast Bonanza." Ike chuckled. "You've never seen a live wire first thing in the morning till you've seen your grandfather. You'd get up and stagger down the stairs trying to see through your eyelashes without letting the sun in, and there he'd be, crouched at the table, supposedly eating his French toast, but really just waiting for you. 'What's the capital of

Maine? What's the Spanish word for bacon?' Then, while you were trying to wind up your brain, he'd kind of bounce a little in his seat—yes, you did, Daddy, as if you had so much energy that you just couldn't contain it—and pretty soon he'd say, 'Your sister got it in fifteen seconds!' "

"Can't blame a fellow for wanting to stir things up a little!" laughed Ike, pleased with the memory of himself at forty, crouched.

Christine lay back against the arm of the couch. "Was it fun? It sounds like *Cheaper by the Dozen*. It must have been wonderful with so much going on."

"A dozen would have been just about enough for Daddy," remarked Anna. Everybody sighed.

In a few moments, Anna laid aside her knitting. "Would you like some dinner, Ike?" she offered, but he waved the suggestion away. Lately he'd been very coquettish about food, pretending that he wasn't hungry and wouldn't want to put her to any trouble. She rather thought he liked the martyrdom and so didn't press him.

Ike looked around, and Claire rose to the bait. Anna pursed her lips, picked up her knitting, and began to count stitches with elaborate care. "You must be hungry, Daddy. Please let me fix you something." Anna cleared her throat. "It's no trouble," persisted Claire. "We had pork chops for dinner."

Ike deflated a little. "Pork doesn't agree with me lately."

Claire was on her feet. "How about a little fruit salad and some slices of chicken from last night? I could warm them up. Or some yogurt."

"No yogurt."

Claire headed for the kitchen. Anna knew Ike was looking at her, but she stared steadfastly at her knitting, moving her lips as if counting, although she'd counted them twice already. What? Would he believe in her concern if she forced him to eat? Finally, he said, "Well! Christine!" He leaned toward her and began to whisper. Christine laughed and demurred. Ike whispered some more. Out of the corner of her eye, Anna could see him jerking his head in her direction and winking at Christine, who laughed again and then nodded. She came up behind Anna's shoulder. "Grandma? Grandfather would like me to give you something."

In the time-honored tradition, Anna said, "And what might that be?"

Christine laughed and put her fingers gently over Anna's shoulder. "The old eagle's claw!" She squeezed lightly, Anna squealed in the expected manner, and Ike slapped his knee. He had been sending Christine to her in this fashion since the girl was three years old—twenty years now, almost exactly. And he always did it for the same reason, because she wasn't paying attention to him and he couldn't stand it. Anna dropped her knitting in her lap. "Some dessert? Helen? Susanna? There's ice cream in there, and I made a new kind of coffee cake yesterday; it's got Cheerios in the topping."

"Cheerios!" howled Christine. "Grandma, I'm ashamed of you!"

"I cooked on a wood stove too long to be ashamed of convenience foods, believe me, young lady. Anything in a box with a long shelf-life is fine with your grandmother."

"No ice cream for me," said Susanna. "What kind is it?"

"Cherry something. Cherry delight?"

"Mmmm."

"Come on, Aunt Susie, live it up."

"When it comes to food, Chrissy, I live it up every day." But she heaved herself out of the deep sofa.

"I'll get it."

"I'll get it."

"Let's both get it. Mom? You?" Helen shook her head. Christine threw her arm over Susanna's shoulders and guided her out of the room. Nelson clicked at their heels.

Ike turned immediately to Helen, who was leafing through a magazine. "What's the boy's name again, Helen?"

"Do you mean Todd, Daddy?"

"That's it! I couldn't remember that damned name if my life depended on it. I always think Frank. Why's that, Mother?"

"Wasn't there a boy named Frank, Helen?"

"I don't think so, Mother. Susanna had a boyfriend named Frank, though. Remember him? He bought that airplane after the war, some old piece of junk. You never would let Susanna go up in it. She did, though. They flew to Chicago once and visited me at my studio. I don't think it was the only time, either;

Susanna was very blasé about the whole thing."

"What did she say, Mother? Susanna went up in a plane?"

"After the war, Ike! Susanna took some plane rides with a boy!" Ike wasn't always hard of hearing, or perhaps they were accustomed to speaking up. At any rate, the things he seemed to have difficulty with were always the things he shouldn't have heard in the first place, so that the embarrassment of shouting them out was doubled.

Anna remembered that Frank quite well. Ike hadn't liked him because he was short—almost shorter than Susanna, who was the shortest of the girls. And Ike's distrust of the man's shortness hadn't masked any deeper feelings. In her life with Ike she had found that his prejudice in favor of tall, burly men like himself was as simple as it was pronounced. Anna, on the other hand, had liked Frank, who was self-educated, without pretension, and plainspoken, a more spirited and substantial man than Hanson Gilbert, Susanna's ex-husband, a doctor. It was too bad about Frank. Ike had taken every opportunity to poke fun at him, until Susanna finally gave up. Anna smiled to think of Susanna, blasé about flying. Iowa must have been so beautifully green and simple just after the war, a tablecloth of old-fashioned crops like oats and rye in addition to the eternal corn; barns and houses white and blocky; clusters like jewels, of black-and-white cows, glossy draft horses, and even mules. People must have waved to Frank and Susanna as they flew over; and Frank and Susanna, perhaps watching their shadow

24

skate over meadow and wooded hillside, must have waved back. Anna caught her breath sharply and quickened her knitting. Such thoughts filled her with yearning to have been asked along.

"What boy? Mother? What boy?"

Helen interceded. "Frank Somebody, Daddy! He was from Council Bluffs or Omaha. You didn't like him!"

"Little shrimp of a guy?"

Helen nodded.

"No," said Ike. "Couldn't see much in that punk. Not much at all."

Anna knew that Ike was teasing a little, but she couldn't help flaring up. "No, Ike, you didn't see much in him, and you were wrong. He was a good boy, and he had lots of get-up-and-go. I knew that boy was going to be a big success, and he was crazy about Susanna." Not many had been. Every time you took a step in those days you stumbled over some kid who was dangling after Helen or Claire, or both, but Susanna hated to wear dresses, and she hated to fix herself up, and she was relentlessly competitive. She could apply any racket or stick or mallet or club to any ball, and the ball would fly like an angel. It never even occurred to her not to win, and a lot of first dates ended on the front porch, with Susanna shaking the boy's hand, saying, "Thanks, and sorry I beat you."

"So what'd he do, Mother?" Ike leaned toward her. She should have foreseen this.

"I don't know, Ike. Flew off into the sunset, I guess." Ike sat back triumphantly and Anna leaned forward.

"But what does that matter? Hanson Gilbert was a big success, and you could hardly open your mouth, you were so impressed with the notion of a doctor, and look what happened!" Hanson was now married to the woman he had taken up with while still married to Susanna. Anna understood that they had something like four or five children, perhaps more. Susanna had none. Her marriage had ended so early—during Susanna's twenty-seventh year—that Anna had felt certain she would marry again and have five of her own. She loved children, especially little girls. But nothing happened.

"Frank's one we lost track of completely, isn't he?" remarked Helen, and picked up her magazine again. It was a *Family Circle*. At home Helen received *Gourmet*, and *The New Yorker*, and *Archeology*. Here she always picked up the *Family Circles* and the *Woman's Days* and read while others talked.

Anna said, "There's a cute sweater pattern in there, Helen. Man's pullover with a real smart cable. I thought I'd make a couple for the twins."

"You'd better ask Claire, Mother. I don't know if the twins wear the same clothes anymore."

"Ask me what?" Claire bore a small flowered tray on which she had arranged a dish of fruit salad and a plate of chicken slices bedded on a lettuce leaf, two neatly bisected pieces of toast, a linen napkin in a napkin ring, a glass of bluish skim milk, and a knife and fork—the good silver—Anna noticed. She exchanged a glance with Helen, who also noticed, then said, "There's a lovely sweater pattern in that magazine Helen's reading. I thought Jimmy and Jeremy each might like one."

"Don't ask me, Mother!" She set the tray on Ike's lap. "Buying clothes for them is like sticking your money in a slot machine, as far as I'm concerned. Picky, picky, picky! Jimmy's the worst. He could lead me by the hand to the very item he wants and then decide that the stitching around the buttonholes looks funny before we get to the checkout counter."

Ike began to eat. The plate was too far from his mouth, and Anna could not help falling silent and staring as the fork wobbled and shook in its ascent. The others, too, were mesmerized, and before Claire could leap to amend the problem, Ike put down his fork and declared that he wasn't hungry. Claire offered to put a pillow on his lap, but it was too late. The peculiar sound the fruit made as it dropped onto the tray had done its damage. By the time they were finished discussing it, the peaches and pears would be warm, the chicken dry and unappetizing.

Claire's face fell. Helen peered studiously at the magazine. Ike picked up his plate to put it on the table, and Anna sat up. "Eat it, Ike!" she commanded. "Claire put herself out for you, and it's the least you can do!" Ike looked at her. Claire put a sofa pillow on his lap and balanced the tray on it. In a moment he began to eat. Anna realized she was breathing rather quickly. In years gone by such a tone would have earned a retaliation, and it was hard for her to get used to her new power.

In a few moments he had finished the fruit and was

safely to the chicken. She pushed her glasses up her nose and went back to her knitting. Ike said, "Thank you, Claire, that was delicious."

"You're welcome, Daddy." Claire took the tray.

Helen threw down her magazine. "Christine and Susanna are taking their time," she observed. Helen gave off a sense of laborious nonchalance when Christine was around that was almost an odor. With Anna, Claire, Susanna, even Ike, Helen was the most independent, the least likely to find family gatherings alluring, although she preferred to be present in case her name came up in discussion. Her feelings for Christine, however, were hot and possessive. It was at times amusing and at times discomforting to watch her arrange herself into the cool, detached being Christine both assumed she was and insisted she be.

When she stood up, Claire turned deftly in the doorway and blocked her exit. "Helen," she said, "why don't you show me the pattern mother was talking about?"

"It's right there, you'll see it."

"Is there anything else in there you like?" She put down the tray and half pushed Helen back toward the couch.

Helen sidestepped, saying, "You know homemade isn't my style." The phone rang. Even as Claire was saying, "I'll—" and Anna was hoisting herself out of her chair, Christine flashed past the kitchen doorway and caught it on the third ring. Helen plopped on the arm of the couch, took up the magazine, and turned to the requisite page. "There!" she said. "Now get out of the way!" But Claire didn't move. Everyone strained to hear who it might be. Christine's voice murmured steadily, deepened by the tunnel effect of the back hall.

"It must be for her," said Claire. "I thought Jeremy might call over here tonight if he couldn't reach me at home." Christine hung up the phone. There had been no pause in the murmuring, and Christine's face was red as she passed the back hall doorway on her return to the kitchen. Helen followed her and Claire sat down on the couch with the dirty dishes in her lap. "Mother," she said, "I think Christine has some news for us."

"Speak up!" said Ike. "What about Christine?"

"She's got something to tell us!" exclaimed Anna. Ike nodded. Already he was tired. His skin was pale and he let his head rest stiffly against the back of his chair, ashamed, perhaps, that a half-hour with his family could tell upon him so, or perhaps afraid that she would make him go back to bed if he let on. He lifted his leg to cross it, and Anna vowed to get him a half-dozen pairs of new, thick, very thick, socks. His ankles thrust out of his trousers like bamboo. Perhaps it was a baby.

Anna remembered each of her babies perfectly, more perfectly at times than she remembered her daughters' current selves. Having babies seemed to her the essential activity of youth, and she always felt sorry for mothers who were too old to be energetic and playful with their infants. She'd been only twenty when Helen was born, twenty-one with Claire. She'd attributed the difficulty of her third pregnancy to age. Now it made her laugh. She'd been twenty-five! Claire was the easiest baby. Any object would fascinate her, and she could occupy herself by the hour with a strip of fabric, changing it from hand to hand, flicking it with her index finger, folding it, pulling it, bunching it, laying it over her head or chest. Anna would come in from another room and see her seated on the floor. From the back, the great curve of her head with its brown-gold curls would taper into the hollow between the tendons of her neck, and somehow the tendons themselves would bespeak concentration. Although Anna loved Claire's, and each child's, smiles and waves and kisses, loved too the stroke of a little hand on her breast while the child nursed, chancing upon this quiet business with a piece of cloth had touched her the most. It was so mysteriously inward when you hardly yet believed that the child had an inner life.

These moments were invariably brief. Helen, who would be with Anna, who was always with her at that age, would run over to see what the baby had and if it was worth demanding for her own. Even if it were not, the fight would begin. And Claire, with her sturdy grip and vigilant concentration, was no mean opponent. Fights, yes. All the time. But better still Anna could perfectly remember the intent angle of the head and the apparent fragility of the pale infant neck.

Susanna came in from the kitchen, followed by Christine, who struck a posture in the doorway, tapped her chest with her fist, and burped discreetly. "Oh, Grandmother, delicious! I outdid myself. I even outdid Susanna, didn't I? She had three scoops, I had four." Susanna groaned.

Ike said, "Remember when Abel and I used to sit down with a five-pound box of chocolates and finish them before bed?"

"Grandpa! Did you really?"

"Sure! Whitman's Sampler we'd always get. Abel liked the creams and I liked the nougats. Of course, if your grandmother got there first, there'd be holes in all the bottoms where she'd stuck her thumb to see what they were. Had to have all the caramel centers, or we'd never hear the end to it. She's got a sweet tooth!" Ike dislodged his false teeth and pushed them out of his mouth in a picket-fence grin, then drew them back in. Christine and Susanna laughed, Helen and Claire smiled.

Anna said, "Now, Daddy, you never ate five pounds in a night, that's for sure."

Nelson, who had fallen asleep in the kitchen, came to the dining room doorway and yawned vigorously. "Nelson!" exclaimed Christine. "Are you a good dog?" Nelson wagged his tail and barked once. She squatted down beside him, saying, "Pleased to meet you!" Nelson gave her his paw. "What brings you to our fair city?" Nelson barked twice. She went on in an elaborately solicitous tone, "Ah, poor Nelson had a hard day, didn't he?" Nelson's paws crept forward until he was down, then he flopped over onto his side and closed his eyes. Christine cooed, "Night-night, Nelson. Sleep tight." Ike laughed. In a moment Christine jumped up, "Morning, Nelson! Breakfast time!"

31

Nelson jumped to his feet, then carefully sat back on his haunches and began to lift his front legs. He lost his balance immediately. "Good try, doggy, okay!" said Christine. Nelson wagged his tail and went to the front door, where he lay down.

"Very good!" cried Helen. I had no idea you'd taught him all that! He's very smart, isn't he?"

"Todd did most of it, but I taught him to bark when I ask him if he's a good dog. I don't like the begging, frankly, but Todd's been trying really hard to teach him to get his balance."

Anna glanced over at Ike. His head was back on the chair, and he had closed his eyes. He'd been up for nearly an hour, and not a quiet hour. He looked at it. "Daddy?" She leaned over and poked him on the knee. "I think you should go back upstairs." It alarmed her, how long he took in rousing himself. In a moment he had apparently fallen asleep, and now he was drowsy and disoriented. He looked toward her, mumbling that he was fine, but his eyelids fluttered and white shone beneath them. "Come on!" She stood up, Claire and Christine got up to help her. She hoped that they hadn't seen the look he gave her. The weakness in it gave her something of a turn.

"We'll do it, Mother," said Claire. "You lead the way."

When Ike was seated on the bed in his musty, messy bedroom, Anna sent the others away, for she was newly conscious of the smell and she suddenly didn't want either of them associating it with Ike. Though each had visited him in this room without a second thought, the smell seemed to close in when he was weak and tired like this, to reinforce his age and underline the distance he had fallen from good health. It was a dusty smell, still benign, still not rotten. But the potential was there, was everywhere in the house. She vowed to open all the windows tomorrow, cold or no cold. Ike lifted his feet one by one. She removed his slippers and pulled off his thin Banlon socks. He sat, docile. She unbuttoned his shirt and slipped the cuffs over his speckled hands, pulled the sleeves down over his arms. Underneath, he still wore his pajama top. The sight of its tiny red-and-black print saddened her. It seemed like a person with more hope would have removed one to don the other. And now the pants. Anna took a deep breath. When had she ever been comfortable removing his pants? Girls of her time, girls who left their mothers at eighteen, weren't expected to be comfortable with a man's pants, either button fly, as they'd been in the first years of her marriage, or zipped fly, as they were now. And yet, how could it be that now, past seventy, she still fumbled at the fastening, not because it was familiar but because it was momentous. Even now anything could happen once the belt was unbuckled and the zipper opened. Ike began to sink back against the pillows that propped him day and night, made it easier for his heart to go than to stop. The zipper disclosed further pajamas. Relieved, Anna grew businesslike, though she panted with the effort of lifting his pelvis and sliding the trousers beneath it. And then they were on the floor. Anna flopped down in the chair and took several deep breaths. Ike had fallen asleep. His sheets would have to be changed tomorrow, and his blankets ought to be washed as well. Anna sighed. The girls were right in most ways—this illness of Ike's was literally at the limits of her strength. It was difficult for her to move his bed, difficult for her to carry trays up and endless laundry down. A big strong nurse, preferably European and not an English speaker, would be a great help. Even the footsteps of someone who could only work and not hold conversations would wreak a transformation, though, and it was unthinkable that this room, her room, the bathroom, and the hallway, a space that had closed about them like a cocoon or a beaver lodge since Ike's first heart attack, should become public domain. It would be like sleeping outdoors.

Ike groaned and scowled in his sleep, no doubt because the light shone in his eyes. Anna tugged the covers from beneath him and spread them over his legs; then she switched out the offending lamp. Ike turned toward the wall and his pillow, knocking the book be had been reading off the bed. At the noise of its fall he said, "Mother!" but when she answered, he had already gone back to sleep. Since the hospital he had taken to calling her in the same automatic way that babies cry out as soon as they awaken, or as soon as they feel the least discomfort or fear. She had not thought in the old days, when he ignored every illness and growled at every incapacity, that he would ever get this way.

She looked down upon her daughters from the

staircase and knew something had changed in her absence. Christine and Susanna were petting Nelson, Claire had turned on the television and was flipping the channels, Helen had picked up another magazine, this one a *Good Housekeeping*. Clearly, though, the primary occupation of each of them was thought. Helen's abstraction, in particular, was rigid as a clenched fist. "I got him to bed, for now," said Anna.

"Will he sleep through the night, Grandma?"

"We'll see." She settled into her chair. They would tell her soon enough. And soon enough they began to look at one another, to shift about where they were sitting or standing. Nelson whined. "Later!" snapped Christine, getting up and brushing her hands on her jeans, then flopping into her grandfather's chair. Susanna sat down on the piano bench, opened the piano, struck a note, and closed it again. Claire turned off the television with a decided click and put herself next to Helen on the couch. Helen cleared her throat and coughed to show that she wasn't about to say anything, that her throat really did need clearing.

"Grandma," said Christine. Nelson introduced his muzzle between her hand and her leg. She scratched his head, then rubbed the knuckle of her index finger on the bridge of his nose. She went on at last. "I just told Mom that, uh, Todd and I have decided that things aren't right, and we're going to get a divorce." Helen coughed again.

"Well, Christine!" Anna answered. "Is that your news?" Christine nodded. "And here I thought—" But she stopped herself.

. . .

When Anna headed for the kitchen to begin on the supper dishes, Christine, and inevitably Nelson, followed her. Anna said nothing except, "The dish towels are in the middle drawer now." She was annoyed. Susanna had stacked everything helter skelter on the kitchen table, leaving knives and forks between plates, and serving spoons adrift in congealed butter and cold potatoes. A napkin had been thrown onto the pork chop platter and its cotton threads had soaked up much of the grease. "I swear!" exclaimed Anna. Christine began disentangling silverware with an air of apology, as if the mess were her fault. Anna ran the water steaming into the sink. After all these years of housework, she could stand it much hotter than anyone else she knew, and she had gotten particular about having it as hot as possible, especially with Ike ill. "But germs don't cause heart attacks!" expostulated Claire. Anna didn't care in the least. Having an invalid in the house meant striving vigorously after cleanliness wherever and whenever possible, otherwise illness might become entrenched.

"Grandma, don't you need rubber gloves?" exclaimed Christine, when her fingers touched the water.

"With these claws?" Anna waved a hand. "Pure horn, honey, pure horn."

They'd gotten through plates and glasses before Christine broached the topic. There had been no discussion of Christine's news after Anna's response. Ostensibly, the decision was made, and everyone knew

36

everyone else's feelings in the matter. What need for discussion? It was apparent to Anna, though, that Christine wanted to talk and that Helen wasn't going to give her the satisfaction of doing so. The girl sputtered even more than she had the first time. Finally, she said, "Mom's pretty mad, I think."

"I don't know if anger is what she feels, Christine. You had a large wedding, and we were all very hopeful that you had made the right choice."

"Nobody ever liked Todd really, did they?" Although Christine paused belligerently for an answer, Anna made none. "I don't see why not! He's very smart, and he's funny, once he gets to know you, and he's very kind as well. I tried to tell Mom that he's shy, not standoffish, but she always thinks that if someone can't make small talk, they must be a boob."

"If he's so terrific, then why are you divorcing?"

"I didn't say he was terrific! I said he wasn't a bad choice. He was a good choice."

"Then why are you divorcing?"

"Well, maybe because he's not terrific! Maybe because I'm not terrific! I don't know!"

Anna continued to wash, swirling soapy water around in the measuring cups, then the coffee cups, then the ice cream bowls.

"Grandma?"

"Hmm."

"You stayed with Grandfather all these years. Do you think worse of me because I can't do the same with Todd?"

Anna submerged a cookpot in the now greasy water.

"Your grandfather and I had your mother before the first year was out, and your aunt Claire at the end of the second. It doesn't seem to me like we paid all that much attention to one another. Your great uncle Abel owned the ranch with us, you know, and he was there all the time. When we moved back here, there was my sister for a long time. All along people were all over the place, especially in Wyoming. Hands and hired men." She paused. "I don't think life with your grandfather was what I expected. For one thing, the day after we got married, I had to wash every dish and pot on the place, just to make breakfast. Those men hadn't touched a plate to water in four months. It wasn't like that at my mama's, I can tell you. Anyway, so much happened so fast, and there was so much to do, I couldn't even remember what I'd expected after a while. I'm not saying that's good."

"But will you think less of me?"

"Life with your grandfather wasn't all that easy. I don't think you can expect a marriage to be easy."

"I don't, but I want to be happy." Christine spoke softly, her face red, her manner chastened.

"I don't know, Christine."

"Will you think less of me?"

Anna did not answer.

With a sigh Christine finally said, "Tell me about life on the ranch, Grandma." She took a handful of silver and began to wipe the utensils one by one.

"I cooked all the time. That was life on the ranch. Bread and pie and steak and chicken, day in day out."

"Did you raise your own chickens?"

"Of course, and your grandfather was too squeamish to slaughter any. If ever we were having chicken and he wasn't out in the fields or looking after the livestock, he'd hide so I wouldn't ask him to kill me a chicken."

"Do chickens run around with their heads cut off?"

"They squirm a little. Only one that I killed ever took any steps."

"Couldn't he stand the sight of blood?"

"I don't know. He'd slaughter a hog or a steer. It was something about chickens. He didn't like to go into the coop. It was pretty slippery and smelly in there. Abel would do it sometimes, though."

"What else was it like?"

"There was always laundry to do. Mrs. Dawson from the next ranch would come do it with me sometimes, especially after your mother and your aunt Claire were born. She had a little boy, Patrick his name was. I didn't mind laundry especially. I liked being outside. The sunlight would be pouring down, and the sheets would shine and snap in the breeze. After we'd finished the laundry, we'd take the babies up in the meadow above the house and sit them down in the wildflowers. We'd talk about what we'd done before coming to Sheridan, and look down at the lines and lines of sheets. It was almost blinding. Your mother and Patrick would walk all over and then kind of sink down and fall asleep in their tracks. It smelled real good, like the beginning of the world."

"It sounds idyllic."

"It wasn't."

"Tell me more."

"Your grandfather used to go into town whenever he could and play on the baseball team. Every town had some kind of team in those days, and your grandfather was nuts for it. He was good, too. He was always leading the team in hits or runs or some such thing. He ran fast and had great big shoulders, and he'd swing at anything. One summer he led the team in hits and in strikeouts. That was the year before we had a car. Anyway, we'd make a bed in the back of the wagon for your mother, and Claire, and pack a big picnic, and go down to Sheridan for the game, or even over the mountains to Basin, and sometimes your grandfather would take the train to Buffalo or Billings. We'd meet everybody, and the game would be played, and then we'd eat and eat. You've never seen so much food as was brought to those baseball games. We didn't get home before dawn, but I think that's when I liked the ranch best, coming up the road and watching the sun hit the tips of the cottonwoods, making the leaves look like they were their own lights, then turning the trunks silver, then falling over the house and the barn. All the angles looked so straight and true in the dawn sunlight. Ike used to tell me to imagine we were all inside, and that strangers, ourselves, were passing on the road, and he'd say, 'Don't you wish we were us?' "

"It sounds wonderful!"

"It's just stories, Chrissy. The light was pretty, though."

Anna let the water out of the sink and wiped her hands on her apron. Christine put the last pot in the cabinet beside the stove, and Nelson, sensing a change in activity, stood up and went to the back door, whining. "Nelson's going to burst," said Christine. She got her coat from the back hall and let herself out into the damp air. Anna could hear her voice, muffled, shouting, "Come on Nel! Run! Nelson!" Her daughters would be expecting her to come make her report. Their discussion could be heard from the living room, clattering like a Ping-Pong tournament. It was not adventures of the ranch that Anna had intended to talk about, but it was hard to seize the conversation when you didn't know what you wanted to say.

"Did she talk about it?" demanded Helen, as soon as she saw Anna.

"She asked about the ranch."

"The ranch! What about Todd? Is she serious about this?"

"She said we should have liked Todd more."

"I like Todd fine for someone who's impossible to get along with."

"She says he's shy."

"That's what she's always said. I don't believe in 'shy.' People with good manners are pleasant company. That's what manners are for."

"Quote unquote, Isaac Robison," observed Claire.

"Anyway," continued Helen, "has she decided to divorce Todd because he can't keep up his end of the conversation? I've never heard of such a thing!"

"Obviously she doesn't know what in the world she's doing, Helen," said Claire. "What twenty-three-year-old ever does? I'm sure it will all pass."

"I think she's serious," offered Susanna. "Maybe he's stepping out on her."

"Oh, come on," replied Helen, "that stick in the mud?"

"Every law firm has secretaries."

"Oh, for Pete's sake!"

"Don't 'Oh for Pete's sake' me, Helen. I bet every man in my real estate office has been unfaithful to his wife, and if he hasn't it's only for want of a chance."

"All I can say," said Claire, "is that when I was in college I went out with a boy once who asked me if I thought most of the girls on campus were virgins. After I said that I did, he said that he always asked that question because the girls who said yes always were and the ones who said no always weren't."

"So what does that prove? I've worked with these men for more than ten years now, and I've played golf with most of them. I should think I would know something about their habits."

"Nonetheless," put in Helen, "here we're talking about Todd, who's twenty-seven, not forty, and who's married to a perfectly attractive, vibrant, intelligent girl."

"And nobody eats out when dinner's best at home? Well, I think you've got your head in a pillowcase, Helen, but I doubt if we'll ever find out."

After a moment Claire announced, "She ought to go back to him anyway. He's her husband. It's that simple."

Helen scowled. "Everything's simple to you, Claire."

Claire lifted her chin to reply, but the door crunched and opened with a protest from the weather stripping. Nelson bounded through, his curly coat dewy. "Grandma," panted Christine. "You should see. It's like wet laundry everywhere. It's wonderful! The neighborhood looks incredibly exotic, and my voice sounds like I'm shouting into drapes or something." It was easy now for Anna to see that Christine's manner had been overexcited all evening long. Her voice had been too pleadingly elated, her hands had fluttered too frequently about her face. She had goaded Nelson into a small frenzy, so that now the dog trotted restively from room to room, pushing his nose at objects he normally wouldn't have noticed. When she ordered him to come to her, her tone of voice excited him further, so that he bounded in from the dining room and knocked a glass off the coffee table into the wooden leg of the couch. The glass broke. Christine was upon the fragments in a flash, apologizing frantically. Nelson pressed in to see what was going on. Finally, she turned on him, screaming, "No! Go away! Lie down! Bad dog! Bad, bad, bad dog!" Nelson dropped, put his nose between his paws, and in the ensuing silence, Christine picked up the shards with elaborate care.

"Christine . . ." began Helen.

"Why can't I just be like Aunt Susanna?" Christine wailed. "I have a perfectly good job, I can find another apartment easily enough! It would be so wonderful to be alone! I feel like everything I do is hemmed in by Todd's desires or his disapproval or his expectations. I realized a few months ago that I was getting nervous and even wringing my hands as evening approached, and it was because I was about to see him, and I was afraid something would be wrong and he would be in a bad mood again. The things that go wrong for him at work just flood our lives every evening. I can't describe it!"

"He's not violent—" Helen hesitated.

"No, he's not a bad person, but he's always there."

"Being alone isn't—" began Claire.

"But it could be fine. You could make it fine. You wouldn't even have to eat dinner if you didn't want to, or you could have pizza right before bed. You wouldn't believe this routine we've got. He has to have eight-and-a-quarter hours of sleep between eleven and eight, otherwise he thinks his sleep cycle will get off and he'll go back to being insomniac! Then there's breakfast, not after eight-thirty, even on weekends, and then lunch not more than four-and-a-half or less than four hours later, then dinner six to six-and-a-half hours after that. He lives in terror of something happening too soon or too late and ruining everything. And he's right. If the routine goes off, everything is ruined because he can't stop talking about it. If we get up at eight-fifteen, he talks about it all day, and plans how he's going to avoid the same mistake the next day and tells me all about the importance of routine until I could die from listening to it. All day!"

"Darling, men all have these petrified idiosyncrasies when they first get married," replied Helen. "They wear off."

"And then we discuss his lunch, every morning. Maybe I should fix him a sandwich and put in a pear, or maybe he should go out for cottage cheese and he could pick up a pear there, or would an apple be better. He loves the taste of beer, but beer for lunch makes him sleepy all afternoon, so perhaps a coke. I don't care! Do I have to care?"

Anna said, "How did he get like this? Was he like this before you were married?"

"A little, but it just made him seem unusually solid, you know, I mean, everybody else was sleeping till noon and cutting weeks of classes, and Todd, who was just as much fun and wore the same kind of clothes, was getting As. He seemed sort of brilliant. Anyway, marriage changed him. Now he loves suits and comparison shopping, blah blah blah!"

"Chrissy, when I first married your father, he had fourteen white shirts. Every two weeks, on Sunday night, I set up the ironing board and pressed those fourteen white shirts. Along about number ten, he would go to bed, and then, every ten minutes or so, he would call from the bedroom, 'Done yet, Elly? How much longer?' "

"What did you do?"

"I found a laundry that did hand pressing with light starch, and I paid seven dollars a month to have them done. That was the year we couldn't even afford to put a license on the car and always had to drive on the back streets, but it was worth every penny. I'll never forget, 'Are you coming to bed? I can hardly stay awake!' and me pressing and pressing—tabs, collars, cuffs. Ugh."

"Your mother's right," said Anna. "He'll come around eventually."

"Any man," said Helen, "is better than none."

"And you like his family," put in Susanna. "And they always get to be more and more like their families."

"I do like his family."

Anna shifted in her chair, waiting for the qualifications.

"I do like his family." Christine looked around at each of her relatives. "But they aren't like us."

"Who is?" said Claire.

"Thank God," added Susanna.

"No, really!" exclaimed Christine. "Nothing ever seems to have happened to them. They've always lived in Aurora; Mr. Walker's always grown steadily more prosperous; the cupboards are stocked with years of food; and when you walk in the door, you feel like the world could end but the Walkers would go on, concerned but not affected. They don't talk about anything. They don't seem to have any history. At family reunions they get out the old games and play them around the dining room table."

"It sounds very wholesome to me," said Claire.

"I wish I were back in college," continued Christine. "I wish I could be a sophomore for the rest of my life. I think so much about the single room I had that year that I can almost smell it. I had these awful red-and-black curtains that someone gave me, and there wasn't a bedspread, and I only had an overhead

46

light, but I loved it. I sat up and I went to bed and I listened to music and read and took baths in the middle of the night. Some days there was such a mess you couldn't even see the floor."

"I'll bet," said Helen.

"And others I would scrub and wash and have this incredible sense of imminent perfection. There were a lot of other things about college that were exciting and even inspiring, and the campus was very pretty, but lately I just think about that room. The walnut furniture we've collected and the Dansk pots we got for our wedding seem sordid in comparison."

Helen said, "You'll be glad to have nice things. I think it's awful to look around and not see anything beautiful that you own yourself."

"I had beautiful thoughts."

"Oh, come on!" Helen's contempt sang.

"Possessions *are* sordid! I can't stand listening to Todd talking about the things he wants to buy. He thinks he deserves only the best."

"What's wrong with that? He has an eye for quality."

"Maybe, but what has he ever done to deserve it? I mean, deserve it! My God!" Nelson began to whine. She stroked his nose and scratched in his curls. "Nelson knows I'm talking about Todd."

In the silence that followed, Anna's peripheral vision glittered and the room floated away from her, bright and hot. She closed her eyes and was terribly tired. They, whoever they were and in whatever gathering, seemed to have been wrangling all day. She touched her fingertips to her temples, and her body unfurled beneath her, a banner of aches: insteps, heels, calves, one wrist, lower back, shoulder, neck, even the muscles of her jaw where she'd been clenching them for the last few minutes.

"Oh, God!" said Christine, and her tone was such a mixture of anger, disgust, laughter, and hopelessness that Anna kept her eyes closed until the tears, tears of fatigue more than anything else she was sure, dissipated. All her life Christine's voice had carried this odd note of merriment, so that even now, knowing her as well as she did, Anna couldn't be sure of the girl's real mood. It was disconcerting.

Susanna settled into the couch. With a large sigh and a great creaking of couch springs, she shifted position and uncrossed her legs. Anna opened her eyes, and in the coruscating heat of the room, she realized that Susanna was fat. Her cheeks were red, her breasts were full and heavy, and her blouse had caught in a fold of flesh at her waist. As she shifted position, she automatically pulled it out and smoothed it down. For years Susanna had been talking about food, for years she had declared that she simply had to lose some number of pounds. She was fat. Yes, she was fat. Anna wondered why she felt so surprised. At twelve, coming in for lunch after three sets of tennis, before running off to find a softball game or go swimming, Susanna had solemnly sworn off desserts, bread, mayonnaise, Coca-Cola. "You're just getting your figure," Anna had said. "Don't be ridiculous." And she'd repeated something similar all these years: "You're filling out"; "you're big-boned"; "muscle weighs more than fat."

And now Susanna, who once pedaled her bicycle twelve times around the neighborhood park, no hands, was fat. She began, "If you ask me—"

"A basic desire to provide well for his family is nothing to sneer at, Christine," said Helen. "If you buy something good the first time, then you don't have to buy it again."

Susanna sat forward and looked idly into a coffee cup left on the end table. "I think—"

"Furthermore, it's more economical to establish some sort of taste at the beginning, so that things go together as you acquire them. I—"

Susanna raised her voice. "Helen!" Helen glanced at her. "May I say—"

"Christine," said Claire, "it seems to me that you've made your choice. It was your idea to get married, and you were full of arguments when your mother showed a little opposition. And it's not as if any other man is going to suit you better than Todd does. I frankly don't think there is better or worse, only different. If you make up your mind to the idea that this is what you've got, then you can make the best of it."

"I didn't know!"

"Who does? If anybody did, do you think they'd choose anything?"

"*May I say something?*" Surprised at the loudness of her own voice and the silence it produced, Susanna flushed and then giggled. "I'd like to get a word in. Okay, Helen? Okay, Claire?" She cleared her throat.

"Aunt Susanna, I think you live the most perfect life. You love your job, and you're the best salesman in

49

the office. You know all the houses around, and you're terrific with ideas about fixing them up. The men in your office give you lots of respect, and you've gotten to develop lots of different kinds of talents. Your free time is your own, you have your own house and car, you travel. You know, I hate traveling with Todd. He wants to stop and check the map at every corner, and I can't wait to get lost and find something unexpected."

"Shut up!" exclaimed Susanna.

"I'm sorry! Really, I—"

"Why do you consider me the great example of single success? I mean, yes, my job is fine, houses are fine. Money is fine! If I were married to Gilbert Hanson, we'd have four kids, constant fights, and utter chaos. He'd be some high-powered, silver-haired staff physician, and I'd be an alcoholic with a Mercedes for going to the grocery store. Looking back, it seems like my choices were that and this. This is better than that."

"But it's not just the money and the house!" cried Christine. "Don't you all see? When I'm alone I feel like anything can happen! No, hush Nelson. Go lie down." Nelson lay down, flopping over onto his side with a thud that made Anna wince.

Susanna ignored Christine's enthusiasm. "I always think that maybe there could have been something else to choose, like another man."

Helen rolled her eyes.

"Just one."

Helen waved her hand. "Don't be melodramatic."

"Helen, men were never a problem for you."

"I don't know about that."

"You know what I think?" Claire uncrossed her legs and spoke imperiously. "I'll tell you." She looked around. "I think you can only really choose what presents itself to you at the moment. You can't say you're going to divorce one man and find someone better. You can only say that you can have the man you've got now, or no man at all. If you're willing to have no man at all, then maybe that's the right choice for you, but the real question is married or not married. Maybe someone will come along and then you can say again, married or not married, but you can't say, this one or that one."

"Claire, some people make sure they've got the next one on the line before they let the first one off the hook, you know."

"There's many a slip twixt the line and the lip, Helen."

Helen had been married twice. Anna had found the men, both of whom drank with the casual abandon that seemed characteristic of Helen's generation, remarkably charming. Both were now dead. This year Helen would turn fifty-two.

"I didn't divorce Hanson Gilbert because I had another man on the line, Claire, but because he had another woman on the line. So there. I made just the choice you say we have to make."

"You couldn't—"

"Besides, you're always setting up these rules to live by. You never actually look at a situation, you know.

51

Helen's right. Everything is simple to you."

"I was going to say that you couldn't make any other decision at the time because at the time, you had some self-respect."

"A half an hour ago, you said something about, 'He's her husband, it's that simple.' "

Claire's face was red and her toe tapped with measured severity against the leg of the coffee table. "A dalliance is one thing. A loveless marriage is another."

"Pardon me?"

"Hanson didn't love you."

Susanna coughed. In a moment she said, "I know that." Anna was surprised by the ensuing silence. It had an air of shock about it, as if the events, and the knowledge they forced upon everyone of betrayal and jealousy and sadness, were not nineteen years in the past. Susanna coughed again, then she said in a trembly voice, "No one ever did."

Claire said, "Oh, stop feeling sorry for yourself," but Anna thought, Why should she stop? Why? Why? Susanna spoke again, her voice even more teary, "I wanted a baby." Helen got up and went into the kitchen. In a moment Claire followed. Fifty years of prickly rivalry had never prevented them from despising Susanna's difficulties and using her admittedly frequent self-pity as an excuse not to sympathize.

Anna could say that she herself had sympathized continually, and say so with honesty, but looking back it seemed that the words had been routine, the willing ear only half-attentive, the embraces, when Susanna was young enough to welcome embraces, perfunctory.

52

Hanson's departure had been so perfect in its way. Even Susanna had recognized it at the time as a development uniquely to be expected, its timing a relief, as there was little property to be divided and no child to worry about.

Susanna delivered herself of two or three shuddering sobs, Christine looked on sympathetically, and Anna sighed. How could she say, after all these years of reassurance, that yes, all those things Susanna had feared at fourteen, twelve, even as young as six, when she worried that the other first-graders did not like her, had come to pass? How could she admit now that the pain was real and that nothing had, or would, compensate her for it? Her daughters were so unhappy! Was it her fault, after all?

"You know what?" remarked Christine in her half-humorous way. "I was just thinking about the best time Todd and I ever had together. It was about a month before we got married. We'd gone out for dinner and shared this big shrimp salad, then walked back to Todd's apartment. Well, I have never had such a stomach ache as I had by the time we got there. I could hardly stand up straight. Todd, too. We turned out the lights and lay down on the couch, and then Todd began to do impressions. He sniffed my ear and mouth like a dog, he pretended to be a hard-of-hearing old man, he imitated a whole group of foreigners from different countries meeting at Disneyland and trying to have a conversation, he even pretended he was the chef who made our salad. I laughed and laughed. God! It hurt so much and I laughed so much! I didn't know it was going to be the best time we would ever have until the next morning, when he told me that the whole night he thought we had dangerous fish poisoning from the shrimp. He seemed so funny and heroic to me. I never thought I'd mind about the pear and the beer and the sandwich ever again."

Anna looked toward the clock on the mantelpiece; the delicate miniature of the room reflected in its bright glass dome triggered the old hot glitter in her vision. It was nine-thirty, time for everyone to go home, time for relief from the cacophony of her daughters' superabundant opinions. "Oh, me!" she said, elaborating her sigh. At last the headache came on. Anna inhaled sharply, but the air in the room was tepid, unrefreshing. These headaches made her forehead seem like a bank of bony knobs played on by the pain like organ stops. Her hearing sharpened. In the kitchen Claire and Helen were opening and closing the refrigerator. Every one of them approached her refrigerator with a ten-year-old's belief in treasure boxes; none of theirs gleamed and flashed with ice cream, Cokes, caramel upside-down rolls, brandied fruits, butterscotch sauce, and stored icebox cookie dough the way hers did. The sucking creak of the heavy door sounded again, followed presently by its muffled slap. Anna bit her lip. She had not stopped feeding these women for half a century. She was furious. She had to go to bed. Why did they treat her house, her larder, her furniture, her effects as if they owned them? And her life, too! A nurse! Contemptible! The pain narrowed to two awl points above her nose.

Christine picked up the magazine Helen had put down. Susanna said, "I remember the best time I ever had. I was nine, and we were down at the playground, swinging." As she spoke, Anna's headache seemed to open into a memory: the elm-ringed pavement with its rooted jungle gym and chinning bars and swings. The brown painted benches in the horseshoe about the sandbox. "Jeffrey Neal and I used to meet there every afternoon, and the other kids would come from school to watch us. We'd draw straws for the best swing, because one was about an inch and a half lower than the others; then we'd get on and start pumping. We were the best pumpers in the grade school. I was better than Jeffrey, for that matter. I always pumped so hard I lost my shoes. You'd go back and forth and back again, and after a while, on the back swing, you'd be looking at your hands, and it would seem like the crossbar was below you, and you'd know that if you made a certain kind of kick at just the right time you'd be up and over on the front swing." Christine's mouth had dropped open, and Susanna, smiling, was gazing at her knees. "Sometimes I dared myself not to kick at the right time, or I made myself think about what we were going to have for dinner, but it was like my body couldn't be distracted. My legs would kick, and the swing would seem to shoot straight up, and then the board seat would sort of smack against my behind, and just when everything was upside-down, I'd sort of settle into it, and it would carry me down and around.

Hmm!" She paused. "I remember the way that pavement looked to this very day. It looked like a target. Anyway, then the chains would be wrapped around the crossbar, so the cat would die, and we'd get off. All the other kids would take turns throwing the swings back to starting position. I remember we always wanted to go over right together, but I don't think we ever did."

Anna thought she might throw up. She had never heard of this before. Christine exclaimed, "Aunt Susanna, did you really go over the top of the swing set?"

"Like a bucket on a rope."

"How often did you do it?"

"At least once every school day that fall, until Jeffrey ran into the bathroom door in the dark and knocked out one of his front teeth. He didn't want to do it after that, and it wasn't as much fun alone. I bet I did it fifty times."

"My God! I can't believe it!"

Anna could, though. She could imagine it so vividly that she knew it had happened, precisely as Susanna related it, once or twice between three and five in the afternoons, while she, three blocks away, housed, pre-served from knowledge, baked a pie for dinner, nagged Claire to set the table, thought continually of money, worried about Ike driving home from work and stopping at a bar. She wanted to jump up now and slap Susanna senseless, but also to crush her in an embrace. It was impossible that she was still here, still safe and intact. She shuddered and said, "Susanna, you must be immortal."

"It wasn't hard if your timing was right."

"What wasn't?" Helen stood in the doorway, sensing she had missed something.

"Aunt Susanna used to swing over the top bar of the swing set."

"Really?" But Helen had already lost interest. "That's a pretty quilt, I think." She pointed to a page in Christine's magazine. "Not so old-fashioned as most. I think this kind of fabric sculpture is rather interesting, actually."

"Mother! Aunt Susanna went all the way around, over the top! Don't you think that's amazing?"

"Oh, she did that kind of thing all the time, didn't you, Susanna?"

Susanna shrugged. Still caught up in the pleasure of the memory, she did not care, for once, whether Helen was impressed or not.

Claire pushed past Helen, saying, "Mother, I'm just bushed! Is there anything I can do for you before we go? Do you think Daddy's all right? I cannot sleep past five-thirty these days. No matter what time I go to bed, bingo, five-thirty rolls around and my eyes pop right open."

"That's secondary insomnia."

"Thank you, Helen. Insomnia, huh?"

"No, really, it's called that. I read it in the Sunday paper. Primary insomnia is not being able to get to sleep in the first place."

"I swear, Helen, you're such a patsy for any pseudo-scientific jargon."

"That's better than not taking any interest at all, I should think."

"Mom," said Christine, "was there ever a time when you and Aunt Claire didn't argue?"

Claire jammed her arms energetically into the sleeves of her coat. "Sure! When we were in high school. We always had to do the dishes together, and that's when we practiced our tap routines. By the sink. We figured if we got up a good team act, someone would discover us and take us away from all that. Your mother wasn't half bad, actually."

Christine snapped the leash onto Nelson's collar and he stood up. Helen said, "I don't think we argued much after we were married."

"Now I'll go lock the back door for you, Mother. Claire can give me a ride home, and Helen can go with Christine."

"Maybe our arguments are just another sign of our eternal youth," laughed Claire.

As if on cue, Helen said, "Now drive carefully, Claire."

"Yes, Daddy!"

"Well, it's foggy!"

"I've got perfectly good eyes in my head."

"People who don't care don't worry. Good night, Mother. Call me if, you know."

Anna nodded. Claire kissed her on the cheek, smiling and rolling her eyes at Helen. Soon their argument had floated away into the fog.

"Goodnight, Grandma. I'm glad to be home. Come on, Nelson."

"Now Mother, the back window was unlocked, and I almost didn't notice it. It's not that safe around here anymore. I locked the door and latched the storm door. I've got to be at the office early tomorrow, but I can come by before lunch if you need anything. Thank you for dinner. Please don't forget to think about the nurse. I hate to think of you and Daddy alone here, I really do. Goodnight, Mother." Susanna paused to reach for pins in her hairdo.

"Susanna?"

"Mmm?"

"Would you rather have been pretty and popular like Helen and Claire?"

"I don't know, Mother." She shrugged, unwilling to think of the question.

"Would you?" Anna thought of the pavement flying up, a target to be averted; of the earth like a laden table and the horizon all around.

"Mom, I really don't know. I really don't."

Anna kissed her goodnight. Her cheek was powdery and soft, like Anna's own cheek.

Two

*T*he bathroom had once been pink and white, the boundary between the two colors a strip of shoulder-high carved molding. Over the green tile, twenty years ago, Anna had thrown a thick pink rug, and from the old-fashioned porcelain towel racks she had hung her first matched set of towels, pink, complete, a Christmas gift from Susanna and Hanson. Washcloths, hand towels, guest towels, bath towels, bath mat, each monogrammed with her initials: *aRg*. The rug and remaining towels were now thin and clingy with use, and this winter she had supplemented them with new thick towels of bright red and cool white. Ruffled, bleached muslin curtains of the same vintage as the towels had given way to a crisp strawberry print, and for her birthday she'd received red heart-shaped bars of translucent soap that smelled pleasantly of fruit. Her bathroom, long a place of utter indifference to her, was now something of a nest, and she had taken to indulging in long baths, the sort of baths where she would add hot water as the tub cooled, and leaf through more than one of the novels and magazines piled near the big tub.

While the tub was filling, Anna opened the window and leaned into the fog. Anna was a lover of weather. When something odd happened, like a large snowfall or a heavy fog, her spirits lifted at the simple novelty. In addition she had never fully believed in the dangers of snowy roads or diminished visibility. These were the dangers of the automobile age. Her heart believed in staying at home with a full larder, shoveling a path only as far as the barn, where hay would be piled up for the horse, leaving the mail at the post office for days on end. Perilous weather, to Anna, was an endless series of clear and breezy days, when people tended to grow too independent and self-assured. The fog gusted and puffed. Margaret Lacina's house, next door, could just be discerned, and her own sideyard, below, was shrouded in the smoky warmth. Soon, in six weeks, the apple trees would blossom, and the apricot after that. With Ike sick, the spraying and pruning would of course be too much work. She lifted her arms to the wet breeze. Mama had believed that night air could cure anything, clean it out of you, and Anna still thought it uniquely present, tangible and almost visible, ready to enfold one, or buoy one up. The fog seemed very personal, almost cozy. She leaned farther out the window, stretching her neck and opening her mouth. The fog parted, and she saw that Margaret Lacina was still up and downstairs, for a single light shown in the bay window. Margaret's bathroom was directly across from hers, and Anna thought how convivial it would be if Margaret flung open her window, leaned on the sill, and told her all the neighborhood gossip she had missed in the last day or so. She had had a friend like that once, a neighbor who wrote messages in lipstick on her own bedroom window for Anna to read across the way: *tomatoes up* or *bread delish*. It would never happen with Margaret, though. She was from North Carolina, and her house was hermetically sealed, year around.

Her bath ready, Anna closed the window, drew the shade, and began carefully to take off her clothes. Old age sometimes felt like a course she had to thread between various attacks of pain, and her evasions and retreats were now habitual. Certain movements she avoided, or made deliberately, testing. When she saw others on the street doing the same thing, she knew that she was old, as they were. She exhaled, pulled in her stomach, and unhooked her foundation, grimacing at the flow of her flesh as it took its natural shape or, she thought, smiling, shapelessness. Her breasts had gotten so large that it hurt to go without support, so she lifted them as she stepped across the new cherry-colored rug to her bath.

She had never looked like any of her daughters. In her youth she'd been white and slender, with little pubic hair, and no hair at all on the rest of her body. After a while, when she was no longer so slim or pale or smooth, she had occasionally recalled herself as "petite" or "delicate" with "good legs" and "nice skin," but at the time she'd assumed her looks depended on "a pleasant expression" and "good grooming." Ike had never mentioned what he saw in her. She remembered thinking at seventeen that if she didn't wear a pretty dress, no one would see her at all. Mama had thought so, too. Anna had any number of pretty dresses. Mama could make a pretty dress out of a bedsheet and a yard of drapery trim.

Stepping into and out of the bathtub had become disagreeably suspenseful, in spite of the white rubber daisies stuck to the bathtub for traction. Nothing worked right. Her legs were heavy as she raised them one by one, her knees ached slightly, as if bones abraded each other. One-legged, she always felt precarious and stuck. Fear of falling combined with fear of being unable to move. But then she was in, both calves baptized in warmth, both hands securely gripping the edges of the tub. She lowered herself to kneeling, then to sitting. Her book, she discovered too late, was across the room. For a moment she considered it: torchlit, velveted Italy, sixteenth century, boar hounds in the dining hall. But the characters were too young, and their concerns actually rather contrived. Not worth another in, another out. She slipped down, the warmth rolled over her shoulders, dividing around her neck as around a boulder in a stream. The water was so deep that if she pressed her arms and back to the bottom of the tub, only her head and the crook of her knees jutted through the surface. She was reminded of something Helen liked to do years ago, to hold so still that the water would cease absolutely to move. "Mother," she would utter in a pressed-out voice, "do I look like I'm trapped in a block of ice?"

She could easily envision herself as she had been at

first, though not as one always saw oneself, chest, belly, knees, from above. Instead she saw herself from across the room, as Ike might have seen her, or as she would appear in a photograph or a mirror, except that she never looked in the mirror if she was naked, and of course there were no photos of her without all her clothes, and a hat and gloves for good measure. Still, she believed that what she imagined was somehow herself, and no wonder Ike had been frightened of it, so thin and pale and hairless, so unlike his own ruddy flesh. Perhaps she had frightened him more than he had frightened her, after all. As for their life in bed, they had done their best for a long time without ever saying a word about it. She suspected they'd done better than her own parents; in the winter, Mama wore as many clothes to bed as she did to the store. Even so, maybe they hadn't done well enough. You never knew how such things exfoliated into the lives of your children.

Helen's life, for instance. Helen had been a lovely child, with Ike's height and without his big bones, her hair the color of some pale wood like pine or maple, her posture and the set of her limbs easy and straight. A perfect first child in a way, for with her they'd had time to marvel at their own cleverness and to anticipate with enthusiasm the certainty of engendering a race of such beauties. She had not been obedient, but the fact that she did not toe out, that she could see and hear perfectly (and look so effortlessly beautiful doing it) was full compensation. Ike had taken her over early, partly because of Claire's instantaneous appearance, but partly because of his own enchantment.

Anna shivered, splintering the solid water, and manipulated the hot tap with her toe. More warmth plunged to the depths of the tub, then eddied to either side of her buttocks and over her belly. Helen had been a great runner-away. Anna always said that she took a step one day, walked across the room the next day, and ran away the day after that. The exaggeration was only slight. Thereafter she'd been found any number of places on the ranch: headed for the horse corral, in the doorway of the barn, toddling down the dirt road, toddling up the slopes west of the house, even as far as the wildflower meadow overlooking the house. She had been found with shoes and without, without a coat, without a sweater, once without a stitch of clothing. No toys or games or adjurations to play with Claire could keep her in the house, and one summer they'd actually harnessed her to a post in the backyard, following a neighbor woman's advice, but the harness had seemed cruel, and after a week or so had fallen into disuse. Miraculously, she had never gotten hurt, at least on the ranch. If Anna or Ike or Abel put on a coat, Helen would beat her or him to the door, saying, "Go? Go? Bye?" It was funny how you didn't attribute any human significance to these infant predilections. It wasn't until years later that Anna even suspected that home repelled Helen as much as distance attracted her.

When they moved off the ranch, the fascinations, and dangers, of Helen's journeys multiplied. Anna considered herself fortunate if Helen went to the playground by herself and could be found there when her absence was discovered. At six years of age, since the crossing of only one small street was involved, she was allowed to go on her own. One small street. Nevertheless, it was enough. Helen stepped into the street, was hit by an oncoming car, which threw her into a telephone pole, dislocating her shoulder. She picked herself up, eluded the driver who had stopped to investigate the small bump he'd felt, and ran on to her destination. Only after playing in the sandbox, hanging by her heels from the jungle-gym, teeter-tottering with a neighbor child, and trying to swing, had she come home, her arm dangling at her side, and reported the accident. When asked if it hurt, she'd said, "Yes," and fainted. Anna could even remember what she was cooking that evening (knockwurst and sauerkraut, pungent and nearly ready) when all of a sudden her green-clad child was slumped on the brown-painted floor. Her first thought had been to turn the pot handles toward the back of the stove, as if boiling cabbage might leap off the burner and scald the prostrate form.

Anna's heavy eyelids closed. And Helen was six years old in her green coat, arcing through the air like a baseball, and then the car had stopped and the driver was scurrying around it double-time, looking for Helen, sniffing her out, but Helen had disappeared. Anna shifted position and her shoulder came out of the water into the chilly air. She woke up, turned on the hot water again, slipped down. Behind her lids was a pleasant, warm brightness, given color by her awareness of the red, white, pink, and green she knew was there. She sighed. Her headache had gone. The water was blissfully warm. She closed the tap. It was then that she heard his call, "Mother! Goddamn it!" He had obviously called before.

By the time she got there, he was florid with impatience. "I'm thirsty!" he snapped. "Can't you hear me? I must have called ten times! What were you doing?" It was only the weakness of his voice that kept her from barking back at him. After a pause while she suppressed her annoyance, she said, "What would you like to drink, Ike?"

"Chocolate milk!"

Anna tied the knot in the belt of her robe and turned to go."

"I'm freezing!"

"Yes?"

"I'm freezing."

"Would you like some hot chocolate, Ike?"

The old man settled back against the wall and put his hands under the blankets. "If it's not too much trouble," he said benevolently. In her fatigue this remark struck her oddly, since it implied some choice on her part while at the same time removing all actual choice from her power. Only a churl would respond that indeed it was trouble, great trouble, to go downstairs into the darkness, round up the milk and the cocoa and the sugar and a pan and a cup and a spoon, apply them all to one another in the proper fashion, and then balance the cup through the darkness, back up the stairs, only to be faced with perplexity about where to put it. It was trouble. But was it too much trouble? In what context? In the context of his illness? Of their marriage? Of her delay in responding to his wish (need)? Of her tiredness? There were cases in which no trouble was too much. Perhaps he was so ill already that the greatest pains and inconveniences would be merely sufficient, merely humane. Perhaps they had been married so long (fifty-two years!) that no trouble was too much trouble in light of all the trouble that had been taken already.

Actually, it wasn't much trouble. She could find her way easily among her things in the dark, the milk and cocoa and sugar and utensils were immediately to her hand. Cooking anything was second nature to her, and she filled the cup, a large mug, only three-quarters full. There was even a marshmallow, in a bag right there on the kitchen table, and she plopped it in. How much trouble was too much trouble? "Thank you," said Ike.

"Anything more?"

"I'm wide awake."

"You'll go back to sleep."

"Anna."

"What?"

"I'm wide awake."

She heaved an ostentatious sigh and fixed her hands upon her hips. "Well?"

"Will you read to me?"

"Read to you! It's the middle of the night. Anyway, you always say you hate to be read to when I offer."

"It's ten-thirty. Well, twenty to eleven."

"Hand me that book!" She reached for his chair.

"Something of yours."

"Something of mine?"

"I don't care what."

"A sweater pattern?"

"Oh, you know."

She pursed her lips, but she went into her bedroom and found some Dorothy Sayers stories she had been reading the day before.

"What's that?" he said.

"Some mystery stories."

"I don't like mystery stories." He glanced at her. "Usually. Okay."

She began. "The gate on whose peeled and faded surface the name *Scrawns* was just legible in the dim light fell to with a clap that shook the rotten gatepost and scattered a shower of drops on the drenched laurels." Ike tipped his head back against the wall, then sat noisily upright again and reached for his cup. The girl in the story turned out to be a parlormaid. Ike sniffed, hawked, and swallowed, then reached for his teeth. The habitual clack with which they went into his mouth reverberated above the drone of her own voice. She heard every squeak of his bed as he settled himself again. ". . . giving to that side of the face a look of blind and cunning malignity."

"Mother."

" '. . . acutely on Susan's face.' What?"

"Is that door still locked?" He pointed to the door joining their bedrooms.

" 'I'm Mrs. Jarrock,' said the woman in her—' "

"Is it?"

"It never was locked, Ike. It's tied with a stocking to my bedpost. 'It was incredible to Susan that any man who was not blind and deaf should have married—' "

"Why?"

"Because it always has been. I can hear you."

"You didn't."

"I was in the bathroom with the water running. I can hear you fine in my bedroom."

"Then how come you don't come sometimes?"

"I always come."

"Anna, you know that's wrong."

" 'She said: "How do you do?" and extended a reluctant hand, which Mrs. Jarrock's vast palm engulfed in a grasp unexpectedly—' "

"Why didn't he come?"

"What? Do you want me to read this to you or not?"

"With Christine. Why didn't he come?"

"If you mean Todd, he had to work."

"I'd like to see him one more time."

"You will." She lowered the book and glanced sharply at Ike, who was rolling hot chocolate around in his cup. His wrists were as stalklike as his ankles, and the tiny dimple at the tip of his nose had deepened to a crevice. Anna's hands trembled for a moment. "Lots more times," but the way she said it sounded as if she were scooting it by him.

"He'll be rich."

"I suppose."

"He'll be rich!" The anger in his voice was thin but real, and touched off an answering anger in her, as it always did. Once again it seemed possible after all these years to discuss the relative value of wealth, to change Ike's attitude, rectify his notions. And simultaneously it seemed impossible that she could have lived so long with someone who could insist so triumphantly and resentfully that a relative of his was going to be rich, just a relative, not himself. "So what," she snapped. "You won't be here to enjoy it." Her sight dimmed and brightened. What was she saying? "And neither will I." But her fingers crept over the upholstery of her chair and touched the wood. She said in a more solicitous voice, "Do you want me to go on reading this story?"

"Nah."

"Can I get you anything? More hot chocolate?"

"Nah."

"What?"

He waited expectantly. Anna tossed her head in the direction of the bathroom and lifted her eyebrows. He nodded.

When he shouted that he was finished and she opened the bathroom door to retrieve him, he said, "Are you sorry I was never a success?"

"What's a success?"

"Don't foist me off with that damned nonsense!"

"None of your children died before you did. You lived to be an old man. You kept your job during the Depression. You think Christine's father was more of a success? Or Alfred? You think a man who takes his first drink before breakfast is a success just because he has lots of money and charm? You think Helen thought

71

being left a widow a second time in ten years was a sign of success?" She should have stayed away from Alfred. How to regard him was an ancient bone of contention between them.

He clenched his teeth. She could see them working inside his thin cheeks. She knew he'd always seen this attitude of hers as intentional perversity, taken to be ornery, and from time to time be had argued bitterly that she ought to blame him for their modest life, their small yard, their single car. She could not. She could, and often did, blame him for many things, but never for these broad movements of fate. He paused to speak, and she half dragged him through the door of his bedroom. He was panting.

"Ike, you've been a good provider," said Anna, conciliatory.

"Seth got to be a rich man. Ben, too. Of the five of us boys, I did the least."

"Ike, times were different when Seth and Ben were starting out, and Seth's money went in the Crash just like everybody else's even though he wasn't here to see it."

"Mama thought I would do the most."

"I know, Ike." Her mother-in-law's preference for Isaac, the youngest of eight, had been a well-known joke in the Robison family. Abel was his brother too, although Anna didn't dare mention it. The rumor was that Abel spent some time as a hobo on the railroads during the Depression. Anna sighed and lowered the youngest Robison, who was seven years older than she, down on his old man's rumpled bed.

"You should have had a big place, Mother, with some women to help you with the work, and a big terraced garden, and some real good things for the house. Crystal and china. What's that stuff Helen has? That stuff in the shape of flowers sort of?"

"The Belleek?"

Ike nodded. "And Persian rugs. All that stuff."

It was almost funny. Not only did she recoil from the very idea of bouncing from wall to wall in a big house, trying to think of something to say to the servants, not only did she shudder at the thought of garish Waterford and gold-bedizened Wedgwood, she also recognized that this pet fantasy of Ike's, that he had not given her what she wanted and deserved, was a sentimental and determined rearrangement of what he knew to be her character. While she enjoyed as much as anything the knitting of sweaters and the slip-covering of chairs, the redesigning of old clothes and the stashing away of tomatoes, potatoes, and squash from the garden, Ike hated it. To him handmade was always homemade, while to her homemade was something you knew everything about, a contribution you made to your own history. But it was not funny, either. She said, not in a sharp voice, because this was something she really meant, "Ike, I wish Seth and Ben had never made a cent. I really do. It's poisoned the whole family. They weren't happy because they had it, and everybody else was unhappy because they didn't have it. Helen is a prime example."

"You always say Helen's just like your mother."

"Well, that's true, too."

Ike waved his hand, dismissing her remarks. It was probably just as well. After a while he said, "Everything makes me so dog tired lately."

"I know, Ike. Me too."

"Remember that time Abel and I went out looking for those four head of cattle? Abel rode that roan horse Bucko, and I rode Sassy. Remember Sassy?"

"Yes, Ike. Sassy was a lovely mare. You got yourself a real bargain there."

"Three days. We were gone for three days. It snowed. I remember it snowed, and we dug down in the snow and camped."

"You didn't! You found a little cabin! That's what you told me."

"Not the first night. We didn't find the cabin till the second night. The first night it was snowing and we couldn't see. We dug down in the snow. I've never been so cold." He paused for a long time. "Abel and I slept in the same bedroll in a hole in the snow." The beginnings of a snore ruffled in his nose. "We were so tired." Anna leaned forward. "I was never so tired as then." She pulled the covers up to his chin and turned out the light. The glow from her hot bath had worn off, and she was chilled again. Fog drifted pale outside the window, cut by the single branch of a black tree. The night was so thick that the other limbs had disappeared. Anna drew the curtain.

In the dark bowl of her own soft bed, Anna imagined a big yellow fire, consuming seasoned apple logs with a crackle like laughter. She curled up, shoving her hands between her thighs, trying never to touch the cold rim of the sheet. She imagined the fire glowing on her face, reddening her hands and the bodice of her garments, toasting her toes, initiating a glorious sweat at her hairline, at the line of her throat (which, she noticed with a start, she still imagined to be a hollow at the meeting of her collarbones). She imagined throwing even more logs on the fire, and then turning to bask her back in the mounting blaze, careful not to stand too close. Drawing her head under the covers, she imagined turning back to face the conflagration, lifting her arms so that her hands were almost over it, almost in danger of burning. She imagined herself as warm as she could be, warmer than any sensible person would ever want to be. As warm as warm as warm, but the pocket she lay in under the covers was slow in giving up its chill, and close around the fire in her mind was Ike's midnight snow, so cold that he and the brother he feared and disliked had to cuddle together for survival.

The fire had become almost a dream, almost the awareness of huddled, not quite warm but welcome sleep, when the phone began to ring. Her first thought was to ignore it, but her second thought was of Ike. If he were to wake, he might be up for hours yet. The phone continued to ring, imperious, clattering. On the floor of the hall, it was somewhere. She stumbled over the phone. The receiver knocked to the floor. Before she could even say "Hello," a man's voice demanded, "Who is this? Who are you? Hello?"

Anna caught her breath. "Who are you?"

Delighted with a response, the voice became at once

purring and meaningful. "I have your number. This is George. Who are you? This is George." He continued to identify himself and ask her who she was in a tone of voice that implied obscenity, but he said nothing obscene. She hung up, instantly regretful that she had not at least slammed the phone in his ear. More than once she had had obscene phone calls: men who declared what they wanted to do with various parts of her body before she even had the presence of mind to hand the phone to Ike, who said in his naturally angry telephone voice, "Who's this?" An obscene call without obscenities, though, was perhaps more disconcerting, because it had no reason. "George" had said nothing, only his own name. She wanted to have asked him if he was so stupid that he couldn't even make a proper obscene phone call, or to have threatened him somehow. She was shaking with cold. She dialed Helen, who answered sleepily. It was not exactly embarrassment that made her unable to speak about the caller after all. She was not exactly lying when she said, "I just feel funny. I can't describe it."

"How's Daddy?" Helen asked suspiciously, as if Anna might be leading up to telling her something.

"He's asleep. He's fine. It's me."

"Do you want me to come over?" She sounded decidedly reluctant, but then she repeated the offer, this time more genuinely. Yes, Anna did want her to come over, along with Christine and the dog, especially the dog, but in Helen's voice she heard the putting on of underwear and slacks and coats and hats, the opening of the garage and the warming up of the car, the drive through the forbidding fog, lights and activity and sleepiness everywhere, cups of coffee in the middle of the night, and her own embarrassment at being able to produce nothing to justify all this trouble. And Helen would call Claire and Claire would call Susanna, and everyone would be seized again in a tangle of speculation about what was really wrong, what should really be done. The nurse. Anna coughed briskly into the phone. "It's nothing. Hearing your voice is enough. It is nothing, really." It wasn't nothing, but how to explain the odd effect of all this reminiscing: Susanna hurtling over the crossbar on that swing, Ike and Abel clutched together under a cold and starry sky, Helen herself flipped against a telephone pole like a tiddly wink? How to explain the cold she could not get rid of? Some silly caller who didn't even say dirty words was the least of it. "Nothing, Helen."

"Do you think you can get back to sleep? Call me anytime and we'll come over, really, Mother."

"Thank you, Helen." Was it clear to Helen how heartfelt this small phrase was? How very unconventional Anna's gratitude?

"Okay, Mother. Call me in the morning."

"Yes, Helen."

When they hung up, Anna crept down the stairs, unaccountably afraid both to turn on the light and not to turn it on. She checked each window and door. Locked, bolted, the windows reassuringly taped against drafts. She wedged a chair against the basement door and at last, in the kitchen, turned on the light. There was nothing she wanted to eat or drink, but she opened the oven door and turned the dial up to 450. The flame came on with a whoosh, and she stretched her hands toward it.

Helen had been beautiful. One of a kind. No, they had not engendered a race of her; no, people did not say about the Robison girls, "Each one prettier than the last." Even Christine, daughter of Helen and her certain match, Sam Lakin, was only normally pretty, normally graceful, normally compelling. Christine and Todd were a handsome couple, but nothing like Helen and Sam. Helen had found Sam by running the farthest away, to the Army, to Europe, where the war was ending and Sam was returning after recovery from a chest wound. They met on a troop ship (Helen, two other WACS, and three thousand soldiers). They met again in London, and again in Bavaria, where Helen was photographed engaging in winter sports for army brochures, and Sam was assigned to provisioning refugees and displaced persons. The war was over. When Anna leafed through *Life* magazines and saw pictures of flattened Europe, every emaciated, homeless human figure reminded her of Helen, sleek, rosy, blond, whose running away had been eminently successful, who wrote, "Saw Geo at last, on our stop over in Paris. He was just walking down the street. He was with Bill Nolan, in fact, and they had seen Frank Miller. I hear that Les Shorter was killed, though. He was in Frank's regiment. It seems like the whole world, including all of Des Moines, is right here. In Paris saw Notre Dame from a distance, and some other places

78

up close. Lots of destruction. Learning to ski."

Claire, who missed Geo and was in a snit for two whole years, said, "I don't see how she can sound so happy when she's surrounded by misery and destruction. I think it's heartless." From a dry distance, though, Anna thought that Helen must surely have found the center of life in the Alps of Bavaria. Mama had loved the Alps. Up until she decided to tell people she was really from Paris, she had always announced her birthplace as Munich, even though everyone knew she had lived her whole childhood in Hamburg. In Garmisch in 1945, everyone was free, including Helen. All her dreams of the exotic and adventurous had been realized. Anna sighed, though she did not know why. Helen rarely spoke of Germany, and her thoughts did not seem to linger over that time. It was as if Anna were nostalgic in her behalf.

At the end of her hitch, Helen came home single, cool, and European. She gathered up her paints and drawing supplies, and moved to Chicago, where she rented a small studio and supported herself doing drawings for newspaper ads and department store flyers. Ike was furious. Girls stayed home until they got married, as far as he was concerned, and furthermore, they got married at a reasonable age (younger than twenty-five). Claire was married and living in West Des Moines. On the first anniversary of VJ day, she was pregnant. Not Helen. Ike would grit his teeth and say, "She's just determined to be different, that's all it is."

Anna went to the studio once, an invited guest, offered tea with bread and butter. It was a pleasant place, with cider-colored floors and a bank of south windows. The telephone rang incessantly, and Helen was proud to show papers and materials and tools she had been secretive about while living at home. Her friends were hardly bohemian. The two Anna met were pregnant, in crisp white piqué maternity blouses of the purest Midwestern style. Her bed, Anna noted, was narrow and virginal, and there was no coffee in the kitchen cupboard. Anna thought Helen might clear away any masculine signs in the bathroom, but surely she would forget that her mother knew she hated coffee. Ike was not mollified when Anna told him these things, and so she didn't mention Helen's endless birdsong of plans about going back to Europe to study art, to see the great pieces when they were back in their museums, to immerse herself, simply immerse herself. She would never get married. It wasn't a vow, just a considered opinion, London, Paris, London, Paris. Susanna got married to get out of the house.

Anna yawned, at last, and then yawned again. The warmth of the bright blue gas flames crept around her, and their sound comforted her, a low roar. It was not midnight yet. Her eyes drifted closed with the thought of all the luxurious sleeping hours ahead, deep in her old sunken mattress, covered with quilts she had sewn herself, her nose poked into pillowcases she had cross-stitched. It was remarkable how well you could equip yourself over the years, how many stitches you could take in whatever colors you pleased, how many things were left after you had given any number away. Anna turned off the oven, then shoved her hands into the sleeves of her robe. Now, of course, though unmarried and possessed of the wherewithal for any number of years in Europe, Helen was unhappy. Ike had asked about that adjoining door. "I'm cold!" was what he used to say when she awoke to find him creeping into her bed. "Brr! I can't sleep." "Go back to your own bed," she would snap, pretending her anger was the fruit of sudden awakening. Anna put her hands on her knees, and pushed herself to her feet. The night twenty years ago when she tied the doorknob to her bedpost with a stocking, she heard Ike pull at it, making it rattle, and then curse once in a whisper. They never spoke of it afterward, and he never invaded her nest again.

She left more blankets at the foot of his bed.

In her socks, in her robe, in her bed, Anna admired the mammoth comfort in the way her knee was drawn up just so, the way her toe was pointed. One arm, the underneath arm that so often posed difficulties, fit neatly and warmly around her pillow. The other arm balanced first along her hip, then on the bed in front of her, but at last, perfectly, half across the pillow with her fingertips below her chin. She groaned without meaning to; it wasn't often that she achieved such a posture, achieved the ease that presaged inevitable sleep. She appreciated it, and then she was asleep.

Her first dreams were nothing: fragments of color, an emphatic word here and there, mostly a sense of enveloping darkness, similar to the darkness of bedclothes and curtains at the windows. She dreamed of her body moving and knew that it moved smoothly along the sheet like a snake stretching in the grass, and then she fell more deeply asleep and dreamed that she said very clearly, "Father, today is my birthday," something that she had never said. Her birthday appeared, 11 02 00, a rack of bright numbers, and then other numbers appeared, but they were not the birthdays of anyone she knew, although it seemed to her in the dream that they were birthdays of importance. She dreamed that she had a pleasant gift to open, but that she kept putting it in a sack and then dropping groceries on top of it. Soon she would remember that the bow would get squashed, and she would take the present out and begin to open it, but in a moment she would be putting it back in the sack, and tossing sausage and green peppers in after.

Simultaneously, another self in her dream was saying, "This is like your dream of Helen. You used to dream that you put Helen in a sack and carried her home with your groceries." A third dream voice remarked how interesting it was that these themes were repeated, and suggested that she remember this dream in the morning. Underlying everything was the importance of birthdays, of times, days, months, years. "Ike was born on July 4, 1900," she reminded herself, while knowing all the time that it was wrong. She spoke more loudly, as if insistent, "Father! Today is my birthday. I am—" but her dream voice forgot to finish the sentence and instead exclaimed, "I *am* happy to meet you. My husband works at the works." And then she laughed. It was the sound of her laughter that woke her up without waking her. Her eyes opened, took in the darkness and a pale shape next to the window, but her body seemed dead and her wits scattered, too scattered to close her eyes for her again, and the pale shape would not resolve itself into anything. She was not exactly frightened.

The first thing that she could think of was that Ike's birthday was January 14, 1895, seventy-seven now. His mother would have been a hundred and seventeen. Her own mother was born in 1866. Three miscarriages had preceded baby Anna. And her grandmother, 1837. Her grandmother's brother, James, 1833. Anna shook her head, trying to free it of the numbers, and a picture came instead, a picture of old hands holding little James, in his little cap and his little lace mittens, hands born in 1767. The pale shape became a curtain and she forced herself to think of something else: Christine and Todd and their baby. No, they weren't having a baby. The baby would certainly be alive in 2037, just eligible for Social Security, younger than Anna was now. But they weren't having a baby! Anna shook her head and coughed, but no sound came, only the repeating numbers: 1767, 1867 (Mother was eight or nine then), 1967, 1837, 1937 (Susanna on that swing?), 2037. And the baby would, of course, know someone who would then live until 2067, or perhaps the baby herself would live until then, drawing Social Security, being photographed in her bed, recalling that her great-grandmother, whom she remembered very well, thank you, herself remembered people who were born in 1837, less than a lifetime after the Declaration of Independence. Anna shivered, and her life seemed dwarfed by memory.

With the shiver her body began to revive. She grew sensible of her robe and nightgown twisted about her waist, of one of her slippers half off. It seemed that if she thought another thought, then she would think only of dead people, and even to think why that would be frightening was frightening. She coughed again, and this time managed to make a rather matter-of-fact, dry-throated noise. She dared not make another noise, though: it might be a groan.

"I need new curtains," she articulated clearly in the silence of her mind. "Green and white with a touch of orange would be bright. Or a nice lemon color." But her own voice modulated into that of her mother: "Anna Gertrude, the first thing I made was curtains, though we didn't have glass yet in the windows. White starched curtains with ruffles. The wind would blow through the house, and these curtains would stick out straight like dinner plates. You could see them from the next block. I washed them every week. Put on your gloves, Anna Gertrude." And she would put on her gloves and imagine those white curtains like petticoats in an updraft, and the Wyoming wind blowing through as if there were nothing there. Even the most specific thoughts were dangerous.

She sat up and turned on the light. "Well!" she said to herself busily, like a saleswoman approaching and rubbing her hands in a department store, "Maybe I'll write some letters! I certainly owe something to

Cousin Jean, at least." But her fingers, as she rummaged for a pen on her dressing table, knocked things over that she hadn't meant to touch. "There *was* a pen!" Her voice strove for cheeriness. A pen at last, though red, and lined yellow paper. Jean, who prided herself on her "correspondences" would infer haste and skim the first page for bad news. *Dear Cousin Jean Fountain,* she wrote, adjusting a magazine on her knee.

I should have written sooner, but Daddy got sick in February again, and I have had my hands full. It is his heart mainly, and he does not look very good at all, but I think he is better than he seems, and perhaps as the Spring wears on he will return to his old self. The girls are very helpful—they come in every day and also do much of my shopping. Helen's daughter Christine has just come for a visit, bringing her dog, Nelson, who is an Airedale, I believe. Perhaps you knew that Christine was married two years ago September. Todd Walker is the boy's name, and he is a young lawyer. They live outside of Chicago.

Dead people. Papa was born in eighteen seventy. He would be over a hundred now himself. Anna pulled together the lapels of her robe and looked around the dressing table for a safety pin.

We have heard on the television about your cold winter, and have thought of you so many times. Just the other day, Ike asked if I had replied to your last.

I swear, he keeps better track of my letters than I do myself!

This was not in fact true. Ike had mentioned Cousin Jean, but had forgotten the letter she'd read him after Christmas. He thought Jean still lived in Pittsburgh, when actually she had moved back out to Wyoming to stay with her son and his wife in Laramie five years ago. After Ezra died. Of a heart attack. At only sixty-five. Dead people. Anna turned over the page. Her red pen wanted to dash over the yellow surface, spill something about the number nightmare, about the unknown caller, about Susanna's revelation, about Christine's divorce. She wanted to ask why all bonds seemed as tenuous as dewy threads to her, to ask if Cousin Jean had learned anything more than she had in the last fifty years. But Jean had a tendency toward religion; it was hard to tell what she knew.

We've had only two snowfalls since Christmas this year, though the weather has been plenty wet. Tonight there is quite a fog. Earlier on, I could only just see the house next door. I can't say I've done much in the way of needlework this winter. I had to slipcover Daddy's chair. I've been slowly knitting an afghan for Christine and her husband, but now that won't be—

She broke off and recollected herself.

finished until next winter.

. . .

She read over the sentence. It sounded normal. The evening's events beat about like a flight of starlings in her head. She bit her lip and waded in.

It is a funny thing about getting old . . .

This was a convention. It had nothing to do with her but with the old age of everyone around her. She snorted resentfully.

. . . everything seems smaller. Have you noticed this?

A pious remark rose in her mind, Jean's inevitable response. The truth was, though, that she hadn't seen or talked to Jean in five years, since her trip across country, and so there was no telling what her response would be.

Except me, that is. I don't even get on the scale anymore.

She read this joke over and grimaced. She had not intended to step back so soon from the topic she needed to discuss. But there was no discussing it! She might as easily waken Ike and open these fears and this strange excitement to him, even though she had always told her daughters that the one great marital truth was that those fears which don't repel one's husband insult him. She tried another approach.

. . .

I had a dream about Mama tonight.

But she hadn't dreamed of her mother, or of any one person. There had been no scenes, no fractured dream-drama, no characters of any sort, only numbers, or rather years, spinning by, as dark as her moonless room, terribly distinct and far away. Thinking of her dream brought it back, and she imagined all those ancestors and all those descendants sleeping through nights that flipped by like shuffled cards. She shuddered. It was like dreaming of outer space or of time itself.

I wonder if you remember Mama's forever-white curtains? She was very proud of them. She always hated the West, I think, even though she talked about Basin till the day she died.

Anna sighed and set down her pen. She had made it almost to the bottom of the second page without saying a thing, and yet the letter was a perfect example of everything she had written to Jean, one of her closest friends, certainly her oldest, in the fifty years of their correspondence. She cleared a space on her dressing table and lay down the paper, covering it with a blank sheet. She began to massage her shoulder, reaching under her arm and pressing her fingers into the muscles of her neck. The pain had come over her stealthily, a hard punishment for the small sin of sit-ting too long in one position. This was being old, she thought, kneading the shoulder and pressing her fin-gers into the muscle next to the scapula. Massage never worked—the problem was in the joint—but sensations in the muscles distracted her from the ache in the bones. She wished she could take another bath. One of her earliest memories was of having her bath outdoors under a cottonwood tree with Jeannie Schlatter while Mama and Aunt Eugenie (named for the Empress of France) talked about the family. Mama was a good deal older than Aunt Eugenie, Papa's cousin, and she always adopted an instructive tone with her. Jeannie and Anna were almost the same age, but almost automatically Anna had adopted the same tone with the other child, and almost automatically Jeannie bowed to it. Anna could remember leaning back, naked, in the slippery wooden tub, pointing out and identifying rocks and birds and plants to her cousin, informing her soberly of categories and natural histories that she herself made up. After her fourth birthday, Mama had begun teaching her how to read, so Anna promptly introduced into her lessons small quizzes that Jeannie was at pains to answer correctly.

Anna closed her eyes. By concentrating on the thought of that slippery tub, she could bring to mind the exact toothed line and hyacinth color of the mountains in the morning light, and the flat golden prairie dotted with sage brush that broke against them. In the other direction marched a row of blue-roofed white houses whose backyards lay between her and "downtown" Basin, where Papa had the newspaper. Just when she needed it, Mama would bring over the kettle and pour in more hot water. In that dry air, anything that dripped in the dust evaporated in a second. Mama talked very emphatically, Aunt Eugenie nodded, and the girls soaked in the tub most of the morning. Summer. Anna sighed, opened her eyes, and sighed again. In light of such a common experience, couldn't she tell Cousin Jean what was borne in upon her? Wouldn't one word, or at most a phrase, be sufficient to force a bloom of feelings in her cousin akin to those in herself? But it seemed that the contrary was more true: that shared experience precluded the sharing of experience totally new.

The tub Aunt Eugenie had gotten from Great-Aunt Clarice. Mama had no such inheritance, for she was from Germany; she had come over with two blouses and a pair of white gloves, by herself, at sixteen. The tub, after many washings of sheets and towels and work clothes and children, had the feel of brown velvet. You lolled against the staves, sensing in the flesh of your back the smooth scalloped edges of the rim, taking your hand out and putting it in, watching the edge of the water break your arm, watching the water itself turn from white to blue as a cloud drifted over, finding with turnings of your head the sun in the surface of the water, although forbidden to do so by Mama, who predicted consequent blindness. And all of the time you were talking. Although unable to remember the words, Anna could remember the yeasty pleasure of saying them, the sensual appreciation she had felt for herself as an intelligent being. At that time she had appreciated Mama, too, and had admired the hitch of her accent as she lectured Aunt

Eugenie in the background. And then, "Ach!" Mama would say, "these girls have been in the water for two hours! What are we thinking of? You can get bloated from soaking it up, Eugenia. I knew a woman who lost ten pounds when she stopped taking long baths. Anna Gertrude, don't splash, please!" Anna could see herself stepping out of the tub in the long perspective of the Big Horn mountains, and hear Cousin Jeannie say, "Mama! You got the corner of the towel wet!" Aunt Eugenie died long before Mama, of lupus erythematosis. Dead people. That was what you got when you indulged your memories at her age: advance notices of mortality.

And the telephone rang. Its clatter, though she had turned the dial down to "soft," was shocking in the quiet house, so shocking that she didn't even consider not answering. As it was, she didn't catch it until after the third ring, and she could hear Ike rustling in his bed. She answered with the same annoyance she'd once felt toward people who threatened to wake the baby from one of those longed-for naps.

The voice said, "Who is this?"

"My word!" She hung up.

It rang again. The voice said, "I have your number. Who are you?"

"I've called the police. Don't disturb me again!" Slamming the receiver to its cradle, her hand trembled, more with anger than with fright, although she wondered if the caller had her address as well. She dialed the first three digits of Helen's number, then pressed down the disconnect button, so vivid was her

91

picture of Helen's abandonment to sleep. Oh, sleep! The very idea flooded Anna with the foreboding peculiar to insomnia. The day ahead seemed fearsome in its length and darkly circumscribed, as if seen through a tunnel. Anna lowered herself heavily to the step and leaned her head against the wall. The man would call back. He would come by, large and black, and rattle her windows, break them. Mindful of Christine's disapproval that she still used the word "colored," Anna quickly reimagined the intruder as blond. Had she barricaded the basement door? Why hadn't she called someone to fix that basement lock? But they could get in anyway. They could cut the telephone cord and break the windows. Houses two blocks down had bars on the first floor windows, the leading edge of danger creeping from downtown. Or they could smoke her out—spill gasoline all around the periphery of the house, and then set it afire. How long would it take this old frame house to go up? Long enough for agony? What would they do to her if she got out? Ike was too sick to run. If he called back she could blow a high-pitched whistle into the mouthpiece, or scream right into that intimate ear. How she wanted to hurt this caller, to deafen him. She didn't want the police, the courts, the prisons, she wanted the act of calling itself to scar him for the rest of his life. Many years ago, a man in a public library exposed himself to her. She had been looking through a big picture book of needlework designs, and he walked by, his face impassive, his genitals swinging. Shock had rendered her motionless, but after that, what she had wanted more than anything to have done was to slap that book shut as hard as she could around those red organs. She had never told Ike about the experience, but she had carried the anger of doing nothing and the satisfaction of what she might have done with her for weeks, until they faded in the business of life, only to reappear, fresh as ever, for the first time now. She was breathing hard. That man, too, would be dead. Anna took off her robe and wrapped it securely around the phone.

The house was cold. She could not go to sleep. She was not hungry. She was fearful and full of hatred, so that when Ike suddenly cried out, "Mother! Mother!" she pressed herself closer to the wall, and thought, Go to sleep! I've had enough out of you! Do for yourself for a change! As if in response there were no more cries. She heard him turn over, groan once, and begin to snore. His covers, she knew, would be down around his waist. She made herself think of them there, but she did not go pull them up. She shoved her arms between her knees and hunched her shoulders. She was too cold even to go to bed.

And then she drifted off, because when she stood up at last, she had the distinct sense of waking up, and of the sleeper's compulsion to do what had to be done with the smallest exertion of energy and the least possible arousal before toppling into bed. She scurried through Ike's room, covering him as she went, then, eyes down, slid over to her dresser light, turned it off, and fell toward the bed. It was chilly. So what? Her eyes closed. Her foot thrust out of the covers and jerked in again. She was asleep.

. . .

"Mother! Mother!" The whispering voice detached itself from her dream and she opened her eyes. Ike was standing above her, his bedspread half falling off his shoulders, his eyes wide. He poked her again.

"I'm awake, Daddy. You don't have to whisper." He bent down and peered at her eyes, probably to make sure she wasn't talking in her sleep. When he straightened up, he staggered, but caught himself on the bedstead. "Did something wake you up, Ike? Did the telephone ring?" She thought of the caller, and felt oddly protective of Ike and the caller as well. She didn't want them to speak to one another.

The old man shook his head impatiently. "I feel funny," he said. "I had a nightmare."

Anna closed her lips together, annoyed. "Well, what was it about?"

"Pain. I mean, it was a bad pain. It was gone when I woke up."

She sat up.

"How come you've got your slippers on?"

"I was cold. Do you feel it anywhere now?" She touched his left side, near the armpit. He jerked away.

"Nah. It wasn't that kind of pain."

"What kind?"

"You know. I called you. You didn't hear me. I told you we ought to keep the door open."

"Daddy, it's freezing. Come on, I'll put you back in bed." He leaned heavily on her, more so than usual, and he stopped once, suddenly, as if startled. "What's the matter?"

"Nothing. I thought I stepped on a cat."

"Ike, we haven't had a cat since Underfoot died, remember?" But she led him carefully, all at once a little worried. She spoke brightly. "Remember on the ranch when there were so many mice we thought they were going to carry us away? You got that big tortoise-shell tom from somebody on the baseball team and brought him home in a basket. Remember? He was so mad that we had to take him upstairs and let him out in the bedroom. I closed the door and was only about halfway down the stairs when I heard the first pounce. Remember? He had those mice cleared out in three days. Remember? Ike?"

Ike nodded. She set him gently in his chair and turned to the bed, which was quite disarranged. It was terrible in a way, as if he had been thrashing about in pain. She smoothed the bottom sheet and tucked it in, then flipped the top sheet with a practiced snap of the wrists, the blankets, one by one. She made hospital corners and tucked everything in, then arranged the mound of pillows. Ike hadn't slept flat in two years, almost. She loved a newly made bed in the middle of the night. It so benignly promised a fresh start. "There you go!" She raised her voice. "Your bed's ready. Do you have to, um . . . ?" She waved her hand toward the bathroom.

"Huh?"

"Daddy, are you all right?" She peered closely at his slumping form. "I'm going to turn on the light." Ike sat up carefully, then pushed himself out of the chair. "I'm tired," he enunciated. "Just tired."

95

"Did that pain come back?"

"No!"

"Ike, are you telling me the truth?"

"Just forget it."

"Ike, you came into my room."

"Can't a man come into his own wife's room once in a while?"

"It's the middle of the night."

"I called you. I thought something might be wrong with you." His voice had dropped.

"What?"

"I said I thought something might have happened to you."

"Is that all?"

"Well, Mother, what would I do if something happened to you?" He spoke angrily, some of his old temper coming back at the thought of dependence on her.

"The girls would be happy to take care of you. They're practically running the show now, to ask them, so get into bed and don't worry about it."

"Anna?"

"Get into bed! It's cold!"

"Anna, I never thought of divorcing you, not ever."

Anna set her hands on her hips and regarded her husband. Her eyes were so accustomed to the dark that she could see his face perfectly, and it held a look of fear and sadness that she had never seen before. The idea of divorce reminded her of the times he had hit her, and the times he had strapped the children. With weakness, his impatience had subsided into an old man's crotchets, but once he had beat Claire into a state of absolute silence, a silence that lasted for three days. Helen and Susanna he had knocked across the room, herself he had slapped, pushed, and kicked. He had never broken any bones; no one had gone to the doctor. After Claire's insensibility, he had never again laid a finger on her. But such occasions were numerous. He had been a violent man. She answered lightly, "I wish I could say the same." He smiled weakly, but she knew that she had misspoken herself and she would regret it. She sighed. Ike turned on the bed where he had been sitting and inserted his legs between the smooth sheets.

"Is there anything you want, Ike?" As she spoke, he started again, and turned his head quickly toward the window. "What's the matter, Daddy?"

"I . . . Nothing."

"Are you sure?"

"Dammit, Anna, stop asking me if I'm sure!"

"I'm going back to bed. I've had enough trouble trying to get to sleep tonight!" She spoke belligerently, but did not move. Her worry about Ike could not help spreading, like a little stain in the corner of a linen napkin. His behavior was not so much symptomatic as it was strange, as if illness might somehow have affected his attitude instead of his body. "Let me cover you up."

"I'm going to read."

"You can still read."

"I can't read!"

"You'll get cold!"

"You women want to take everything away from me! I can cover myself up! Next you'll have some god-damned nurse in here, turning me over like a veal cutlet and spilling soup on my chin! I tell you, I can read, and turn the pages, and hold the book all at the same time, plus I can decide when I'm cold and pull up my covers if I need them." He shivered, but remained adamantly still, refusing to touch the covers until she was gone.

"Good night, then."

"Good night!"

She stepped out of the room, then peeped around the doorway. He was scooting down under the covers and shaking his shoulders to arrange them across his chest. "Well, go to bed then," he cried, without looking in her direction. She smiled. The worry shrank to its normal size. He was obviously feeling good enough for healthy impatience.

In her own room, though, on the other side of the wall, she sat quietly on her bed, listening, staring at the bar of light beneath their adjoining door. The violence had slid away without a trace, hadn't it? When she threw the coffee pot across the room, plastering the wall with coffee grounds, when she flourished the sizzling frying pan, dumping chicken on the floor, hadn't these extravagant gestures punctured their anger and whirled it away? Now she rarely remembered that time, thinking of it as a phase, as part of the Depression, as a holdover from Ike's years with Abel. The blows had vanished as their anger had vanished, hadn't they? Hadn't it? Christine wanted a divorce.

Helen, Susanna, and Claire seemed at times desperately unhappy. The door between their rooms was tied with a stocking to her bedpost. She did not want a nurse to hear him, to help her with him. Anna sighed. She could not follow all the threads through the tangle, she simply could not.

And besides, it was he who didn't want the nurse. Here was the answer for Helen, Claire, and Susanna: "Your father won't stand for it." It would take them a couple of months at least to work up opposition, and so she had a reprieve, the reprieve she wholeheartedly wanted. The house around her seemed dark and desolate and empty. The red-cheeked Danish nurse she didn't even know she had imagined, quick-fingered and redolent of anise, receded. A woman who would hand her apples and sit her by a fire and read her Victorian fairy tales. Anna had been grown up for a strangely long time, longer, perhaps, than she would have chosen had she known everything then that she knew now.

Mama had not been kindly or Danish, and she had read Anna Struwelpeter's cautionary tales, but she had smelled of anise and cardamom seed and cloves, especially at Christmas time, and she had dried Anna after herbal baths in front of the fire on a big red rag rug that still seemed to Anna the perfect symbol of hospitality—more Christmassy than the tree or the candles or the Buche de Noël Mama learned to bake from Adele Miller, who came from France. In the winter, before bed, she gave Anna a mug of tea, spiced with cinnamon and dried lemon peel, sweetened with honey, and sporting a sprig of crystallized, summery mint. This was Anna's drink. Mama made it for her alone and brought it to her on a little tray with a napkin, even though for the rest of the day, the rule was that she should do things for herself. And where was her father? Anna did not remember, and did not remember wanting to know.

The bar of light had gone. Anna got to her feet with a loud creaking of the bedsprings and sneaked around to Ike's doorway. Without disturbing the book (he would remember she had left it on the bed and accuse her of babying him), she pulled up the blanket and then felt his head. It was very cool. She reached for his wrist, but he pulled his hand away from her and shoved it under the covers between his knees. He was breathing calmly, though, with just the ruffle of a snore every so often.

With her Buche de Noël and her long candles brought from Denver and her white gloves and white curtains in the middle of the sagebrush, Mama had been so like Helen, with her Croquembouche and her English antiques and her silk underwear and her Italian wallpapers. And her running away. It was as if Mama had skipped a generation and reappeared, softened by beauty. In that studio after the war, there had been no mess and no making do. In one of her two silk blouses and one of her two woolen skirts, Helen had served Anna tea in one of her three Meissen teacups. Anna had sat in Helen's single chair—pecan, pressed back, neatly canned—and Helen had sat on her painting stool. Hanging on a hanger behind the easel had been Helen's smock, which she wore over one of her two cotton shirts and her single pair of twill slacks. She washed everything by hand. Anna, whose own house testified only to what sort of project she'd like to try next, marveled that such care and taste could have grown up before her very eyes, without encouragement and without practice. It was conceivable only in terms of an inherited drive.

"Oh, my!" Anna yawned tears into her eyes. Funny how that drive had flowered so completely into a house full of belongings valuable enough that the police had to be contacted if Helen left for the night; strange that Helen was more careful than anyone about locking doors and installing grates and burglar alarms; that she spoke so knowledgeably about every mechanism whose purpose was to keep her, the ultimate runaway, inside, at home, secure.

It was also strange that after turning up her nose at meals not taken in restaurants (she had once told Anna admiringly of a friend of Alfred's, who ate out with his wife every night—their townhouse contained a coffeemaker as its sole cooking utensil), she had blossomed into a cook much like Mama—painstaking and almost pretentious, who served the freshest vegetables and fish, the silkiest sauces, the plumpest poultry, even to herself, when she was eating, "dining," alone. Her desire to paint great paintings had ended in a desire to create in every particular the fantasy life of luxury that she had missed by Alfred's premature death, and to present herself with it daily, her own servant to her own brilliant self. Anna shook herself, trying to shake away her thirty-year-old habitual resentment of Helen's breezy and total rejection of Anna's taste in furniture, ideas of color, notions of arrangement. More than once Anna had thought that any cruelty, any abandonment, would be more easily forgiven than this unspoken slight of her womanly eye. Still, thinking of Helen's house was like thinking of an opulent toybox. While the many-windowed brick had never been professionally decorated, it had also never become a cluttered monument to changing tastes and expectations. The idea of a Parisian mural above the sofa or wrought-iron wall sconces beside the door had never appealed to Helen. Her house looked Oriental and European, tasteful and light, expensive but not imposing. Anna fixed her mind on its happy glitter in hopes of inducing sleep.

"Come here!" said Helen to the doorway. She was wearing a dress that matched the printed wallpaper— white figures dizzying against a navy background, and she had to stand in front of the window in order to be visible. "Come here," she said again, this time more softly, more coaxingly. Christine came toward her from the right in the same print, with the same wide-frilled collar and the same covered buttons. Anna was about to say that the idea didn't work somehow when the door, also covered with wallpaper, swung inward, and Sam stepped through, naked and netted with fine cracks, like an old painting. He was carrying his briefcase. To greet him, Helen had to traverse a long wall with many windows, and with each step she disappeared and reappeared, except that when she had disappeared into the wallpaper her face and hands were still white and visible, and when she reappeared in the frame of a window her face and hands were black in the bright light. The dirndl skirt of her mother-daughter dress swung like a bell as she walked. Sam smiled, and the closer you got to him the more cracks appeared, ramifying over the lines of his face and contours of his body. Anna was so happy to see him! She held out her arms as if she herself were Helen or Christine, and when he moved toward her or away, the air between them contracted and expanded, as if he were a suction cup. "I'm fine," was what he said, "I'm fine!" Anna was about to speak when Christine pulled the iron off the ironing board, and then what had happened could not be seen. A chair was in the way, the ironing board itself, nothing really, she simply could not see, and there was no sound, no indication whether the iron had sailed point first into Christine's little head.

There was a great deal of light, and Anna could barely open her eyes. She had Christine by the hand, and in the other hand she carried a chicken, her forefinger between its legs and her hand closed over its bony feet. They were walking down a slope, toward a picnic, and both Christine and the chicken struggled in her grasp. She wanted very much to open her eyes, but she could not because of the light, which spread insistently under her lids anyway. She was barefoot, and the soles of her feet were as sensitive as fingertips. She marveled, even as she snapped at Christine and cursed the chicken, that her insteps could make out clover and violets and wild strawberries, that her toes acknowledged vetch and chicory and purslane. She took a deep breath.

She did not open her eyes, but she felt the little bump of wakefulness. Her mind stretched to retain the pressure of Christine's toddler fingers on her palm and the fragrance of the wild plants all around her. The dream melted into a memory of Ike and Sam pitching Christine back and forth across the living room, or so it had seemed, though perhaps three feet separated them. The child left one pair of hands half a second before the other pair grabbed her, but it was enough. Her mouth was open, her arms spread, her body rigid with delight. After two or three tosses she began to squeal, and Ike and Sam, too, were laughing. Helen stood apart, but leaned toward them, a smile fixed on her face, her hands vigilant at her sides, but they never dropped Christine, never so much as let her slip. Everyone thought that he or she loved Christine the most.

Her cheeks were so fat that when she slept, a tiny prone infant, her head turned to one side, you could see both cheeks as you looked down adoringly, and the bee-stung lips sandwiched between. When she held her head up, then sat up, and stood up, those cheeks seemed to ride on her little neck by a special dispensation, and her smile, all horizontal, surprised and ambushed you every familiar time. Anna had been happy with Sam who, having lived in London, Hong Kong, Lahore, Florence, New York, and Washington, could think of nothing he wanted more than to settle down in Des Moines and regale himself with family dinners, baseball games on the radio with Ike, large cookies at Anna's kitchen table, and long filial talks that he had never known with his own parents, who worked for the State Department and were always shipping him out of sensitive parts of the world.

In Helen's manner, now that she had made up her mind to accept Sam, was not a settling down but a gearing up. They bought a house so that they would have something to show for it when they moved away. They invested in a few nice pieces of furniture, things that would look fine anywhere in the world, and wouldn't be too hard to ship. She read the fashion magazines and collected silks and linens and woolens that would look good after years in New York or London, or wherever. She professed no interest in the local schools, wondered aloud about nannies in far-off places, talked continually about the garage sale they simply had to have. Most important, she smiled upon Sam's infatuation with "Americana," as she called it, with the indulgence not only of love but of pure self-confidence.

And a great compensation was Christine, who need not have put her feet on the ground until school, so readily was she passed from hand to hand. Helen was much avider for Christine than Anna had thought she would be. In her vaguely European tones and the girdle and stockings she put on just to walk two blocks, Helen chattered endlessly about Christine's idiosyncrasies and accomplishments. Claire, who had miscarried once and had not been able to get pregnant again, was furious, but Sam was enchanted. The mere existence of Helen convinced him that he could have everything that was stylish and everything that was homely right here on East Walnut Street. It was a bustling, peaceful time, the turn of the forties into the fifties, when the family was full of men. Babies, it seemed, could be counted on. Every romper and toy that Christine outgrew Anna put carefully away in a box labeled: "Six mos." or "Rattles etc." and stored in her attic. Only the sturdiest items were purchased; who could say how many kids there would be? Claire, for instance, might be having trouble, but surely there would someday be three or four.

And Helen had a different kind of marriage from Anna's, one she seemed to have made with her own two hands, a ship she would soon ready for launching. It seemed rooted in their house, where she and Sam spoke always in pleasant voices, whence, it seemed, she and Sam always issued forth together. Sam had his cocktails at home, with his wife, and never even once came bowling in drunk and violent, as Ike had done so often. Even Papa, who abstained, spent most of Anna's childhood away from the house. With the Men's Choir, and the Basin Improvement Society, and the Professional Men's Social Club, plus everything he had to do for the paper, Papa put his coat and hat on every night. Mama would have worried about his standing in the community had he failed to do so. Helen and Sam went out together, alone or with another couple or two. She seemed to be practicing for when their destinations would be Carnegie Hall or Maxim's. And each time she paraded her clothes and jewelry in front of Christine, wanting Christine to be proud that her mother was slender and glamorous, wanting to instill, by example, taste and a sense of wonder at the mystery of the adult world.

Sam drank a lot, perhaps more in a week than Ike had, but it didn't fall into him and explode as it had with Ike, so after the fatal car wreck, when they tested his blood for alcohol content, it was a great shock, almost an insult, that they referred to him as intoxicated. Christine was three, and though Claire was pregnant for the second time, soon to bear twins, Anna could not get over the notion that the charm was broken, that for each man and each baby there would be a hard fight, that the family would never again be in the midst of busy, bubbling fertility. Instead of cruising on Helen's great ship of the future, they had scrambled: the twins were small, and Jimmy almost died. Claire herself was very sick, and the obstetrician discouraged more pregnancies. And then Hanson divorced Susanna, and Helen met Alfred—older, already successful and disillusioned, the father of three teen-aged children by his first wife—Christine was enough for him. Helen and Christine did then move away, first to Chicago, then to New York. And they lived in Paris for a year. But Helen's confidence had been devastated by Sam's death. She saw every yearned-for prospect with the eyes of worry and of cynicism reflected off Alfred. The schools were terrible, the baby-sitters suspect, Christine reacted badly to the food.

At home, the toys and clothes so carefully chosen and put away slipped everyone's mind, and never came out for the twins, until at six they raided the attic, broke into the boxes, and spread everything far and wide. How to control them became a bit of a sore point between Claire and her parents.

Anna's memories were very still, and when she heard a sound—a groan and the creaking of bedsprings from the adjoining room—she realized that she had been holding herself completely motionless, so given over was she to visions of Helen and Sam. She got up. "Ike?" From the doorway, the lightest part of the room, Anna could see nothing, so she went to the window and pulled back the curtain. She had forgotten the fog, pale but without light. She shivered and drew the curtain again, half expecting Ike to speak to her, but when she could see him, she saw that he was still sleeping. The covers had fallen down, and his pajamas had come unbuttoned. As she touched a button, he frightened her with another groan, and his eyes opened white in the darkness. Her hand flew away. "Ike?" Still he hadn't seen her.

Once, in school, on a sledding trip, some of her friends had run into an empty house ahead of her, and when she came to the black doorway, she had been unable to enter, so thoroughly did the noises she heard them making seem transformed by the strange place into the creakings and bangings of ghosts. She had grown afraid even of their reappearance, so that, though she was straining her eyes after them, the sight of their faces had shocked her heart into pounding so hard that her body trembled. She felt on the verge of such fear now, afraid of touching Ike, yet wanting to grab him, afraid of his eyes opening again, yet wanting to yank him safely into wakefulness. The book he had been reading so long ago teetered on the edge of the bed. Ever so carefully, muffling even the rustling of her clothes and the cracking of her bones, Anna leaned over and touched it. It retained its purchase. She touched it again, hoping to precipitate it to the floor with a sharp smack. It slid on the bedspread, balanced on its end, then tipped over onto the rug with hardly a sound. Her annoyance pushed back the fear so that she could breathe "Ike?" once again, and then the sound of her own voice enabled her to stand upright, put her hands on her hips, and pretend that he was merely inconveniencing her. In a moment, she was briskly buttoning and smoothing and patting, arranging his clothes and the bedclothes as well as she could around him, jostling against him half on purpose so that he would snap at her for waking him up. And he did wake up, but the process was so slow, his disorientation so complete, that she failed in her busyness again, and caught herself watching, sensing in her sudden self-consciousness that her brows and lips were screwed into concern. "Daddy!" she barked. "What's the matter? Wake up! You're okay, aren't you?"

"Ahhn-nnah?" He spoke as if he couldn't move his mouth, and tossed his head from side to side.

Gripped by anger and fear, for he was so odd-looking, so weak and unlike himself, she con-

109

tinued to order him to sit up, to tell her what was wrong with him, to become healthy. Hearing her own harsh tone, she thought, Oh God, oh my God.

He took a deep breath, which she instantly echoed. "Mother?" He spoke in his usual voice, a trifle subdued.

"Daddy, you've been . . . talking in your sleep. You woke me right up. What were you dreaming about? You see, I heard you fine. Now sit up, and let me button your collar right and straighten your sheet. You keep kicking the covers off, and lord knows, it's plenty cold tonight. It must be the damp from the fog. just seems to get in everywhere. How's that? Now, look, even the sleeve is all twisted. Would you like some aspirin? There, now. How about a little glass of water, anyway? Daddy?"

He coughed and drew his lips in over his dentureless gums, then reached both hands to the top of his head and patted down his hair. Still his motions were so slow that Anna bit her lip. "You know who I've been thinking of tonight? I can't sleep a wink." She hastily thought over everyone they had known. "Remember Jane Pownall? I suddenly just thought of that blue dress she made, with the pink squares on it and the giant bow in the front. Remember how she wore it to that grange dance we went to, and it was cut so low in the back that you could see goose bumps? Remember, Ike? I do think she was sweet on you."

"Who, Mother?" His tone was annoyed.

Anna sighed and smiled slightly. "Miss Jane Pownall! Jane Marie it was."

He grunted.

"Daddy, I'm going to turn on the light. And remember Ida Franks? She just couldn't stand me after I moved to Sheridan. Now shade your eyes. I do believe she had her eye on you all along. She married that boy from Green River who looked just like you from the back." Oh, the spectacle of him, covering his bony eye sockets with his livid hands, his shoulders still flat and broad like a shelf, but his upper arms so thin that it seemed you could see the hinge of the shoulder joint open and close like a drop-leaf table. He brought his hands down from his face and put them in his lap. Electric light in the middle of the night gave his lips and cheeks an odd clayey color, and brought out the liver spots on his forehead. Though she knew it must be the light, she was taken aback. She pressed her mouth to keep talking, as she pressed her hands to keep picking things up and putting them straight. "Oh, and I haven't thought of Bertha Carswell in years!" The name sprung straight from nowhere. Anna had never spoken it, and no one had ever teased with it. Bertha Carswell had been younger than Anna by twelve years, the daughter of a neighbor when they first moved to Des Moines, a student at Drake. She had fallen in love with Ike, but only Ike knew what happened then, and why her name disappeared. Not even Claire and Helen, who surely remembered her, ever reminisced about whom she had married or what she had done after the war. She taught them all—Ike, Helen, Claire, and Susanna—to play tennis. Anna, beginning to get heavy and to feel middle-aged, refused to learn.

111

She sat down on the bed next to Ike, whose response to Bertha's name was invisible but absolutely certain, and said, "I thought Bertha was a very nice girl, you know. Smart, pretty, and athletic, too. She didn't make a fool of herself like all those others that were crazy about you." And a knife stood up in the back of her throat, just for a second, the same knife that stood there nearly forty years before, and she almost felt young again.

Ike groaned.

"Well, maybe I shouldn't have mentioned those women. But I haven't slept a wink, and they just came to me. It was funny."

Ike waved his hand, dismissing all the women, even Bertha Carswell.

"Are you okay, Daddy?"

There was no response, no angry denial. Anna bit her lip, wishing she had never heard the groans, never gotten out of her own bed, never turned on the light. Especially never turned on the light that made everything about their whole lives seem worse than it could possibly be. "I'm going to get you some of that stuff we got from the doctor. It'll make you feel better."

Ike nodded a centimeter. His eyes were closed.

The medicine was just in the bathroom, but Anna wanted a clean glass and water from the kitchen. She set the house ablaze with light: the bathroom, the hallway, her room, even the guest room, the living room, the dining room, and of course, the kitchen. And she did not shut them off behind her. Without letting herself know what she wanted, she turned up the

112

heat. Then she gave Ike his medicine with more equanimity, briskly, with confidence, as if it were aspirin and he had a cold. "Feel better?" she demanded, before it even had time to take effect, and when he nodded and muttered, "Mmmhm," she felt vindicated, triumphant, annoyed that she still hadn't gotten any sleep, and god knew what time it was.

He said, "Mother?"

"Yes, what?"

"Funny, Bertha looked so much like Helen."

"Well, Ike—" Bertha hadn't looked a thing like Helen that Anna could remember. Bertha was just a blond girl. Helen at eleven looked sleek, like water was running off her somehow.

"You don't remember. Do you think Helen loves me?"

"Of course, Daddy."

"Don't palm me off, Anna! You always palm me off with some—"

"You should see them downstairs! All they talk about is you!"

"She never wanted to be at home, remember? And it wasn't boys, either. Even when she was little. You'd bring a toy home to her from town, and she'd meet you at the front door, and you'd give her the toy, and always, even while she was squealing and grinning, she'd be looking over your shoulder, out the door."

"Helen's just like that, Daddy."

"No, I think—"

"Ike, she—"

"Don't interrupt me, dammit!"

113

"I'm sorry."

"When Claire came, it was all different when Claire came. Maybe she didn't think it was her home after that. You don't know what kids are thinking at that age."

"Remember Mama, Ike? She was the same way. It's the pioneer spirit or something. Mama always used to say that."

"You never thought that if she loved us—Helen, I mean—she would have wanted to stay home?"

"I never even thought about it, Ike."

"She was so pretty. I never saw anybody who was so pretty."

There was no possible reply. Anna shifted her position and pursed her lips. Ike closed his eyes, as if the effort of speaking had exhausted him. Finally, Anna said, "How's that medicine working?" He waved his hand.

"I'm going to bed then." But something held her in the room, possibly concern, though possibly simple curiosity. The stark change in his appearance seemed to be a moving thing, like a snake slipping its skin, which she might witness if she watched. She watched. Although he twitched under her gaze, his usual challenge was not made; his lifelong annoyance at being the object of any observation that was not admiring had vanished. He wanted her to stay. She did, pushing aside the pile of clothes in his armchair and settling down there. In order not to make him uneasy, she directed her gaze to various parts of the room, but she didn't really see anything until she realized with a start that the place had gotten very dingy.

The wallpaper, once a rose and dove gray stripe, had darkened to charcoal and maroon. The arms of the stuffed chair had frayed and the door of the closet bulged ajar with coats and bathrobes and outmoded dresses. The little rug she had braided needed washing, and interspersed with his books were letters and papers and old bills. She could not help thinking of the refurbished bathroom, the neat downstairs. She had pushed the television back to the wall, recovered his chair in flowers, rearranged the record player and the objects on the coffee table. She had removed his old cigarette box to the mantelpiece, out of the way. The changes recurred to her vividly, as if lit by accusing rays of light. She remembered how she came down the stairs first thing each morning, the way she glanced around the room with a smile and even, sometimes, spread her hands a little, as if embracing her domain. Surely she hadn't shouldered him into this little room? It was he who had gotten sick, he who preferred his sickness to be private. She remembered her sense of spreading out, like a person suddenly alone in a big bed, and cringed. Her pleasure, in retrospect, seemed too ready, too greedy. The rest of the house was light, neat, colorful. Only in this room did the overhead light have a parchment shade, hastily painted with a few dots of violets.

"Ike . . ." Of course, you could set against this her constant attendance; for example, the cup of cocoa she had made earlier in the evening (grudgingly), the trays and drinks and newspapers and magazines, the

115

endless trips up and down the stairs (complaining more often than not), the night wakings (resentful). She thought again of that sunny moment when she stepped off the last riser, when the living room blossomed in her eye, her little knickknacks and projects set out, neat and sparkling like round dew drops. Of course, Ike's things had been everywhere for years, golf clubs on the couch, tennis racket on the kitchen table, hats, sweaters, dirty socks on the steps, on the dining room table, on the floor of her room, but that was ages in the past.

"Oh, Daddy, I—"

"Anna, dammit, this mattress is slipping again. The whole damned foot is cockeyed!" His voice was weak, but he managed a snort as eloquently put upon as ever.

He was settled again, in clean pajamas in a straight bed, covers off the floor, the light off. Anna perched on the edge of the armchair, not quite certain about going back to bed. Actually, she was hungry. She tried to imagine, without really wanting to, eating something delicious. In fact, she could not not imagine it. The lighted house outside this room promised a quiet, orderly pleasure that further attempts at sleep denied. Ike was at rest. His breathing, while not robust, was smooth and even. Still she perched. His breathing calmed her, distanced the fears she had just felt, that in retrospect seemed disconcerting, like coughing and hiccuping at the same time. The thought of going into the kitchen pleased her. She could imagine the refrigerator and cabinets, arrayed neatly, modestly, like a bank vault. She could make something with onions, which Ike hated, or with lemons, which he maintained he couldn't eat.

She could get out a cookbook and try something new, always a risky business with Ike to think of. He liked beef and potatoes, chicken once in a while, the infrequent pork chop, and plenty of pie, as well as ice cream (but not sherbet), saltines, and milk with white bread torn up in it. He did not like different types of food mushed together and masked with a gravy, and he could detect the merest fragment of garlic in any dish. Her gorge had risen (she did not know what a gorge was, but did know that sense of the heart and lungs beating up into the windpipe and catching) an insane number of times in the past fifty years, whenever she had said, "We're having a big salad," or "I thought I'd try a souffle just this once," and his response had been a curse or an argument. He saw dinner as the food he had a right to enjoy after a hard day at work. She saw it as a theater of activity. She had persisted ridiculously, it seemed looking back, but every single time, from the first curse to the last, she had caught her breath in anger, thinking he was going to doom her to a life of meat loaf. Now, with him safely medicated and asleep, she could mix up anything and eat it by herself. Since his illness she had stocked the house with ingredients. In the dark she crossed her arms over her chest and smiled, thinking of the household magazines, with their recipes, in abundant splendor on the coffee table in the living room.

117

But then it came over her again. Possibly it was the thought of the coffee table given over solely to her activities. At any rate, her insides dropped together in a feeling much like fear, and she saw herself loading the kitchen shelves, leafing through cookbooks, and passing Ike off with oatmeal and bananas and vanilla ice cream. She imagined, or remembered, her own hands, competent and fatly satisfied, measuring and leveling off, stirring, pouring. They had characteristic little motions when they chopped—short synchronized scoopings and graspings that she could see perfectly, and the image shocked her with its horrible eaten-up complacency. Only hands; where was the thought in cooking? Where were the ears to hear Ike's shouts, the eyes to see what he needed? How had she made the whole garishly lit house her own, and relegated Ike to this black cubicle? Already?

"Mother?"

"Huh? Ike? I thought you were asleep."

"Unhuh."

"Daddy, I've been sitting here thinking, and I think we should move—"

He did not even seem to hear her. "What was her name?"

"Whose?"

"That woman who came over all the time.

"Margaret Lacina?"

"Who's that?"

"Listen, Daddy, I've been thinking about your room, and—"

"That other woman."

"I don't know who you're talking about."

"You do! Mother!" His voice rose angrily, like a fist being lifted.

"Ike, explain to me. Where were we living?"

"In that town!" He cursed in a weak but vehement undertone. She saw that he couldn't remember even simple things, things that he had remembered a day or so before. She made her voice as soothing as possible. "Sheridan, Daddy? You mean Sheridan?"

He shook his head.

"Ankeny? Hiawatha?" They had lived outside Cedar Rapids for not more than eight months.

"Yeah! That woman. You know! She came every day. She had brown hair, and kind of a funny name. You know. Goddammit!"

Anna knew. Elinor Onley. She felt her scalp grow warm at the roots of her hair. "I know who you're talking about. What about her?"

"Well, what was her name?"

"I don't remember."

"Noley, it was, something like that."

"Daddy, it doesn't matter."

"You say you were thinking about all those women, Bertha Carswell and those, well, I was thinking, too. Just kind of to remember the names."

"Onley. Elinor Onley." She said it because she hated to imagine him shuffling through the names, testing his memory and finding evidence of age, or worse, but she hated, too, to say it.

Childless, her hair knotted around a knitting needle on top of her head, always trousered, Elinor had swept

119

into Anna's new house on the day they moved in, and disconnected her. Right out from under the noses of Ike and Dolores, Helen and Claire and Susanna, Elinor Onley had prodded Anna through the door, chattering all the while, and taken her over to her place, where she lived in virginal socialist splendor with her brother. "At last!" she sang, "Somebody with a frontal lobe! Don't contradict. I've been waiting for someone like you forever."

Her certainty that Anna was her predestined bosom companion was compelling, and her ordered, book-lined house was alluring. She worked in an electronics factory, was a graduate of Wellesley, prickled the side of the League of Women Voters, idolized Eleanor Roosevelt. She was the only person who had ever shamed Ike for mocking Mrs. Roosevelt's looks. She referred to the path they pounded between their back doors as her "umbilical cord." She never stopped talking, and Anna went from being perplexed to being fascinated to being enamored. Mama had instructed her, Dolores had complained and gossiped to her, sometimes Ike had ordered her around, and the children had asked her questions, but no one had ever talked with her as Elinor did, explaining and doubting and seeking her approval all at the same time. Ike wouldn't have liked her except that she made an effort to charm him. Anna and Helen and Claire and Susanna spent entire winter evenings in Elinor's kitchen, where she had a fireplace and kept toys and books for the girls.

Then, Anna was not sure what happened. Elinor's

ardor cooled. Anna remembered saying something like, "I do think Ike's right about that, though" (about what, she could not now recall), and seeing Elinor's eyelids flicker with annoyance. Could that really have been it? Anna had expressed agreement with Ike's admittedly rather Republican ideas before. At any rate, for some unknown reason the welcome had ended, Elinor had grown extremely distant, and before Anna could circle in again and find out what might be salvaged of their intimacy, Ike had taken a job in Ankeny, and they had moved away. It was the only time Anna had ever been plucked out of her family by such a friendship, and its uniqueness made the sudden end to it uniquely mysterious and shaming. The only person she could have mentioned the pain to was Elinor, and so she had never mentioned it. It seemed odd that to Ike she was only a name in a naming exercise, along with Constance Logan and Frank Hunt and Hack Maloney, representing no more than a button in a box of buttons.

Ike rasped out a chuckle. "There was a crazy one!" His breath caught, and then he chuckled again. "She had that brother of hers scrubbed down to a shadow, all right! 'Hoe between the rows, Dickie, and watch out for those shoots. How glorious to dine on our own baby peas!' "

"Richard was a quiet man, Ike."

"How could anyone tell? He probably didn't know, himself."

"Daddy, I—"

"And she looked like a piece of beef jerky."

"Don't talk about her!"

"Well, she—"

Anna jumped up. "I said don't talk about her! Just don't! Just don't!"

"That was nineteen thirty—"

"So what! Go back to sleep! I haven't slept all night! When do you think I'll have time for a nap tomorrow? You think I can clean house all day, and cook meals, and run up and down the stairs, and argue all the time with the girls, not to mention listen to them day in day out, remember so and so, wasn't it this and that, no you're wrong, Mother you should blah blah, and then stay up all night like I was eighteen years old? I'm seventy-two! My legs hurt and my shoulder and everything else just about! And then I've got to sit here and listen to you make fun of the only friend I ever had? I'm sick and tired—"

"She didn't bid you a fond adieu when we moved to Ankeny! She didn't even cross her yard to say goodbye!"

"You remember plenty when it suits you, don't you? Go to sleep. I'm going to bed." Ike had shrunk into his pillow in the face of her wrath. He probably didn't know why she was so mad. She didn't either, but glorying in the power, she turned and thumped out of the room. In a moment she hit the hall switch with a decisive click, and plunged him into darkness.

Anna stood at the back door, dressed. The churning set up by this name Ike had retrieved made her breathless. There had been an endlessness to her conversations with Elinor that she had adored, more safety in Elinor's firelit kitchen than she had ever felt in her own. And Elinor pried. There was nothing so flattering as having your life pried into by someone whose own life fascinated you in turn. Certainly the worst thing about being old was that she would never know. In books and on TV there was always a letter or a dying explanation, but in her experience, motives were never explained. Few people could even remember what they'd been thinking then, and if you tried to remind them or prod them or tell them what you had thought, distance gaped wider, and even rudimentary cooperation came to seem a miracle. There were little burrs she had turned over for her entire life—slights she had been unable to forget, rudenesses unresolved, hurtful remarks that no one remembered uttering, but that had worked their way into her like shards of glass. Mama was like that before she died, brimming with the insults of a lifetime. Even Mama, who had embraced America alone, sixteen years old, in a pair of white gloves. Anna sighed. They were always left. No matter how much of the brain got washed away, little granite pinnacles of what people had said, how they had crossed the street or not come to the phone, stood glinting in the sunlight.

Oddly, Ike didn't figure in these recollections. Thoughts that brought her needlelike breathless pain were always of someone who had vanished twenty or thirty years before; things Ike had said or done that hurt shockingly at the time, that she had sworn never to forget, always to take into account, had been for-

123

gotten, had failed to figure in the account, did not affect anymore the mixture of exasperation and custom that was their marriage. (Did they?) That Helen had once laughed at a picture she bought and was proud of, and that Claire had accused her of always giving the twins Cokes when they were supposed to have juice rankled more often. Anna turned the lock and pushed open the heavy back door. The fog, perhaps, had diminished, perhaps had not been so thick after all. In any event, she could make out the garden, and it seemed open, fresh, alluring, free of indoor memories, maybe free of all memories except those of corn and beans and kale and chard, hoeing and watering and harvesting, life's most innocent work.

She was not as fanatical about a clean garden as Ike was, and in the past few years she had persuaded him to leave the old stalks, roots, and leaves on the ground over the winter. She liked to see them rot, turn black and soft, replenish the soil. And she liked to see in them the ghost of last year's plantings. Something had gotten the peppers and, to a degree, the tomatoes. The leaves turned yellow and the fruits were small. They'd had glorious squash, though. Hot-dog sized zucchinis became torpedoes in a day, crooknecks inflated like balloons, there'd been pumpkins for every kid on the block, rolling in the dying garden like basketballs, more exciting in their exuberant way than carrots or corn. Potatoes were her favorites, but they'd stopped growing potatoes after Ike's first heart attack. Potatoes were good every minute of the summer—easy to plant, quick to sprout, green and sparkling with white flowers, ready to eat as new potatoes, then heavy and moist like huge rubies when you dug them up in the fall. She also loved peppers in a good year, when they clustered eight or ten to a plant, and you could sit in the garden and eat them from your hand while the shade from the house made even August cool. There was broccoli, too, and cabbage. The solidity of cabbage always amazed her, its crisp resistance to the knife and then its cranial involutions as the two halves fell apart with a thump. And peas were good, and pole beans, too. And marigolds around the border, and muddy baseball-solid onions. Anna dug the toes of her shoes into the soil, wondering if she dared to plant a little early this year. It had been such a mild winter, and she had no feeling of blizzards lying in ambush. She bent down. You could almost work the soil already. She pulled up a couple of old zucchini stalks. Maybe they could do something with the raspberry patch this year, too. It had become so brambly and overgrown that she didn't let the neighborhood children go back there anymore. God knew if there were any berries at all. Ike was a fruit person. For dozens of Junes he'd eaten nothing for breakfast except a bowl of strawberries, gritty sweet with granulated sugar. He always wanted to plant another dwarf something or a new variety of berry. Anna, though, saved her greatest fondness for simple green vegetables, flavors as daily as air and water.

The shovel and hoe would be in the garage. In the predawn darkness it would be a pleasant blind work to dig a little and plan a little, corn where the peas and

125

beans had been, tomatoes across the garden from last year, garlic and onions bordering everything. She shivered, having forgotten how chilly it was, even that it was chilly. When she lifted her eyes above the earth, she saw that the fog still settled in, and she could see nothing of the house except the light in the kitchen window. Upstairs, her room and Ike's faced the street.

She'd not gardened before Iowa, had in fact disdained Mama's turnips and cauliflowers in favor of Papa's mushrooms. Every summer, in the mountains above Kane where they had a small cabin, Papa would promise her fields of mushrooms, and for a few summers, anyway, there were none to be found. Papa was a city boy. There were terrific wildflowers, though: Indian paintbrush, wild iris, acres of poisonous cerulean lupine, buttercups and alpine daisies. There were meadows higher and more cleanly washed with air than she could have imagined had she not seen them, and there were the peaks, named by her four-year-old self, "Goose" (for the fire scar that curved like the neck of a Canada goose) and "Sun" for the way the ball of the sun in June teetered on the summit just before bouncing into the blue sky and bathing the cabin in light. Papa knew the names of flowers and trees and lichens and birds, but produced no mushrooms until the summer of Anna's ninth year, when they came to a meadow near Teardrop Lake (as they called it), and had to find refuge from a sudden storm. Papa pulled her under a big overhanging rock and rubbed her hands between his to keep them warm. When the rain had blown across the mountain and the sun was throwing their shadows along the face of a big cliff, they finished up their sandwiches and stepped into the open. Bubbled out of the meadow grass by the hundreds were the pearly crowns of baby mushrooms. The thrust of peaks all around held them tilted, as in a hand, toward the sun.

After that, they were mushroom psychic, and until going off with Ike, Anna had felt as if to wish for mushrooms was to have them. Later, Ike hadn't liked mushrooms, and it seemed as though they were not something to be pointed out as attractive to little Helen or to Claire, who put everything in her mouth. Nothing twisted her with longing like thoughts of the mountains. She understood from Christine, who liked to backpack and had been to Yellowstone, the Tetons, and the Beartooths, that the strands of cobweb roads she remembered, and the cabins perched like dewdrops, and guest lodges no more permanent than little piles of sticks, were now hammered into the rock itself, weighted down by visitors. That was okay. Who didn't deserve to see it? But it was finished for her.

Whenever Ike said that life was too hard there, thinking of Abel and the ranch and the disease and death of cattle, Anna thought not of her first married years, but of Mama and Papa, who attained an Eastern smoothness of routine; ironing followed washing followed baking just as summer in the cabin followed school in town. One wore gloves for shopping and a smock for spring cleaning, and calicoes were folded and set aside in a rainbow of dresses-to-be. Ike's life, she had always thought, would be hard anywhere, for he hadn't the liking of routine that could eventually smooth it out, and she had no patience with his impatience. Her daughters' childhoods had unraveled chaotically with the failure of the ranch, the uncertainty of the Depression, and then the war. Her own had been a tightly woven piece. She had fought to escape the strands that always looped her back to Mother's rules, but now, at seventy-two, she still could not say what Helen and Claire and Susanna had fought for, or if they had won. And Christine? She shoved her gloved hands into the pockets of her coat. For forty years she had stood in her garden thinking of the mountains, as if earth called up rock, marigolds called up Indian paintbrush, robins called up bald eagles, the trickle from her hose called up the torrent of mountain creeks in June, and she was merely the point where everything touched. To the kitchen or the living room or the solitude of her bed, visions of the Big Horns, the Yellowstones, and the Absarokas would not come, but after a lifetime in the Midwest, she still half expected to look up from the soil she was working and see mountains against the sky.

She glanced remorsefully at the house. Nothing about it indicated what Ike was doing in there, or how he felt, whether he was asleep, or if the medicine had worked. It would be dawn soon, though a somber one. She could call Helen, care for Ike by health-bringing daylight, forget how night and yellow lamplight had sapped him. Christine would come, and the dog, and Claire would take her shopping, and Susanna would bring home something from the bakery, and everything would bump along as usual, busy, tolerable. She fixed her thoughts on this—figures scurrying in and out of Ike's room, handing him the paper, a book, hot chocolate, a pill, running him up and down the stairs, sitting him down and helping him up. She fixed her thoughts on it because she didn't want the image of him as he had looked before, waking up, his eyes rolling, to capture any of them. But it did, and the more she conjured up bustle, the more frightened she grew, until she was stock still in the garden, cold again and afraid to move.

Why did she fail to rise to the occasion of this illness, every day? Why did she meet every demand with resentment and reluctance, or take refuge all the time in gardening plans or sewing plans, or, lately, fruitless reminiscing? Why couldn't she merely pay attention to Ike, her husband of fifty-two years, her patient, her charge? It seemed not a question of will but a question of thoughtlessness or stupidity. Or selfishness. Could a broken hasp will itself fast to the door? He was very sick. Obviously he was very sick and getting sicker, and she acted as if he were merely perverse. She thought of him dead, right now dead in the unspeaking bulk of the dark house, and a greater fear than the one that froze her pushed her toward the back door.

He was groaning, sleeping but groaning. She dared not enter the room, but she could stand just outside and hear him, tossing, snoring, groaning. She went to the phone and unwrapped it.

Just as she noticed her gloves, that she couldn't dial with her gloves on, a voice said, "Hello? Who's this?"

"What? Hello? The phone hasn't rung. Hello?"

"Hello!"

"What are you doing on my phone?"

"This is George! Who is this?"

He fell silent for her answer, but she couldn't say anything. He could as easily have been standing beside her, have stepped suddenly from the closet and whispered in her ear. He would have been on the phone all night, waiting for her to pick it up. Anyone could have tried to call and been unable to reach her. She felt the hairs on the back of her neck prickle, but still could say nothing.

George chuckled. "Just tell me who you are," he said. "Just tell me, tell me."

How could she have forgotten him, have unlocked the door and gone outside in the blanket dark and forgotten him?

"Tell me. Tell me. Tell."

Had she locked the door downstairs? Was that her hand tonight that she remembered turning the bolt, the testing, with a little jerk, whether it caught?

"Tell me."

She croaked, then enunciated, "My husband is dying, get off my line."

There were no clicks, no sounds except a cessation of George's quiet breathing. In a moment, the dialtone blasted her ear. She took off her gloves and dialed Ike's doctor, fingers trembling so that they jumped out of the holes. Dr. Jauss's phone rang and rang. At last a voice clicked in, saying, "You have reached Dr.

130

Edward Jauss. Dr. Jauss has been called out of town until Monday. Patients with emergencies are to call Dr. Simon Clayton, 281-4038. Others may leave messages after the sound of the tone."

She dialed again and reached another recording. "Dr. Clayton's office. Thank you for calling. Office hours for today, Thursday, are from 10 A.M. until 3:30 P.M. Before 10 A.M., Dr. Clayton may be reached at Flowers Memorial Hospital, or you may leave a message and Dr. Clayton will call you as soon as he can. If you have had an accident, please go to the Emergency Room at Flowers Memorial and have Dr. Clayton paged." The bell rang. Anna stumbled over the message, getting out only Ike's name and the fact that he was not Dr. Clayton's patient, when the bell rang again and the phone disconnected. She had not taken down the number. She dialed Dr. Jauss, listened to the recording, dialed Clayton again, drummed her fingers on the phone while the recording wound through the machine. At last. She spoke very carefully.

"Please call Anna Robison. Ike is a patient of Dr. Jauss. Ike seems worse, though maybe not much worse, I don't know. I would like the doctor to see him. I wish Dr. Jauss hadn't—" The bell rang, the phone disconnected, and Anna thought that she hadn't been emphatic enough. She should call again, but again she hadn't written down the number, and it seemed to have vanished in her panic. She put down the receiver and sat on the step. She was breathing very hard and her shoulder was throbbing.

Of course, she should not have left the house, not

131

gotten out of earshot of Ike's bed, perhaps most critically, not raked over still another set of reminiscences, the most saddening of all. The quality of friendship, she thought, or the quality of domestic life, did not change. With each new generation arose new loves and new worlds of memory; what each person had was sufficient, and filled exactly the vessel of expectation, or at least failed to fill it to the same degree in everyone. What was easier than to know people, to think of them lovingly, to distinguish and exalt them in the memory, not, in the end, for a kind manner or a characteristic turn of the head (though that seemed to be the reason) but for their recognition of oneself? It was only human, this endless sociability. The quality of wildflowers untrammeled, of sky unhazed did change, however.

What did she know? She read seed catalogues and planted her garden, pleased as anyone that the tomatoes this year would be resistant to verticillium wilt. She went to the store and bought lettuce out of season, oranges trucked thousands of miles, chickens raised in cages so small that their feet grew around the mesh and ripped away when they were sent off to market. Who knew better than Anna the real cost of chickens that had to be chased and killed and plucked and singed before dinner preparations could even begin? Christine could be rabid on the subject of endangered species; she and Todd had had their most vicious fight, at Anna's dinner table, about tigers, and Christine had gotten redder faced and shriller than wives Anna had known of philanderers and alcoholics and child beaters. Helen had hushed her furiously, and Anna, too, had frowned at the disruption of their pleasant supper, but sometimes as she knelt in the garden, peacefully poking peas into the soil, she remembered the vaster peace of Papa's hired wagon in the mountains, of unhitching the horse at the end of the rutted "road" and hobbling him to graze while Mama and Papa carried sheets and blankets and hampers of food the last mile to the cabin. Helen had attributed Christine's fury to something darkly psychological, but Anna agreed with Christine's fury at never having seen what she had seen, at knowing such scenes had vanished forever. And later on, the hampers and linens would come back down, the horse would be put into his traces, and they would disappear like dust blowing off the mountain. The next spring, the road would be narrower, its ruts more stuffed with moss, lichen, creeping groundcover. "People can't touch these mountains," Papa had said. "Never have, never will." Anna, aged six, had shivered at their power. Papa had, of course, been wrong.

Then Alfred came into her mind again, and she realized that his image had been pressing on her. Her shoulders tightened painfully. Of all the dead people, his death had been the worst, a grand and terrible alcoholic battle against liver disease and heart disease, the course of which was impressed upon Anna and Ike by the intermittence of their visits with him in the last three years of his life, when he looked in his late seventies and was actually in his late fifties. The oddest and most horrifying development was the growth of hair on his face—his eyebrows curved around his eyes, his hairline descended, his beard thickened and encroached upon his upper cheeks. Anna remembered him hearty at the dinner table, casual, very casual with the bottle of wine he had brought, suggesting Helen have a little more, Anna have a drop, it was very "nice tasting, not at all bitter. Practically grape juice, really."

Later, Helen wrote home that he drank in spite of the Antabuse he was taking, and that he threw up in the doorway of his office, under the very eyes of his secretary and the Chairman of the Board. These shocking bits of news were dropped into otherwise light, impersonal narratives about things Christine was doing, plans Helen was making. Anna never quite understood these letters. Perhaps Helen was defying her to sympathize, daring her to advise, or even come. In every letter, she said she thought that the worst was well behind them, Alfred was much calmer now. She seemed horrified that her mother and father might show concern, as if to be unhappy was to prove her aspirations foolish, her judgments wrongheaded. As for Anna, it astounded her as much in the sixties to watch Helen's self-esteem shatter in the face of Alfred's particular destiny as it had in the thirties to watch Ike's crumble in the general devastation. At any rate, Alfred insisted on going to the office the day after he got out of the hospital, even though his weight had dropped to 110. His investments were about to burgeon, he was going to be made a partner, who was more brilliant, in spite of everything, than Alfred Peale

Darlington? Soon they would live like they had never lived before, calmly, carefully, recreationally. They would drive Christine to college and, while some trustworthy young man looked after things in the office, they would take a pleasure trip through New England. They would eat many raw vegetables and swim laps, but Alfred had a heart attack at his desk, someone else was made a partner, and many of the stocks had to be sold to pay for this and that. Christine went to college on the bus, and it seemed wisest to Helen to move her antiques and oriental rugs back to Des Moines, where she could live more cheaply, where she could make friends who didn't belong to the firm and never had. Now, of course, she couldn't understand how she had exerted herself for thirty years and ended up in the same place.

"Mother!"

When Ike's voice broke into her reverie, it startled her upright, startled her into thinking of the phone calls, of how loud her voice had been, or what she had said about dying.

"Are you awake again, Daddy?" she called convivially, as she heaved to her feet.

"I haven't been asleep! Where were you? Turn on the light! Why are you dressed?"

"I went out in the backyard. In the garden."

"What for? I called you!"

"I don't know, Ike, I really don't. I just wanted to get some air."

"It's a pitch black out there."

"I know. I'm sorry I left you in the dark. I really am."

She really was. "I thought you were asleep."

"I'd like to be asleep, but how can I with you traipsing all over? What if something happened to you?"

"Nothing did. Nothing will." She thought of George, of his unknowable knowledge of her, and bit her lip. "Can I get you anything, Ike?"

"No!"

"Are you going to sleep?"

"No!"

"Do you want to get up? You could take a bath. I'll help you."

"No!"

"I won't stay in there with you, I'd just run the wa—"

"NO!"

"Ike, I don't think I nurse you very well. I think I should apologize. Mama was the same way. The whole time somebody was sick, Mama ran around in a temper. Anyway, I've been trying, but I haven't been doing very well. Your room isn't very cheery, and maybe I don't hear you every time you call, for one reason or another. The girls have some ideas. I don't know, Ike, I hate to give up our priv—"

"Unlock that door."

"What?"

"Unlock that door."

"It's tied with a stocking."

"Untie it." His gaze held hers, and she wondered if he could simultaneously take in all of her, as she could of him. It was peculiar how the spectacle of his illness aroused no pity in her, though no horror, either.

136

Mostly it made her want to do the proper thing. She thought of the door open, a breach between the chambers of a heart. "You could move into the guest room, that's right across the hall."

He made no reply, holding her gaze.

"No," she said. "No, I won't untie it."

PART
Three
❦

*C*laire's was the voice of an early riser that could attach itself to the coming day even before dawn. Over the phone it sounded washed, dressed, fed; Anna took as much comfort in its tone as in its words—that Claire would be there soon, she was walking right out the door, she already had her coat on. Putting down the receiver, Anna noticed that the hallway had perceptibly lightened, and suddenly hungry, she thought of food.

When her daughter's arrival coincided with the popping of her toast and the first appearance of the sun, a cueball in the fog, Anna took it as a good omen. The few complaints she had been going to make about her night drained away, and she merely smiled and gestured toward the coffee pot.

"Mother, I'm not going to start," said Claire, "but just tell me if you thought about the nurse since last night."

"Yes, I did. I—"

"No, I promise, I'm not going to pester you. How's Daddy?"

Anna told her briefly about his wakings but did not mention her fear. She could too readily imagine Claire bounding up the stairs and raising Ike's eyelids with thumb and forefinger. Claire did everything with such force and certainty that when she exerted herself to open a reluctant jar, Anna always expected it to shatter in her hands. She had learned to meet the mark rather than exceed it, so that when she jerked off her gloves, they got folded neatly and were put in her pocket, and when she ripped off her coat, it found its way to hanger and closet, but such peaceful results were often surprising. Claire considered herself remarkably calm.

Anna liked to look at her. She had been handsome her entire life. Even in infancy, she'd struck you as handsome, and each year of handsomeness seemed better than the last. Her looks didn't ask you to remember any historic moments of especial beauty, but announced themselves in the present. You always thought, Claire looks very good these days. Oddly, no one had ever compared her to Helen, at least not in front of Anna. She was saying, "I'd love to just tear out the wall, you know. The study is far too small for anything as it is, and if I knocked down the wall, I could throw up some shelves and cupboards, and have a nice storage area right there by the kitchen. I'd like new vinyl, anyway, and I could nail it right over the step and up to the wall. I thought about it all night." But of course she had slept perfectly, Anna thought with envy, wholehearted and even enthusiastic, uninterrupted squarely up to the five-thirty wakening. "This is the last thing I can possibly do to that house, though. If I don't gut the place and start from scratch, I'm going to have to sell it and find something untouched by twentieth-century hands." She laughed. Even during the agonies with Geo, her complexion bloomed, her hair shone, and her teeth sparkled.

Anna must have glanced at the phone, because Claire interrupted herself and said, "It's not even seven."

"You don't think they're up yet?"

"At the enchanted castle? They're lucky to get up at all!"

"Helen is a heavy sleeper."

"Christine does her share." Though Claire's voice lifted as if she intended to continue, she picked up a piece of toast instead and nibbled off the crust. At last she said simply, "Well, Mother," and got up to rummage in the refrigerator. They all knew Claire did not approve of divorce, or any other kind of weakness, either. She bristled with all the views she had to express. Anna, on the other hand, was hard put to find in herself any views at all. Men came and went very suddenly. One was introduced to a fiancé—Sam, Geo, Hanson—and expected immediately to love him, while all the familiar boyfriends disappeared. In the forties she had attributed this to the war, but it was still true. Men came into a family more suddenly and intrusively than babies, with their opinions already formed. Those opinions, as trivial as your own, were exalted and analyzed day after day by the daughter in question, and then you were asked not to serve sweet potatoes for Sunday dinner and not to talk about the

140

Marshall Plan, or the war in Vietnam, which you hadn't intended to talk about, anyway. At Christmas, Christine had been cataloging to Helen Todd's every preference in shirts, ties, sweaters, socks, undershorts, and T-shirts, and now there would be no more Todd. What could be said, after all?

"Frankly, Mother—" Claire found and peeled a grapefruit. Juice spurted out the side of her mouth, and she caught it on her chin with the back of her hand. "Frankly, Mother, I blame Helen."

Anna rolled her eyes skeptically.

"No, really!" Claire swooped down and landed at the table, hunched forward, eager to continue. Anna, too, leaned forward, almost against her will, but the husk of inattention was irretrievably sloughed off. Claire tipped her teacup so that the flower on the bottom appeared, and Anna watched her. This was usual, a ritual to heighten intimacy, lend surprise and insight to the imminent exchange. Mama had been adept at such rituals. As much as Anna didn't want to get into it all, she waited attentively.

"Mother, don't you remember Hugh Pellegrini?" Anna shook her head. "Yes, you do! Helen had a big thing for him right before we went away to college. He had a real bad limp because one leg had been crushed in an accident, and he couldn't be drafted. Don't you remember? We called him Miracle Man, because it was a miracle that the only man left in Iowa lived near us." Anna did remember him—a handsome dark boy who, perhaps because of the accident, seemed older than he was. She remembered that he had been enormously polite, though not fawningly so. "Helen was after him for months! If she thought she might see him the next day, she used to pick whatever bobbie pins she could reach out of my hair after I was asleep and put up her own hair. Remember how there weren't any bobbie pins because of the war? Oh, it made me so mad! I'd wake up half curly and half straight! And she just rifled my clothes and Susanna's, too, because Aunt Dolores had given Susanna that pink sweater with the openwork that was too loose on her. Well, it wasn't too loose on Helen! Anyway, she'd put on that sweater and go down to the drugstore near Leach's Men's Store, where he worked, and she'd thumb through the *New Yorker* and the *Saturday Review.* Never once a *Saturday Evening Post!* He'd come in on his lunch hour, and finally he asked her out. I was there, because after a while she'd been going there so long she looked like a fool, so she'd make me spend a lot of time buying bath salts or picking out a lipstick. 'Now it doesn't matter what you like, Claire,' she'd say. 'Make them show you everything, and try everything, and pretend you just can't make up your mind, and I'll act like I'm waiting for you. If I look impatient, don't pay any attention!' And she did! She'd tap her foot and roll her eyes, and breathe hard the way Daddy does, and then he'd come in and she'd complain about bow picky I was! I swear the salesgirl hid behind the counter whenever I walked by the place for years after that!"

Anna laughed and shook her head, as much at the idea of Claire being bullied as at the elaboration of

142

Helen's act. "And to top it off, she always made me hand over whatever it was I bought, and if she liked it, she kept it! So he asked her out. Remember? They went out most of that summer." Anna did remember that. It had been a pleasure to go to the door and find Hugh, whose smile was so warmly welcoming that it seemed to make him the host and herself, an old mother in her housedress, the greatly anticipated guest. His looks, his dignity, and his limp gave him depth and poignancy, seemed to display something of his soul.

"And you know, Mother, he was terrific! He had good manners and he knew how to talk, and he read a lot, I think. He was pretty ambitious, too. I know he was going to college at night. He was just about perfect for Helen, you know? She thought so, too, and the more she got to know him, the more she thought so. She said it all the time, and I think he fell in love with her. Well, Mother, no matter what she said, it was just as plain as day that everything was downhill after that first date—after he asked her out the first time, even. She talked all about it and about him and about *them,* but the only time she really *felt* it was that first moment. I don't think she's changed, and I think Christine can't help but be the same way."

"Maybe she didn't like him as she got to know him, Claire. Maybe be was boring. Anyway, we don't know what's going on with Todd."

"That's just it! I bet there's nothing going on with Todd. Christine is a good girl, and you know how I've always loved her, but she has about as much persistence as an oatmeal cookie!"

"Well—"

"Mother, listen! Kids need the example of a lifelong marriage, where the parents really stand together and present an undivided front. If they don't see you living together and making it for more than ten years, then they don't know how it's done. Now, obviously it isn't Helen's fault about Sam and Alfred, but still, the example isn't there. At key times in her life, Christine saw her mother living outside of marriage, and so living outside of marriage seems possible to her."

"Well, Claire, it is possible you know."

"I mean as being married, even desirable. Maybe all of this isn't exactly Helen's fault, but that's where the roots of it are." She finished with ringing certainty, licking her lips a little and smiling, and she always did when she had made a point. If there was anything Claire loved to do, it was to make a point.

"Hugh was a very nice man."

"I think he got to be a lawyer or something like that. Can I make more coffee?"

"If you want it. None for me." The fog was beginning, perhaps, to burn away; the sun was completely up. Having seen it rise made Anna feel slightly disarranged and almost nauseated. Her night, by contrast, seemed to have been so black, so constricted. "I'd better check on Daddy."

"I'll do it, Mother." Claire put down the coffeepot.

"No!"

Claire looked sharply at her, seeming for a moment to divine Anna's fear that she might see him disoriented and deathly, as he had appeared (only appeared,

144

a trick of the light) before she went out to the garden, but Claire was in a good mood, pleased with the story she had told, unsuspicious. Anna pushed herself to her feet. In half an hour she would call Helen. Susanna, too. And the doctor again, if he'd not called her back.

Ike lay in a flood of bedclothes, his breathing deeper and more peaceful than it had been lately. He was sometimes like this, wakeful at night, then drowsy all morning. In spite of herself, in spite of her predawn resolutions, she bit her lip angrily, thinking that he knew she couldn't sleep after daylight. He could nap all day, waking luxuriously and calling for food, sliding into sleep after long, pleasant moments of stillness and a few pages of his book, but she had things to do; she had the whole day to wade through before bedtime, and then he'd probably be wide awake all night again! Even as she forced her annoyance to the back of her mind, stopping on the landing to fix the belt of her dress, looking over the bannister at Claire, who was straightening magazines in the living room, she grew frightened of it as of an unexploded shell in a grassy meadow. She said, "He's sleeping."

"Speaking of sleep, Mother, how much did you get last night?"

"A few hours."

"You see, Mother, if you had a nurse, even just a night nurse, you—"

"It was enough. When you get older you stop needing so much sleep." Why was she saying this?

"It's too hard on you—"

"Let's not talk about it."

"We'll do anything you want."

It was on the tip of her tongue to say that she didn't know what she wanted, but such an opening you did not give to Claire, whose certainty abhorred the vacuum of doubt. Were Susanna here, she could say that Ike seemed worse, that she was worried about the doctor not calling, that she was tired to death herself, and a little, just a little, afraid. With Susanna she could sift the justice of these anxieties, consider the nuances and the fineness of these changes. They would sip cinnamon tea and eat muffins, and while Susanna pressed her forefinger onto crumbs and then touched them to her tongue, she would come to a conclusion. Claire was too ready. It seemed to Anna that one word of anxiety would send her caroming around the house, and then about the city, rounding up doctors and nurses and equipment, beating back a tendril of fear with great engines of vehemence. And what did she want, anyway? Only for there to be no need of these worries, for Ike to be healthy and impatient and blamable, an adversary as potent as herself. She said, "Claire, you ought to get a job. You can't keep redecorating your house forever."

"What can I do? Besides, I'm too old."

"You're only fifty."

"Fifty-one soon."

"And you look younger than that. You have too much energy to sit around home—"

"And the money's running out. I know. I've been looking."

"Is it?" Anna could not hide all of her surprise.

Everybody knew that Geo had been so superstitious about an early death that he had vastly insured his life. They'd teased him about it for years.

"College, Mother. I can't stand for the boys to have to worry like we did, every day, about living expenses. I'm not blaming you!" Helen and Claire had gone to college in Cedar Falls together, lived together, shared one allowance, divided their single room so that Helen had the door and Claire had the window. Helen's half was strewn with art supplies, Claire's uncannily neat. The arrangement lasted a year and a half, until Helen dropped out and joined the army. Anna wondered what she and Ike could have been thinking of, why they hadn't borrowed something from Ben, or even Naomi, who had only one child. Sometimes Claire or Helen mentioned, with a laugh, the thin white line Helen had painted down the walls and across the floor of their room and the landlord's horror at it, but otherwise they didn't talk much about college. Jimmy and Jeremy had single rooms, large allowances, fancy bicycles, and a car to share, though Claire often raised the possibility of obviating even that potential conflict. The irony was that Jimmy and Jeremy got along fine, and their single rooms were right across the hall from one another. The ones who ridiculed Claire's automotive notions were Jimmy and Jeremy.

"I blame myself, Claire. Maybe Daddy and I had some kind of vision of sisterly togetherness. Daddy was scared to death of one of you being out alone after dark or coming home to a dark place. Maybe it was just money, maybe we weren't thinking at all. I see

147

how bad it was, though."

"Oh, don't worry about it, Mother!" Claire spoke snappishly, as she always did when someone apologized to her. "Anyway, there are some jobs, and the hospital where I was doing that volunteer work is glad to tell anyone how well organized I got everything. Is that Daddy?" They stilled even their breathing, but no further sounds came from the upstairs.

The telephone roared. Even though the sun had been up for a long time now, Anna jumped and grabbed the arms of her chair. It blared again. She exclaimed, "There was a caller! Did I tell you that? In the middle of the night."

"Did he say—" Claire paused for another ring— "anything obscene?"

"No, nothing."

"I'll get it."

Did the phone always make her this nervous? She wanted to shout to Claire, "Run! Run!" Rings seemed to come at one second intervals. Some people, Susanna was one, could finish a sentence or a cup of coffee or a row of knitting before picking it up.

"It's Helen, Mother!" Claire called from the back hall, then went into the kitchen.

Helen was whispering. Anna could barely hear her. "What, Helen? Why are you up so early? It can't be seven-thirty! What?"

"Threw up."

"What?"

"Christine just went into the bathroom and threw up." The words sounded pressed out, making Anna

148

think of cosmetic tubes.

"So what?"

"She threw up, Mother! She didn't want me to hear her. She kept flushing the toilet. Just a minute." She turned away from the phone. Anna could hear the breathy mumble of conversation. So what? Her own stomach felt uneasy from her long night and the prospect of throwing up seemed almost alluring. And then she realized what Helen was talking about. "Mother!" reverberated in her ear. "Call you back!" Anna could hear Helen's receiver knock sharply against the sides of the cradle before disconnecting. So there was going to be a baby after all! Might be. She made herself think, Might be. She opened her mouth to call out to Claire, and then remembered Christine's other news.

"Don't make them too runny!" Ike said, as if she had ever made them too runny. She sprinkled on salt substitute and pepper, and when she lifted the pan, they slid together on the greaseless surface and buckled. During the winter the doctor had decided to allow eggs back into Ike's diet, evidence of hopelessness, perhaps, though Jauss alluded to recent research. Claire was upstairs changing the bedclothes.

As she turned, Ike lifted his teacup out of the patch of sunlight on the table, and said, "Seth would be a hundred today."

"He's the third, Daddy."

"Ben's the third. Seth is today, March second."

The calculation did not seem right to Anna

somehow, but she dished up the eggs, gingerly, without breaking either yolk, and kept silent. It was remarkable, though she hated to idealize Ike's kin, that the eight of them should so neatly span a century, more than a century now. "Mama was seventeen."

"Tell Claire. Claire'll want to know that."

"You know, my mother was as thin as a whip all her life. We were big like Papa's side of the family, even Naomi, but Mama never did get stout."

"I know, Ike. Claire's going to be like that. She always says she wants her epitaph to be, 'She was thin.' " Anna bit her lip. She shouldn't have mentioned epitaphs.

"Cost too much to have an epitaph nowdays. Where's the salt?"

"I salted them, Daddy."

"Not enough."

She handed him the salt substitute, but he waved his hand and knocked it off the table. "Ike, Dr. Jauss—"

"Dammit! Where's the salt?"

"Daddy, you're not supposed to—"

He pushed himself out of his chair, holding his dressing gown closed with one bony hand. *"Where's the salt! You damned women want to take everything away from me!"*

"The salt we should have taken away from you forty years ago! Do you want to die?" Anna covered her mouth. Ike held out his hand, and she put the salt shaker into it. He let his robe fall open, lowered himself with two hands into his chair. Really, if eggs, why not salt? Sunday she would call Jauss, at home if she

150

had to, and ask him. And she would make him come over, and she would keep him there until he talked to her, until he said something besides, "You can't ever tell," and "It varies from case to case." She would ask him if he had dared to lose hope, if he had dared! Thinking of him reminded her to call that other one, Clayton, who hadn't called back, and instinctively she moved toward the phone, but here was Ike. Deaf as he could be at times, there was no telling how clearly he might pick up his own name, or a tone of concern in her voice. Besides, sitting there victorious over the salt, he didn't look that bad. He had been careful. In spite of his fury, he hadn't sprinkled more than a few grains on his plate. She said, "You want some V-8, Daddy?" He shook his head. He pushed away his breakfast, over easy, peppered, salted, and, as always, abundantly discussed. He had taken three bites. From above came the creak of Claire's tread in the bathroom. She would be straightening up, even though Anna had said, "Don't bother with anything else."

Ike said, "Well, Seth, he would be a hundred, and then Ben would be ninety-five, and Sarah would be ninety-three, and let's see, Rebecca was the one who died as a baby, she'd be eighty-eight herself, and then Naomi'd be eighty-seven, and Joe"—his voice caught at Joe, who had died of pneumonia at twenty, star full-back and third baseman that he was—"Joe would be eighty-six, no, just turned eighty-seven. He and Naomi weren't eleven months apart." He turned his teacup and moved it to the patch of sunlight, which had migrated a few inches across the gingham. Anna wondered sometimes what had happened between Ike's mother and father that they suddenly, after thirteen years of marriage, produced three children inside of twenty-four months. "Abel, of course, eighty-two, and then me." After not hearing from Abel, or writing to him themselves, in thirty-two years, they had gotten a note four years before, announcing his death ("Seventy-eight!" Ike said, "Seventy-eight! That's nearly a hundred!") from cancer. His weight had dropped to under a hundred pounds. When last they'd seen him, his shoulders were so broad that his hands seemed to hang from them like weights on a plumb line. He was a terrifyingly strong man, a bully, and Ike always feared him. Always. Even unconscious in his crib, he'd had reason to fear his angry older brother. It took Anna to hate him, though, on Ike's behalf. She'd forgotten that until just now, forgotten the vigor of her antipathy to Abel, and the enormity of her relief when they sold the ranch and dissolved their partnership. Ike cleared his throat. "If I should live to be the last leaf on the tree . . ." but then he fell silent, unable to remember the rest of the poem. He loved it, had been reciting it since he was twenty-five or six.

"You want anything more, Ike? Helen and Christine are coming over and Claire's taking me to the store. What do you think you'll be wanting for lunch? Tuna? I can get some nice white meat tuna packed in water. Or maybe salmon? How about a good salmon casserole, with little peas and pieces of potato, or noodles. How about noodles?"

He looked at her.

152

She snapped, "Now don't get sentimental, just don't!" He stood up, and Claire came in to find Anna with her hand on his shoulder, pushing him, almost knocking him, back into his chair. Anna didn't know how this happened, how she got across the room, why she was angry again, why she had lifted her hand, what this violence signified, how to interpret the look of shock on Claire's face that filmed over instantly, even before the chair jerked and scraped against the table leg and Ike clattered into it, his hand hitting the teacup, turning it over.

The first sound amid the stares was Ike's chuckle. "Now see?" he said, "I always told you your mother was the most rambunctious person I knew. Once on the ranch I had a fight in the barn with Abel about some tools, and he picked me up and threw me out the door. Well, your mother was standing in the kitchen, rolling out biscuits. It was the spring, so you must of been about six months old. Anyway, she saw me come flying, and she swarmed outside with that rolling pin in one hand and stick of firewood in the other, and she ran right past me, and when I got back into the barn she was waving both arms and shouting that if Abel ever laid a hand on me again, she'd give him a skull fracture he wouldn't soon forget. He stepped back, too." But Claire didn't laugh, and Anna saw Ike push up the sleeve of his robe and run his finger over the underside of his arm. A bruise was beginning to form. Claire said, "Mother, let me take those sheets and things downstairs and throw them into the machine." Anna nodded.

153

When they were alone, when Ike had tottered into the living room to look at the "Today" show, Anna said to Claire "Your father and I have been married fifty-two years—" but Claire cut her off, gathering to her chest sheets and socks and cotton shorts, under-shirts and nightgowns, saying, "Don't worry about it, Mother! There's always a lot of strain." But she didn't meet her gaze, didn't meet her gaze at all.

Claire pushed open the basement door with her hip, and Anna picked up Ike's plate of food, angry and ashamed. The urge to push him down at last had risen out of her fully formed, not feeling like anger or resentment or revenge, but perfectly itself, the simple urge to push him down. It almost had no conscious volition in it, and certainly the great part of her that had stood back amazed while she did it now trembled with regret and horror. But something else in her was a little, just a little, uplifted, curious, intrigued. That was horrible, too. She scraped Ike's eggs and toast into the garbage.

Christine appeared at the back door, ordering Nelson to sit-stay in a high, hopeless tone of voice. She pushed open the door and he leaped through it, but at once hunched down and looked at her when she rep-rimanded him. "Oh, Grandmother, he's driving me crazy! Now, lie down, Nelson, and don't get up!" She took his ears in her hands. "Don't you understand, Nellie? You've got to calm down. I mean it. I really do. Now lie down!" She kissed Anna on the cheek. "Good morning, Grandmother. Mom's furious with me, because he knocked over that big rubber tree in her

154

living room and got dirt on the Persian rug, and then she came into the room and found him lying on the couch when I was in the bathroom. He's got such a kind heart, though. Mom underestimates the value of a kind heart in a big dog like Nelson. Yes! Aren't you a sweet boy? How's Grandpa?"

"He's wide awake. You can ask him yourself."

Christine jerked open the refrigerator door. Anna thought she looked thinner. At the very beginning of each of her pregnancies, Anna had gotten about five or ten pounds thinner than usual. "What's in that foil?"

"Blueberry muffins."

"Really? You see? I knew there would be something terrific in here. Not like Mom, with her half a lemon, six mushroom caps, and used-up tube of anchovy paste. Can I heat them up?"

"Of course. Didn't you eat breakfast?"

"Yes, but I'm starving anyway." Did she glance at Anna just momentarily, speculating on what Anna might know? It was impossible to tell. Anna took the package of muffins out of her hand and turned on the oven. "Chrissy—"

"I'd better go find Grandfather. Okay, Nelson! That's good! Now heel. Calmly! Calmly!"

From the living room came Ike's voice, thin but teasing, and therefore happy. "Chrissy? Got that sorry hound with you, huh?"

"Oh, Grandpa—" Their voices dwindled into unintelligible banter. In the basement, Claire would be soaking this and that, rubbing the stains out of these other things. It was infuriating how you never made a

155

bit of progress, how your own child could make you feel as slovenly at seventy-two as she had from time to time at twenty-five, how your feeling of offense returned freshly, solidly, unchanged by your maturity or hers, untouched by your knowledge of how she was just like that, just energetic and orderly, not unkind, she who'd loved and cared for her own husband monolithically, who hadn't had to be vigilant over her wishes and pleasures lest they, lest her own hands and eyes themselves, betray her into neglect or selfishness. Nursing Ike, keeping her attention on him, considering his welfare, was like training an army of two-year-olds. There was not the perspicacity to see what they were doing or the energy to keep them in line. She arranged the muffins on a plate with a square of butter and a knife.

Anna thought, So what if I've felt violated my whole life by Mama's rules and Daddy's demands. She remembered herself being washed, the cloth rubbed briskly over her entire face, stopping her nose and mouth, damp and chilly, then the twisted corner of it pushed into her ears, then her hair lifted and her neck and the backs of her ears peered at and judged unsuitable. And Mama always inspected her underclothing after she wore it, Anna never knew what for; only tears and signs of wear, or sweat? Stains? At any rate, after inspecting it, Mama threw herself into boiling it and bleaching it dazzling white, cloud white, inhumanly white. Mama brushed her hair, picked through it for nits, probably as her own hair had been picked through. What if she had found one? Thank heaven she never did. Then she dressed Anna in perfectly clean clothing of her own design and manufacture, so full of stitches taken one by one that the fabric between the seams (and there were untold seams, both functional and decorative) had the importance only of paper to be drawn on or canvas to be painted. She could still remember Mama checking the fit of her shoes every day, so that nothing about Anna, no growth or change, would steal up on her. Had there been a hair on Anna's little chin or a pimple on her forehead, Mama would have plucked it or squeezed it. As it was, Anna had countless pairs of snowy gloves for hiding her knuckles, which Mama judged to be a little large, a tad unsightly.

Ike hadn't touched her like that, had almost ignored the details of her appearance, but had never let her ignore a single detail of his. She had admired him, washed for him, bought for him, made for him, inspected the bald spot he couldn't see, judged the growth of his belly, the atrophy of his muscles, and the tone of his skin until she felt that his body was her primary activity. Not to mention feeding it. Her jaw ached from the clenching of her teeth, and she realized she was staring at the plate of muffins. She touched them with the back of her hand. Still warm. She carried them into the living room.

Ike was telling one of his favorite stories. "So, anyway," he said, "most of us must have been about nine, I guess, because Pa was still the doctor for the town. Jake Sumner had found this thing down by the, tracks, see, this black cap about an inch long. And he

157

had it in his pocket. He kept showing it around and then putting it back, and pretty soon we all wanted to see it and hold it—you know how kids are. Well, this little Italian kid whose father worked for the railroad, he got hold of it, and started rubbing it up and down against the brick wall. We were standing out by the side of the blacksmith shop, kind of in an alley. It was a hot day, too. So he rubbed and rubbed, and all at once the damn thing just exploded. It was a dynamite cap, see, and that's how they set off the big explosion, with a little one. Well, that cap blew that kid's thumb off, and damn if it didn't go up his nose. Right up his nose! We could hardly pick him up to take him away to pa's office, we were laughing so hard." Christine had heard it before and began to smile immediately. Anna had heard it so many times that she didn't know what she remembered. When Ike was ten in Iowa, she would have been five in Wyoming, and yet she could see those little boys in their knickers and billed caps, lounging but prickly, ready for something. They seemed big, old, frightening. Perhaps she had remembered them once, maybe the first time Ike told the story, and now remembered the memory.

Ike's voice was weak. He had tired himself with the narrative and slumped against the back of the couch. Christine cast her a sidelong glance as Anna again pointed out the muffins on the coffee table. Christine took one and broke it in half. The smear of blueberry at the center steamed, and Christine inhaled deeply. She said, "Do you feel worse this morning, Grandpa?" Ike didn't answer, instead closed his eyes. Anna turned back toward the kitchen, and Christine followed her, saying, "I'm going to get some juice, Grandpa. Do you want anything?" Ike must have shaken his head, for there was no audible reply.

"Grandmother!" She leaped at Anna, whispering furiously. "Is he always like this in the morning? He seems worse! Have you called the doctor? Are you worried? Oh, Grandmother!" Before Anna could reply, Claire had pulled open the basement door. "Chrissy!" she exclaimed. "Hi! What's up?"

"Well, I think Grandfather looks much worse, Aunt Claire. He seems terribly tired, and I thought we could call the doctor."

"Mother?" But without waiting, Claire shouldered past them into the living room, and they could hear her call out to Ike in a loud voice: interpreting his fatigue as unconsciousness? merely startled?

"I called the doctor and he's going to call me back when he gets the message." Anna wondered if she sounded as defensive as she suddenly felt. "I was going to call back, but Daddy got up and had to have his breakfast. Claire brought him down; she didn't think he was—"

"But I did, Mother! I thought he looked much worse. He should go back to bed right now, and you should get that doctor over here. Maybe even an ambulance. Mother, he would be better off in the hospital, with trained nurses and the doctors right there." Anna could say nothing. She felt fear fasten in her mind the picture of Ike's last stay in the hospital, calling out for her all the time, refusing to cooperate with the nurses and reprimanding them for rudeness when they became impatient, truculent to the interns and residents who came when Jauss could never be found, gritting his teeth continually, and muttering about money. He liked his home and his wife and his room. "I—"

"You've got to make up your mind to do it, Mother! Really!"

"Dr. Jauss is out of town, and I couldn't get the other guy. Clayton, his name is."

"I'll get him, Mother, you can be sure of that. What's his number?"

"I didn't write it down. You've got to call Jauss's answering service." Claire pursed her lips. Anna could not forget that she had seen the pushing incident, heard them yell at one another about the salt.

"What are you women whispering about?" Ike stood in the doorway, frail but upright, still taller than any of them. Nelson was behind him and now pushed his nose delicately between Ike's leg and the doorpost. "Me, I'll bet."

"Grandpa! Do you want to sit down?"

"I want a cup of coffee is all. I'll sit at the table, though." Claire looked hard at Anna, then rolled her eyes in the direction of the phone. Anna nodded almost imperceptibly, agreeing to make the call after all, but really, Ike looked much better. There was color in his face and his shoulders were straight. Coffee was a good sign, too. He never wanted coffee unless he was feeling pretty good.

Christine asked him loudly for another story and in

the midst of his distraction, Anna sneaked away. As she picked up the phone she heard his chuckle joined by Christine's and Claire's, though a moment later Claire came to the doorway at the end of the hall and raised her eyebrows. Anna made the words "It's ringing," with her lips, but she ground her teeth at Claire's checking on her.

The nurse was solicitous. Dr. Clayton was on his way to the hospital; she would leave a message for him there; she was sure he would call immediately; what was the number again? Mrs. Robison had forgotten to leave it before; inside of fifteen minutes without fail, she knew how worrying it was; had the patient taken his medication this morning? She should be sure the patient took all of his medication. She would call Dr. Clayton right now, good-bye. In the kitchen they were talking about Claire's wedding, a day of terrific rainstorms and repeated misadventure. Geo did have the ring, Geo, didn't have the ring. Geo's six-year-old nephew had the ring, to practice with, and then he didn't have it anymore. It was found on the lip of the trapless bathroom sink. And then there were no stockings and then there were no sandwiches for the reception, and then. "I never heard this!" Christine kept saying. "Was it you who got so sunburned the first day of your honeymoon?"

"No, that was Susanna. After my wedding day, believe me, it was a twenty-three year rest! And we needed it! The worst was when Daddy couldn't find a shirt. Every shirt was at the laundry, or at least that's what he told me. He kept stopping outside my bedroom door, where I was frantically trying to get packed and ready because we were due at the church in about three minutes, and saying there wasn't a white shirt in the house, could he wear this Hawaiian shirt he had, or how about just a collar and bow-tie, no shirt at all, he'd have his back to the congregation, nobody would notice. I wanted to kill him for making jokes! Finally I was just about done, and he came in with his jacket on, and I saw that he had on a white shirt, but it was his bowling shirt. I said, 'Oh Daddy,' or something like that, and he said that when the minister asked 'Who gives this woman?' he'd decided that he was just going to throw open his coat, and there it would be, written above the pocket, *Ike*. Meanwhile, mother had been downstairs the whole time, ironing a shirt they found in the dirty clothes!" Claire glanced at Anna as she entered the room and lowered her voice slightly, Anna made a little nod.

"I never heard that!" exclaimed Christine. "That's wonderful."

"Well, you weren't nervous after all, were you?" Ike elbowed Claire in the ribs. "Not really, Daddy," said Claire, and then Ike said, "Where'd you go, Mother? Who were you calling on the phone?"

"Only Susanna. Didn't anybody bring in those muffins? They're probably cold again by now." She made an elaborate face of exasperation.

Just then Nelson stood up, his ears lifted. Half a second later came the sucking crunch of the front door, and Ike said, grinning, "There's Susanna now." He leaned toward Christine. "She's got this phone in

162

her car, you know."

It was Helen, her mouth snapped tight over everything she had to say. When Nelson stepped forward, his tail flicking, to greet her, she ordered, "Get away, dog!" but she did not look at or speak to Christine, whose eyes had dropped to the gingham tablecloth.

"Some coffee, Helen?" offered Claire, holding up the pot. "Daddy thought sure you were Susanna." Helen did not answer and did not look at the coffeepot. She went to the sink, turned on the water and turned it off, looked out the back door, unbuttoned her coat, but then buttoned it again. Anna's gaze met Claire's and Claire lowered the upraised coffeepot. Ike coughed, and Nelson dropped to the floor with a thunk. Helen looked into the refrigerator, reached in, and brought out a pear, which she weighed in her hand, then put back. In a moment, she closed the door again.

Christine whispered furiously, "Nelson, get off my foot!" and Helen glanced at her but still said nothing.

"You going to take off your coat, Helen?" Ike's curiosity was innocent and a bit impatient, but Helen for once paid no attention to him, and he looked in surprise at each of the women sitting with him at the table. "Cat got your tongue, Helen?"

"No, Daddy. How are you, Daddy? Do you feel better this morning? How did you sleep?"

" As a matter of fact"—he settled himself for an extended answer to these inquiries, but even he could see her instant inattention—"fine," he said.

"I'm going shopping. I'll be back for lunch." But she unbuttoned her coat again and half sat on the counter next to the sink. Finally, she joined them at the table, Christine had lifted her gaze hopefully when Helen seemed about to leave but now fixed it intently upon the table. Anna knew that she suspected Helen would expose her secret to Claire, the second to last person she would wish to know it, and Ike, the last. Helen poured herself a cup of coffee.

It occurred to Anna that now was the very moment she had been dreading for years, the moment when the voicing of a single word, although she did not know which word, would work like magic to open up everything—Christine's dilemma, her own fears for Ike's condition, her doubts about her marriage and the rightness of her feelings, Ike's self-doubts and dissatisfactions, Claire's resentments of Helen and Helen's of Claire, Helen's contempt for everyone's taste and manner of living. All the compromises they had forged for the sake of companionship and daily friendship would shatter. Such passion would be expressed as could never be recanted. Ike would die of the fear of death; Christine would get herself an abortion and a divorce; Helen and Claire would never speak again; the family would end, scatter, disappear as if none of them had ever tried as hard as possible to get along, stay in love, do the right thing, remember what it was that held them together. This unknown word could have come to anyone, and now it had come to Helen. Anna held her breath.

"You know what I remembered this morning? I don't know why, but I started thinking about that second winter I was in Germany, after I knew Sam

164

and just before I came home. It wasn't really winter, I mean, it was spring. That's the point. It was April or early May, and I realized one morning that all the snow was melting. I don't think it was very sudden really, but you know how things like that are. You hear the dripping and everything as just a little, continual, unimportant sound, and then it hits you that it's the thaw! The last thaw! Anyway, it was melting! I couldn't believe it. I knew I would never be back, right then, and I ran and got my skis and hiked up the mountain behind the hotel they were using as a barracks. The snow was all in patches, though some of them were pretty big, and I remember that I put on my skis and skied down the patches. Sometimes I fell when I came to the grass and sometimes I didn't, and I got some cuts on my legs and hands, but I'll never forget how desperate I was. I just wanted to ski! And I knew it was the last time, that in fact, I had missed the last time without knowing it. I just cried and cried. I knew I was going to come back here and live here and be a part of this."

Ike was confused and didn't say anything, Claire bristled, as she always did when Helen talked about what a good time she had had in Germany, and Christine was obviously too afraid to even respond to the anecdote, but Anna was relieved. Involuntarily she even smiled a little. The word hadn't been given to Helen after all. She inhaled deeply.

"I just thought of that today," said Helen. "I don't know why. Can I come back for lunch, Mother?" Anna nodded. Helen was gone. Nelson strode to the doorway of the living-room, watched until the front door slammed, then strode back and settled himself at Christine's feet.

In a rather strangled voice, Christine said, "Nelson's crazy about Mom, even though she really can't stand dogs. Isn't it funny how she's always disliked dogs, and they've always been just nuts about her?" She coughed.

"Well, what's her problem?" demanded Claire.

"We'll know soon enough." Anna could not keep herself from sounding sharp. Ike chuckled but then looked around, the whites of his eyes showing anxiously.

"You tired, Daddy? Are you ready to go back upstairs?" He nodded. Claire got to her feet eagerly, and though Anna saw in his eyes that be preferred her, she did not move, not with her heels and knees hurting again like they had the night before, and it was hardly nine yet.

When they were gone, Christine's mouth opened, but Anna forestalled her. "He gets tired really suddenly, Chrissy. It's like a balloon popping or something. Don't worry about it."

"I'll help you with the dishes."

"I wasn't going to—"

"I'll help you. We'll get them done right away."

"There aren't enough to make—"

"Then we'll mop the floor. Please?"

Anna hated to stand up. She had known before joining them at the table that rest at the wrong time of the morning would bring her fatigue down upon her,

166

that her arthritis would quicken, her eyes would sting, her knobby headache would return. She stacked the plates and cups deliberately, putting off the trek across the kitchen. Christine moved with enviable lightness, bending from the waist to wipe something off the floor, rising on her toes to put the sugar in a high cabinet. Her movements around the kitchen were efficient and practiced, bespeaking an inborn orderliness. As a child she had loved dolls, mudpies, helping to bake cookies, having her own cardboard playhouse, where she swept with adorable vigor. She had bemoaned her lack of siblings, and Ike confidently predicted a wealthy husband and seven children, a descending row of heads in matching outfits, like the row of dolls on her bed.

"Chrissy," Anna said, "it takes more time than you think to get used to any kind of life, and maybe you don't even know whether you're accustomed to it until you change it."

"Maybe I don't want to get accustomed to it."

"To what?"

Christine looked at her sharply. "To being married."

"What—"

"It's very limiting."

"You have your job, you have some money of your own. Your mother said you were keeping separate bank accounts."

"We are, but that's not what I mean. I mean I don't have my own thoughts."

"You always have your own thoughts, honey. You've got to. If I hadn't learned to tune out some of your grandfather's cockeyed ideas years ago, I'd be nuts."

"That's not what I mean, either, though Todd hates for me to say certain things in public, and he always tells me after parties how he thought I acted. Even when he's proud of me, I want to smack him one. But don't you remember certain times when you lived alone or something, and you just got carried away on a train of thought, and maybe you stayed up all night, or forgot to make dinner, or spent the whole day outside? It seems like every idea leads perfectly to every other idea, and if you follow it long enough, you'll really learn something, something you'll miss if you stop to go to bed, or even to explain why you don't want to go to bed?"

"I never lived alone."

"When I lived alone it happened all the time. I felt like my mind was just blazing with light, and the room, by being perfectly empty and silent, was crammed with everyone important from my past, completely populated. I would be sitting in a chair, then down on the floor doing exercises, and then taking a bath or making a pot of tea, and moving from revelation to revelation. I thought all about Mom and Alfred, and even remembered a lot about Daddy. There's no other way to recapture him, really, except in that stillness when a well-known memory kind of stumbles on a forgotten one, and if you're interrupted, the thread of the hidden one just snaps, and you may never find it again. I thought about you and Grandfather, and all the stories the twins and I have heard about your lives and Mom's and Aunt Claire's and

168

Aunt Susanna's childhoods. I'm afraid to lose that."

"How you all can be such rememberers I will never understand. Whenever I start, I think it's a sign of old age."

"But I love it. And even though I can remember what it was like to think that way really clearly, I haven't done it once since the wedding. Todd is a very organized person. He loves routine. If a train of thought begins, then he tries to accommodate me, but I know he's trying to accommodate me, and that he's being patient, but that he doesn't understand. Really, he wants his dinner, or he wants me to be in the bed next to him, or he wonders if I am getting cold toward him, and so, sort of automatically, I want to give him what he wants. I don't know. Does that seem stupid to you? Something trivial to be afraid of losing? My mind isn't full like that anymore. I don't love the apartment for all the thoughts and memories I've had there. And I feel like I'm getting colder and colder all the time."

"What fun is it remembering?" Anna shivered to recall the engine of memory that had buzzed her through the night.

"It's not fun, exactly. Sometimes I would cry, even. It's your mind, the sense of your mind working. Work is wrong, too, though. Thinking up the solution to a problem, for instance, is work, but that's more mechanical. This is as if you're laying down new pathways in your own brain, and if you lay them down once now, they'll be there forever. I know that Daddy used to kiss me on the nose before putting me in my crib. Mom doesn't know that, because she was never there. I asked her and she told me they alternated nights putting me to bed. I can feel the kiss, though, on the tip of my nose, and then I can see the crib bars in the dark and the closing of the door. I dredged that up myself from when I was about two, and now I'll never forget it. It was lost, and now it's like a super-highway. It'll never be lost again. And with it is this knowledge of what it felt like to be two, only two!"

"I don't know what to say."

"Don't get up, Grandma. I'll finish this. I just like to have you here. Mom doesn't listen, exactly. I think she listens to what she's about to say."

"Chrissy, did you think of this when you told Todd you'd get married?"

"I didn't think of anything! I think deciding to get married is committing yourself to someone you know a little about, to live a life you know nothing about. How can you make an intelligent decision? How can you even call it a decision? The very word *marriage* is this atomic explosion that wipes out every idea in the vicinity!"

"Chrissy—"

"She told you, didn't she? I can tell by your tone of voice that she told you. I don't care."

"It makes a difference, don't you think?"

"Only if you want it to. You have a choice."

"You had a choice."

"No. It wasn't my mistake. We took precautions every time and it happened anyway. I still have a choice."

"I don't think so."

"Grandmother, you heard what I said. Can I give that up for a lifetime of discussions about beers for lunch and what went on at the office and whether we should buy a washing machine?"

"A child has a mind, too."

"Do I sacrifice my mind to hers? That's what Mom did, and you did. Where does it end? Just when she's ready for her mind to leaf out like a big tree, does she sacrifice that for her kid?"

"Don't make judgments about my life!" The reprimand brought instant tears. "Christine. It isn't so bad to talk about mundane things for a change. Otherwise you might forget you were human, you know."

"I'll tell you the first thing I thought about when I heard it. I'll never be alone again! I'm not alone now! And even if she grew up to be ten or twelve, and I left her with Mom and Todd and went off for a while by myself, she'd be right there, dividing my thoughts, making me worry. Once you let yourself go on with it, then it's like you're pregnant for the rest of your life. That child is never not with you, never."

"I know that better than you do, Chrissy."

"Then how can you stand it?"

"Stand what?" Christine glanced up, startled, at Claire's return, then barked, "Nothing!"

Claire, like Ike, hated disrespect. Anna saw her grit her teeth and inhale deeply. She said, "Claire, Christine and I—"

"If you're talking about this proposed divorce, Christine, I have something to say about it, too. And I have a right to say it, because I've watched you grow up, and I've loved you and cared for you almost as much as your mother and grandmother have, so if you think it's interfering, then so be it. I'm going to interfere. You made your choice. You had lots of dates in high school and college, and Todd was the one you wanted. You knew him as long as I knew your uncle Geo and longer than your mother knew your father. You had time to think about his peculiarities and about the life it seemed like he was going to lead. You knew that changing him was unlikely, because I heard your mother say something about that to you, and I heard you say that you'd take him as is. I heard that! Now things don't seem to be going your way, and you want to get out. You think you can make another choice, one that won't demand as much accommodation or sacrifice. Well, you're wrong. Let me tell you, none of our lives has turned out the way we thought it would, or wanted it to. If the preacher had said during my wedding, 'Claire, do you take this man to worry about money with, to have miscarriages with, to argue about child-raising with, to lose in middle age,' do you think I would have said yes? Of course not! When I was twenty-three I wanted your uncle Geo only to be rich and healthy and happy, always handsome like he was then. But that's not life and marriage is life! You know what getting married is? It's agreeing to take this person who is right now at the top of his form, full of hopes and ideas, feeling good, looking good, wildly interested in you because you're the same way, and sticking by him while he slowly disintegrates. And he does the same for you. You're his responsibility now, and he's yours. If no one else will take care of him, you will. If everyone else rejects you, he won't. What do you think love is? Going to bed all the time? Poo! Don't be weak. Have some spine! He's yours and you're his, he doesn't beat you or abuse you, and you've each made about the same bargain. Now that you know what it's like to be married, now that all the gold leaf has sort of worn off, you can make something of it, you can really learn to love each other."

"That's very nice and idealistic, Aunt Claire, but—"

"Idealistic? Me? That's an insult!"

"Every marriage is different. I don't think you can—"

"Every murder is different, every robbery is different, too. People have to have standards, I think."

Anna's headache tightened around her temples like a wire. She raised her hand. "Claire—"

"Don't give in to her, Mother. You always give in to her and Helen, and I know you don't agree with them! You can't just have what you want all the time. You always want to give them what they want, but they can't have it; no one can, and thinking you can leads you right to despair. That's Helen's whole problem. You and Daddy were never tough with her, not really."

"I don't think Mom would agree with you, Aunt Claire."

"Your mother thinks what she wants to think. Always has."

"I have a headache. I don't want to hear any more of this fight."

Claire took a deep shuddering breath and unclenched her fists. She coughed, then lifted both hands to her hair and smoothed it gently back, exposing the graying roots. "Claire," Anna could not resist saying, "you've had opinions about my treatment of Helen since you were old enough to talk."

"That doesn't mean they're wrong."

"Maybe not."

Claire took another deep breath. "Well! I think I'll go to the store and get some things I need. Let me get food for lunch, and you can put off your big marketing till this afternoon, all right?"

"Fine, Claire. Get what you like."

At the sink, Christine was sobbing. Nelson, who had awakened during the fracas and cowered by the table at the angry voices, went over and nudged her knee with his nose. She patted his head and snuffled.

In a moment, Anna said, "Christine?"

"She's such a bitch! I don't care if she hears me. It's not her business!"

"Honey, I don't think she's exactly talking about you. She sees it as an issue, a sort of political question."

"I'm talking about my life!" She plunked the frying pan into the water with a large splash. "Shit!" She managed to wipe her nose and forehead on her sleeve without losing the dignity of her rage. Anna's headache seemed to burst, turning everything black for a second, but then it receded. She found herself panting.

"Chrissy, she's talking about her life, too." She coughed. "Anyway, your aunt Claire has changed a lot over the past couple of years. She's pretty bitter about

174

your uncle Geo, and she's gotten to be an avid watcher of the news and reader of the paper. When you say *divorce* or *women's lib* or something like that to her, she sees everything all at once—the end of her marriage, the way the house she used to have got vandalized, people burning the flag."

"I don't care."

"Come here, please." Nelson turned his head at the familiar command, then took two steps toward Anna and sat down quizzically. Christine dried her hands. "Sit down. Now, there's been a lot of yelling around here today. First your grandfather and me, then you and your aunt Claire. I don't like it. It gives me a headache. I want you to sit here at the table with me, and not use any more foul language, and listen patiently while I tell you something, all right?" She said it again, raising her voice. "All right?"

Christine sat down sulkily, and part of Anna wanted to shout, "Straighten up, look at me, be my equal, I love you," but instead she marshalled her voice and held her left hand, which was trembling, loosely in her right. She began as calmly as she could. "Your uncle Geo got lung cancer and had to have part of his lung removed. Do you remember that?" Christine nodded. "Well, after the operation, the doctors were jubilant. They said they had caught it in time and that they had done a beautiful job. Those were their exact words, 'Mrs. Crane, we did a beautiful job.' Your aunt Claire had to care for him, but I'll get to that in a minute. Anyway, it was discovered that Geo had a brain tumor not quite two years later, and the same doctor from before said, 'Well, Mrs. Crane, we can't be sure, but it may be that a few cells escaped during the earlier operation. In this case they would go to the brain.' And he smiled slightly. I don't think he meant to. I was there, because Claire suspected what the news would be, and she didn't want to go in alone. I wish I could describe his tone of voice. It was as if he were smiling and saying, 'That's life!' and shrugging his shoulders. And that's when Claire began to get bitter. That very moment. She thought the doctors had blundered the first time, and worse, that they didn't care. I stayed up there, and your uncle died about three weeks later."

"I know. It was very sad, but—"

"Don't interrupt me. I'm going to tell you about the end of Claire's marriage, after the lung operation. Are you listening?"

Christine nodded.

"When your uncle came home from the hospital, there was a place on the right side of his chest where they'd cut away the ribs and then taken out part of his lung. It was about the color of the inside of a chicken, and slick like that, too. When you looked in you could see his lung expanding and contracting, and another kind of vibration that you soon realized was the beating of his heart. Always there was fluid draining into this cavity, and so your aunt Claire would have to clean it out, irrigate it with a solution of some kind, and then pack it with gauze soaked in something. Around the edges they had pulled some of the flesh out to make a smooth rim, and she'd have to rub vaseline on that with her finger, though she had sterile

176

gloves on. At first she had to do this four or five times a day, even getting up at night to do it, and it filled the house with a terrible rank odor. Not only did she never have any help, she wouldn't let anyone watch, because she didn't think your uncle Geo should have to be that intimate with anyone else. For the first couple of days, she threw up every time she had to do it, and lost five or six pounds, and even after that, it was such a strain that she used to call me up long distance to talk about it. She'd do it, and smile, and then go out into the hall and sort of slump against the wall while her hands shook so much that she couldn't even light her cigarette. She didn't want Geo to know how she dreaded pulling off that tape and extricating the wads of used dressing, then having to reach her fingers into his very body, all the time ignoring the odor and making little jokes. It was terribly hard on him, too, and he always used to talk about how when she put the medicine in the cavity, he could taste it in his mouth. Fortunately, after about six months the wound closed, though the doctors warned her that sometimes they never do."

Christine made a face. Anna nodded and paused, not knowing exactly what she wanted to say. Claire had taken Geo's illness and eventual death like a pole vaulter clearing a two-story house, and even as Anna aimed the narrative toward Christine's edification and, perhaps, shame, the memory of Claire's faultless love, of the way she had offered to change Geo's dressings before they could make him at all uncomfortable, of his apologies for having to have them changed, and of Claire's smiling reassurances that she was glad to do it, this memory called up memories of herself and Ike, he calling out, she oblivious. She was panting again.

"In sickness and in health, I know, Grandma, but Todd—"

"No, that's not it." She put her hand to her breast-bone.

"Are you all right?"

Anna nodded and put her hand on Christine's arm, pressing it against the arm of the chair. At length, she said, "It's something I want you to understand about your aunt Claire. After we moved off the ranch, we lived for a while in a great big house with about ten rooms. For almost a year there your mother and your aunt Claire each had her own room, though we really didn't have the furniture to fill them up. Your aunt must have been about five. Anyway, she kept her room perfect all the time. She dusted with a rag I gave her, every day, and even swept, though she was too little to manage the broom very well. Your mother was always out doing something, and her room, well! So, after she cleaned every day, Claire would climb up into a kitchen chair I'd put in there, and she'd just sit, looking around the room. She'd get down and go over and straighten something and then come back and climb up in the chair again, and sit for a while longer. It was cute to see such a little girl be so neat, and Ike and I used to laugh sometimes at her. After we moved again and she had to share her room with Helen, I never saw her be like that, but I think I'll always remember the way she sat in that chair. She wasn't relaxed at all. She was enjoying that orderly room with all her might, like she was going to begin glowing. The wave of pleasure coming through the door about knocked you down." Anna paused again. It was hard to say what she meant, hard not to pile anecdote upon anecdote and hope they'd speak for her, but she did want to draw a conclusion. "Nothing—"

She began again. "Your grandfather loved to play all sports, and Susanna, too. Your mother was forever doing something. If she wasn't painting or drawing, then she was reading or outside getting into trouble. I've got to have some project going or I feel restless, but your aunt Claire isn't like that. It's as if she doesn't have 'passions,' just 'passion.' She's the most single-minded person I ever saw, and if there's no one there like the twins or your uncle for her to be single-minded about, then she'll just be single-minded. Maybe if your mother had more of that, she'd have kept painting, but anyway, Claire has it all, and when the twins were little, they almost used it up. She was crazy about being their mother, hated to leave them off at school. Well, when Geo got that lung thing, that filled her right up. She took that horror and turned it into an act of love, every day, every four or five hours."

"Don't you think most people rise to occasions?"

"Maybe, but they usually make sure you know how high they're rising."

Christine nodded.

"I don't do as well with your grandfather, and I daresay your mother didn't do as well with Alfred."

"It was dif—"

"Different, and not as bad, maybe. I don't know, and anyway, that reminds me that the doctor hasn't called, or did you hear the phone ring?" Anna put her fingers to her lips in involuntary dread.

"It didn't ring, Grandmother. I'm sure of it. And I'm sure Grandfather's fine. I'll go check." Christine stood up with one of those involuntary catching breaths that follow tears. Did she feel as bad as she said? Why did her body move with such spring, such nonchalance? Had Anna, in Mama's dresses and gloves and buttoned shoes, done the same?

The nurse had left two messages at the hospital. She understood Mrs. Robison's concern. What exactly were his symptoms? Was there anything more specific than a funny feeling? No uneven heartbeat? Surely we all sometimes thought we saw things, especially in the middle of the night. And after one or two heart attacks, dreams of pain were not rare. Mrs. Robison was not to worry herself, and the doctor would certainly call as soon as he could. At the worst, he would be in for office hours at ten.

When she put the phone down, it rang immediately, shocking her so that she dropped it and had to bend for it. She had reached such a trough of fatigue that she considered not doing it, though she could hear Susanna's voice quacking, "Mother? Mother?" How could anything be worth so much effort? But she picked it up.

Susanna said, "Are you alone? Is Helen or Claire there? I'm coming over. No, no special reason. Are you going to the store? You'll be home for a while? I'll be there in fifteen minutes." She sounded very suspicious. Anna was too tired to care.

Ike was asleep, Christine was in the attic looking for something, and Anna was thoroughly alone when Susanna came in talking. "It's a tremendous relief," she was saying. "You can't imagine." With her was a strange girl of about thirty-five. Anna looked immediately at her feet, but she wore normal shoes—black pumps with tassels and stacked heels. Nor were her stockings chalky. She looked entirely neutral, not pretty or plain, not chic or unfashionable, not heavy or slender. She held out her hand to Anna and smiled while Susanna said, "Mother, this is Miss Cox."

"Mrs. I'm divorced." She continued to smile. Anna took the hand, which was dry and strong. Everything about the woman was substantive and functional. Anna felt hard put to produce a response. From this more than anything she understood that Mrs. Cox was the nurse. Only Susanna could have come up with her, perfectly opaque, giving off no light and receiving none, guaranteed to skirt as completely as humanly possible the difficulties Anna had presented the night before. Anna asked her to sit down. She took the least comfortable, most upright chair, not Anna's, not Ike's, not a place on the sofa where the girls usually parked themselves. It was as if while not intruding on anyone else's place, she established a place of her own. This would be her chair. She unbuttoned her navy blue coat and exposed a beige cotton blouse and corduroy skirt of the same shade. Susanna at first said nothing,

181

afraid perhaps to mention Mrs. Cox's line of work but not sure how to get around the obstacle.

Anna offered them some coffee. "Oh, I'd love some, Mother! Shall I make it? Let me make it!" Susanna fled into the kitchen.

There was absolutely nothing to say. Anna was certainly not going to accuse her of being a nurse, or enlighten her about the situation. Mrs. Cox said, "Incredibly heavy fog last night. I never expect it in Des Moines, for some reason."

"Are you from around here?"

"Not originally. I was raised in southern Ohio, near the West Virginia border."

Anna had never been there, or known anyone who had.

"My little boy was born here, though. I suppose this is our home, now."

"You have a little boy?"

"A girl, too. She's twelve, not so little anymore. He's nearly six."

For some reason, this information lowered Anna even deeper into her fatigue, and yes, depression. What kind of life could it be, going out to take care of sick people in strange homes, leaving the six-year-old in the care of the twelve-year-old all night, night after night? She wished she could ask without mentioning nursing, without risking a discussion of why Mrs. Cox was here after all. She lifted her gaze from Mrs. Cox's shoes to her face. She was smiling sympathetically. It was an enormous shock.

"I like Des Moines, though. It's terribly bland compared to southern Ohio, but quite prosperous. In a strange way, that's rather a daily relief. When I worked at the hospital, there were magazines in the waiting rooms, good, bright paint on the walls. It's funny what a difference that makes, especially to the nurses. When I was in West Virginia, it got so that every patient looked like he was going to die, even if he was just in for a checkup."

So she had broached the topic. Anna clamped her lips shut. Mrs. Cox extricated her arms from the sleeves of her coat, which fell over the back of her chair. She seemed to be taking root. Susanna would have made real coffee, not instant, just to allow herself more time. For the first time since the nurse's arrival, Anna began to get angry. She said, "It must be extremely difficult to work and have children."

"Oh, they're used to it. I worked even while I was married. They respect what I do. I think it's good for children to know that you exist in order to do something, not in order to serve them."

"Aren't you horribly busy, though?"

"Less so now that Janet is old enough to help. And anyway, I guess I've just learned to be efficient. I don't often feel pressured like I used to."

No, you could tell that. The forthright smile, the firm handshake, the self-imposed—yes, she could see that now—the self-imposed neutrality. Susanna came in at last with coffee and slices of coffee cake, pats of butter, the jam jar, knives, and napkins. She always thought good food nicely arranged ensured peaceful negotiations. But Anna wasn't going to negotiate. She

183

was, however, going to elicit more from Mrs. Cox, who looked pleasingly like she would feel as cool as a bar of metal if you put your hand on her. Susanna's worried expression eased when she saw that they were speaking, and with apparent civility.

"Do they miss their father?"

"I don't think so. They see him every weekend. He's a physician, you see. That's about as often as they saw him when we were all living together. I think the custody hearing was what finally convinced him not to work so hard." She continued to smile.

"I don't mean to pry."

"Please don't apologize. I don't consider my situation a family secret."

"Mother, Mrs. Cox worked for Bill Thirtyacres' sister when her mother-in-law had that stroke."

Anna didn't remember. She poured out the coffee and offered the woman a piece of cake. When she was safely eating and sipping, Anna smiled at Susanna, and said, "What did she do for Bill Thirtyacres' sister?"

Susanna smiled back at her. "The usual things, I suppose. Mrs. Cox can tell you her usual way of working."

Anna continued to smile. "Working at what?"

Susanna said, "Oh," and looked inquiringly at Mrs. Cox, who declined to be drawn into the discussion. Susanna arranged herself once again on the couch and took a bite of coffee cake. Finally, she cleared her throat and said, "Mrs. Cox is a nurse, Mother. She stays nights or days, whatever you would prefer."

"I don't have any preference."

Susanna's mouth curled fleetingly upward, but she did not look at Anna. "I'm sure you'll find Mrs. Cox just perfect, Mother."

"Maybe."

Susanna was visibly relaxing into victory, but Mrs. Cox, Anna could see, knew that the job was not yet hers. Anna wanted to say that if there had been a job, she really would have been perfect. She smiled warmly at Mrs. Cox, but shook her head, just a millimeter to the right, just a millimeter to the left. Mrs. Cox paid attention, as Susanna did not, then folded her napkin into a little square and placed it on her saucer.

"Maybe it's a good time for Mrs. Cox to meet Daddy, mother. Is he awake?"

"No."

"Do you mind waiting? Would you like more coffee?"

"I don't think you should waste the woman's time, Susanna. We aren't in the market for a nurse." Anna stood up. "It's been very nice meeting you, Mrs. Cox."

The others stood up. Crumbs fell off Susanna's skirt, and they seemed to Anna to land in the rug like sparks. It was then that she realized how angry she was. She wanted to shoo these women out of her house like little girls, or chickens, or flies. If they put their coats on as a ruse, and then ran toward the staircase, got out of her range and up the steps to Ike, she would stop them, yes sir! They were very slow, especially Susanna, who had to smooth her blouse, and then her sweater, and then straighten her skirt, front and back. Anna wanted to snap, "Clothes never fit fat people!" but ultimately she dared not. Susanna held the sleeves of her sweater and eased her arms into her coatsleeves one by one, until finally Anna went up to her and jerked her collar up over her shoulders. Susanna staggered. Mrs. Cox continued to smile, though tentatively. Anna wanted to scream at her how cool and refreshing she had been, and how certainly competent Mrs. Cox seemed in every way. Her children were to be envied, perhaps. Susanna stepped carefully toward the door at last, and Anna scuttled to the bottom of the staircase, where she held onto the newel post and guarded the upper floor. Christine came to the landing, looked down, disappeared again. When the women were safely on the porch with the door closed after them, Anna locked it with what she hoped was an audible click and went to the front window. Susanna looked up at her, but Anna did not smile or wave. She got into her car rather sheepishly, and Anna's last view of them was of Mrs. Cox, perfectly upright, gliding away.

The fog had lifted into featureless, bleached overcast. Anna continued to stand by the window, but amazingly she was no longer thinking of Mrs. Cox or Susanna. With their departure they had ceased to annoy her, and she had therefore ceased to be angry at them, almost as if by magic. She was instead listening to the faint click of Nelson's toenails on the upstairs hall linoleum and imagining Christine's mind working, not whirs and taps, light bulbs and gleaming pincers, but a vine. In her exhaustion she thought of a miniature and perfect grapevine exfoliating and curling inside a skull as inside a terrarium, impossibly green and moist, thickening daily. It was almost disgusting, and yet she was attracted to what Christine had said, knew instantly, perhaps by experience, perhaps by intuition, that pleasure of the mind working.

Margaret Lacina came out of her house, gloved, turned to check her door, dropped her keys into her purse. Anna could practically hear the bite of its old-fashioned jaws. She waved to Anna, and Anna lifted her hand. Margaret eased into her twenty-year-old Pontiac, rear end first, knees together, toes pointed as she drew her feet into the car. She had, of course, taken lessons in the ladylike entry of an automobile. Mama would have liked that. In a moment, Margaret pulled out and drove away, a widow for fourteen years, who had sold her house and left her friends and family to come north, no one knew what for, since her new life was mostly an energetic reproduction of the old. With her cakes that Frank would have liked and her minute care of Frank's last car, Margaret often seemed extremely happy. Happier, Anna sometimes thought, with the artifice of this preservation in an alien place than she would have been with remnants at home. What would she do herself when Ike died, when she was no longer in the midst of their lifelong debate? She was too tired to push the notion out of her mind. Susanna and Mrs. Cox seemed somehow to have done her in. She was even too tired to be afraid. She would, of course, die herself. Between now and then, the few years of her widowhood would cuddle against the huge bulk of her marriage like a puppy against its mother. But that was not so, either. Every moment of her widowhood would be as huge, as much everything, as each moment of her marriage was. Life with Ike would come to seem like a long rat's tail leading to the giant present, whatever that might be. The images made her dizzy. She closed her eyes, then opened them on the Paullys' house, across the street. The shrubs needed a terrible pruning. Brutal pruning. Devastating pruning. Their grass was turning green already. Each spring it took about two minutes for grass to turn green. Had she ever loved the workings of her own mind as Christine did? Was Christine a genius? Did her mind deserve to work, deserve to escape the distractions of marriage and children because she was a genius, or simply because Christine took pleasure in it, perhaps only the amateur pleasure of a neighborhood baseball player?

A year after Susanna's birth, Anna had gotten pregnant again. In the midst of their move from the ranch, in the midst of Ike's rooting after some career, some job, in the midst of rice and beans for dinner every night and bare cold floors, and nothing to sit on except kitchen chairs, she had cried and cried, not only because they couldn't support another child but also because she simply didn't want a fourth baby appropriating her womb, then her breasts and her time and the bits of freedom she would soon have now that Helen and Claire were old enough to watch Susanna a little. She had cried her way into a miscarriage, she sometimes thought. If not, then at least she had been sinfully glad at the cramps and the nausea and the bloody tissue. It seemed like nothing; certainly it was not like a baby, whose confused and disgruntled stranger's face was already endearing before you recognized it. She had stood the children in a line against the kitchen wall, then, on the pretext of measuring their height, Susanna in the middle, standing proudly, with her sisters at each hand, and she pondered their faces, looking perhaps for another face, as different from these as they were from each other. A boy's face? She tried to summon up regret for the fourth child, the missing child, but there was no child missing, and she had hardly ever thought of it again. It seemed like her generation had had no choices, only luck, which absolved you from guilt, but Christine could make any choice she wanted, any time. It was never too late to start over, never too early to worry about the choices she had already made. Every plan, every purchase, every lifting of the fork involved a moral decision.

"Did you reach the doctor?" Christine at the top of the stairs again looked carelessly girlish. Without curls, without makeup, without a brassiere, without a girdle, she looked less mature at twenty-three than Helen had at fifteen. "Who was that with Aunt Susanna?"

"Some nurse. The doctor's calling me back."

"Oh, Grandmother!"

"What?"

"Don't you think maybe she should have looked at Grandfather or something?"

"What?"

"Well, did you notice that his hands seem a little

189

swollen? Here's his cup. She could have at least, you know, set our minds at rest, or something."

"My mind is at rest!" After another moment she said, "That hand thing, it's nothing to worry about. He has medicine for that. You don't have to worry." But she imagined Mrs. Cox regally climbing the stairs, placing her cool square hand on Ike's chest, on his forehead, on his wrist. "None of you understands about this nurse thing, none of you!" But she could not help imagining further, imagining Mrs. Cox settled in Ike's bedside chair, knowing what to watch for, exactly when to be concerned.

It was automatic for Christine, although obviously in low spirits, to skip down the staircase, Nelson clattering at her heels. Anna sighed herself into her rocking chair, oddly conscious of the dank street now at her back, the damp houses, the buckling sidewalk, the sodden grass verge, and the great sycamores whose branches tangled into a net at second-story height, and also of her granddaughter, whose arms and legs and back could not help but express elastic youth, who settled unselfconsciously into her grandmother's gaze, used to the many eyes of adult love. Perhaps a lifetime of adoring grownups had produced this refusal to seem suffering, which sometimes appeared as vitality and sometimes as shallowness? Anna closed her eyes, but both Christine in the living room and the street at her back stayed with her, holding her like a huge mixing bowl. She shook her head. Christine would be flipping through magazines. Sure enough, when Anna opened her eyes and picked up her knitting, Christine was glancing at a *Woman's Day*. "You know, Grandmother, Todd is like an open book to me, but he's not a novel or a volume of philosophy, he's more like an auto repair manual or something. Detailed but without a lot of levels. Do you know what I mean?"

Anna could imagine it, although not imagine thinking such a thing, so she nodded.

"When he talks, my mind wanders, but I can't ever think my own thoughts, because he's always wanting my attention. If I settle down to read, he just can't stand it and talks to me the whole time."

"Honey, your grandfather's the same way."

"Doesn't it drive you crazy?"

"I don't remember. Maybe it did once, but after you've been married fifty-two years, it's all a part of you."

"But don't you want to maintain something of yourself? Some pure, independent sort of core, or kernel?"

"You do that anyway. Every time I look at your grandfather, I know he isn't me."

"But you just said—"

"I can't explain." She could not help cutting Christine off, and her tone was annoyed. She knitted a row with quick, jerky strokes, unable to lose the sense that she was exactly the focus of a dome of surroundings, and she felt anxious again. She wanted to speak calmly, without panting. What did Christine think a marriage should be? Perhaps the outside of her own had formed a lot of the girl's early notions, and Anna could not know what that outside was like. She said,

"Your aunts and your mother talk about your grandfather and me sometimes, and they always sound like children in an enchanted forest. Every habit of ours that they suddenly discover, and even most of the ones they remember, seem either magically bad or magically good to them, and every little fact or circumstance has enormous meaning. Sometimes they tiptoe through the forest and sometimes they try to tear it down, but it's always the same huge, dark, important forest, and even when they seem to grasp the fact that your grandfather and I are just two people who have come together and learned to take one day and one argument at a time, they always lose the fact, and go back into the forest, looking for the one mystical stone or leaf, that when they turn it over or pick it up will show them how they came to be them, or even, maybe, what they came to be." What was she talking about? Her marriage? Some definition of marriage? She could only think of Ike, all the years of their married life, telling children and teenagers, and more children who then became teenagers, stories about his boyhood, about his brothers and sisters, about her, and even about themselves—these very children who were listening so raptly—about things they had done and could remember perfectly. He chuckled and rubbed his hands and it all became very interesting in the retelling, things that bored or angered him at the time—fights with Abel, life on the ranch, her idiosyncrasies—got funnier or bigger than they had been. She saw Ike, a well-intentioned man, promoting himself a little bit, but what did the children and grandchildren see? "Honey, anything I tell you about marriage, and about my own marriage—"

She tried again. "It's sort of a matter of smell, you know. And sight, too, and hearing. You look at each other for years, and what you expect of each other, and your life together becomes pretty habitual. The ingredients are indistinguishable. The looking and bearing and whatever, though, reminds you constantly that he is he and you are you, and never the twain shall meet." She thought of the countless times she had caught Ike's gaze, or not caught it. She would have been more like him if they had never met.

"Even though I can predict what your grandfather might do in a given situation, he seems more mysterious to me now than ever, but maybe not importantly mysterious. I mean, he's my husband and your grandfather, and we love him, but he's also just another person who did a few things and didn't do a few others. Do you see what I mean?" Did all of this have any practical use for this granddaughter? This lithe, sad, sulky person who hadn't changed a bit in twenty-three years?

"When your mother and aunts are tramping around in that enchanted forest, what they don't realize is that even though I have seen them every day, just about, since day one, and I saw them born, they are as mysterious to me as your grandfather is." What was she saying? Stay with him? Have the baby? They're all the same? She didn't seem to be. Was she urging any course of action at all, or simply crying out for sleep? She said, "Do you understand?" slightly emphasizing the *you*.

It was not apparent whether Christine, her head on the back of the couch and her eyes on the ceiling, was still listening, and she did not reply to Anna's query, so Anna resumed her knitting, too overcome by fatigue to care whether she had been attended to. The morning was well advanced by now, but without the feeling of morning, or of any time of day. The light in the room was still yellow and diffused. The sun, whose wheel of brightness ordinarily created time and gave Anna a sense of purpose, had not broken through the overcast. Her eyes began to sting and water, and so she closed them, but kept knitting stockinette stitch. Her fingers did it of themselves, as Mama's had, as had the fingers of every self-respecting woman of her mother's generation. Nothing, mere practice. Surely the doctor should have called by now?

Her life was making its usual sounds: the tick, tick, tick of the knitting needles, the voluntary creak of floor boards, her granddaughter's breathing and the brush of her clothes, grunts and joint crackings from Nelson, her own breathing and the beat of her heart that was half sound and half sensation. She could not help thinking herself, because of the darkness behind her eyelids, the black center of all these noises, the body where, regardless of the opening of mouth or eyes, no light penetrated. She could not help thinking her body a room without doors or windows, a hollow, her eyes and ears and nerve endings adrift on the surface, and her mind the most outside of all, filled with external glare, bulbous and doughy, the least capable instrument for probing such an interior vacuity.

"I'm so depressed," said Christine.

"I better call the doctor," said Anna.

"And what is your name?" said Clayton, his voice impersonal and harried, yet reminding her of the midnight caller. "Ma'am?"

"Anna Robison. Mrs. Ike Robison." Ineluctably, they took each other over. Now she would never hear Clayton without thinking of him, George.

"Ah, yes. Coronary thrombosis, eleven-seventy, history of arteriosclerosis? Yes?" He spoke untrustworthily.

Anna cleared her throat.

"Mrs. Robison?"

"Ike feels funny. He seems weaker."

"Have you taken his pulse?"

"It's about as regular as usual."

"Any edema of hands or feet?"

"A little swelling in his hands, not much."

"Patient taking all medications?"

"Yes."

"Any other symptoms? Irregular breathing, pain, undue worry on the part of the patient?"

"He seems as hopeful as usual."

"Well, Mrs. Robison, I—"

"Could you come over?"

"I'm very busy, we have office hours today until—"

"I know, but after that? Just for a look?"

"An ambulance could pick—"

"That would scare him to death, doctor, literally."

"Mrs. Robison, I—"

"When is Dr. Jauss supposed to get back?"

"Possibly late Sunday night."

"And today is Thursday?"

"Mrs. Robison, I—"

"Aren't you ashamed of yourself?"

"No, I am—"

"Think of him as your own father."

"I'm sorry, I—" but then he paused of his own accord, and took what sounded like a puff from a cigarette. "What's the address?"

"Eighteen sixty-five East Walnut."

"I'll try to come between three-thirty and four."

"Thank you."

Christine was right behind her. "What did he say? Is he going to come? You know, Grandmother, this friend of Todd's was in medical school, and the very first day they had a meeting of all the freshmen, and two or three of the deans stood up and welcomed them, and you know what? They didn't mention one thing about helping people or easing pain, all they told these kids was that they were the new high priests of society, their average annual income would be four times the norm, doctors were in demand everywhere, they could write their own tickets." She marched into the kitchen, gesticulating emphatically. "As a rule, you know, they are such evil and hateful people, not even human, really. You know why there aren't more medical schools? Because the AMA won't allow them!"

"He's coming around four."

"I'll bet! He didn't call you back, did he? Even though you've been leaving messages since six o'clock

196

this morning?"

Anna thought of baking bread, imagined the springy, yeasty dough alive beneath her hands, warm with milk and melted butter, honeycombed with gluten. She could roll it out and sprinkle on cinnamon sugar and raisins.

"They love having you in their power. They never tell you anything about yourself, or how you can prevent stuff from happening to you, they just expect you to go in and nod and take your pills and say yessir yessir, and then they complain about how stupid patients are, especially women patients. You'd think because you're paying them, they'd be working for you, but it doesn't work out that way. You're just paying for abuse and ignorance."

"Chrissy—"

"It's true!" Christine turned abruptly and walked out the back door. Anna could see that she was crying again. It would be too late to make bread for lunch. She opened the refrigerator. No yeast, anyway. Christine threw open the back door with a crash, shouting, "They're devils! They profit from our pain! And then they have only contempt and hatred for us! They're evil, horrible, disgusting—"

"Chrissy, they're only human."

"Tell them that!"

Her face was so contorted with anger that Anna was tempted to walk over and smack it. Instead she spoke quietly. "Dr. Jauss has been very good to both your grandfather and me. He's given your grandfather good care—"

"How do you know? How do you know that surgery he had last summer was even necessary? Did you get a second opinion from someone who didn't know Jauss, wasn't his friend?"

"Stop shouting!"

"Well, did you?"

Anna thought of Jauss's pleasant, rather roundish freckled countenance, of the way he pulled his chair up to yours and spoke in a deeper, richer, more kindly voice when he had to tell you anything important, of the way his solid body and short firm fingers seemed competent and human at the same time, and she turned on Christine and put her hand roughly over Christine's open mouth. She said, "Don't speak again. Just don't."

Christine sniffled and shuddered deeply. She shook her head, and after a moment, a moment of relieving silence, Anna said, "I could make popovers for lunch. How would you like that? I have some lovely quince jelly my cousin Jean Fountain sent for Christmas."

Tears were streaming down Christine's face. Anna was afraid to look directly at her. Christine said, "If Grandfather dies, then that'll be the end. There won't be any men left."

Anna's fingers touched the jam keg, sensed its barrel shape, and pushed it to one side. It was easier to stand on her toes peering into the back of the cabinet than to look at Christine. "There's Todd, honey, and the twins."

"I'm leaving Todd! I'm leaving Todd! And anyway, he's not a man, like Grandfather; he doesn't have any history; he's just a nice guy!"

"Oh, Chrissy!" Anna reluctantly grasped the jelly and stood back on her heels, resigned to confronting this anger and grief, but just then the room was full of her daughters, all of them talking, carrying packages, discarding coats, stumbling over Nelson. Christine closed her mouth and banged out the back door again. Anna's daughters made the room smell damp and cool. Their faces, momentarily victorious with shopping, carried the dew of early spring, and looked too young for their three lives, as if the men had never come along, and the most important things in the world were still impressing each other and arguing.

Unpacking a grocery bag, Susanna gave her a side-long sheepish look. Anna smiled. Susanna smiled. "I bought ham," said Claire. Helen flourished her package with a superior chuckle. I bought prosciutto," she declared.

Cupboards gaped all over the kitchen. "Slice it thinner than that, Claire," admonished Helen. "No more than an eighth of an inch. Here's the remoulade."

"Mother, I can't find any oil, is there any oil?"

"Nelson, get out of the way! Where's Christine?"

"You can put mustard on some of that if you want, Claire, but just the remoulade is the way it's supposed to be."

"Mother, I saw Biddy Lane at DiSalvatore's. She broke her arm falling off a unicycle."

"Biddy Lane? Susanna, our Biddy Lane?"

"Claire, those toasts are burning."

"Do you have any garlic, Mother? Cloves, not powder."

"Is that Daddy?"

"Nelson! Go into the living room, for heaven's sake!"

"Where is Christine?"

"Sit down, Mother."

"Daddy doesn't want to come down, but he'd like some kind of sandwich."

"Grandmother, can we eat these spiced apples in this jar?"

"Sit down, Mother."

"Now lay one slice of the cucumber, one piece of prosciutto, a round of onion, then a dab of the sauce. Okay. Now sprinkle on the bread crumbs and run it under the broiler."

"Helen, turn on the fan."

"Shall we use these placemats?"

"Grandfather says this isn't a sandwich, and he'd like two slices of the usual bread wrapped around something he recognizes."

"Wash some spoons, Christine."

"Nelson can eat that."

"Helen, close the freezer door."

"That lettuce isn't dry enough. The dressing won't coat it properly if it isn't dry enough."

"Is this towel clean?"

"Too much salt."

"Sit down, Mother."

"Grandfather wants to know if there are any canned pears. He would like to fling a lip over some canned pears."

"I'm making the tea!"

"I think the sun's coming out."

"I showed a lovely house today. Do you remember the Davieses, Helen?"

"Christine, call this hound!"

"I put them on already, Mother."

"We should wash the windows for spring, Grandmother. We should all get together and wash your windows."

"I like it with the crusts cut off, then the edges buttered and rolled in chopped parsley. The bread has to be really top-notch, though."

"Mr. Scoppino had beautiful standing rib roasts today. Made me actually want to have a dinner party."

"Are those ready, Claire?"

"Is Daddy taken care of?"

"Are we ready?"

"Are we ready?"

"Chrissy, I think we're ready!"

"Sit down, Mother."

Anna sat down. This every one of them was good at, thanks perhaps to her. Perhaps not. Even Christine could dress a salad, splendidly, casually, in passing, a little of this a dash of that while thinking about dessert. Claire sharpened her knives with a manly flourish, unafraid of them, and Helen's julienned vegetables fell onto the plates in patterns of fans and daisies. The hot was hot and the cold was cold. Susanna's lemon souffle was in the oven, certain to balloon, and Anna's own tiny ginger wafers waited to garnish it. As they pulled out their chairs expectantly and looked at one another with greater than usual tolerance, she could see that this was their own feast, made by their own hands for their own eyes, noses, and tongues, and that, in spite of disease and antagonism, divorce, birth, and worry, right now this was enough, the green-and-white trellised placemats, the russet table, the ivory plates and cups with their raised garland design. Radishes and emerald-edged cucumber rounds, beds of lettuce, crisp melba toast, bowls of soup and hard-boiled eggs, pale butter, a cruet of dressing, a pitcher of milk, and a wedge of bleu cheese on the maple cheese board promised for the moment never to give out, to taste in every bite as they tasted in the first, hungriest bite.

"Mother," said Christine, "you have on your food stare."

"What's that?" Helen reached for the pepper.

"It's your instinctual gaze at your prey. You know how when you're in a restaurant and the waiter goes by with food for another table, conversation always stops, and the people at your table always follow his tray with their eyes?"

"Like a cat staring at a mouse?" said Susanna.

"Exactly."

"Oh, Chrissy."

"She's right, Helen. I saw you looking at that sandwich. You were absolutely lethal." Even Helen smiled at Claire's joke and didn't protest. There was a general passing of condiments and opening of mouths. Helen was complimented on the sandwiches. She demurred, saying that Claire had put them together, and adding that the touch of mustard was actually quite tasty. Christine loved Susanna's soup and asked for more. There was plenty more. Susanna said that the tea was still good and hot. Claire disappeared and returned to say that Ike wanted to know what they were talking about. She took him some soup. Christine was asked not to slurp her soup, and she smiled to show that she had only slurped it in order that one of her lifelong caretakers would remind her of her manners for old times' sake. Nelson stood up and pushed his nose into Helen's napkined lap. He was ordered to lie down. He did so, sniffing. Claire poured herself a glass of milk. Anna took a second sandwich. Christine disappeared and returned, carrying Ike's soup bowl and relating that the noise of jaws and teeth was so loud on the second floor, according to Ike, that he couldn't concentrate on his book. "Oh, Daddy," muttered Helen, as if he were at the table. Susanna removed the yolk from her egg, mashed it on her plate with a little of the remoulade sauce, then ate it and licked her fork. "Did you make this sauce, Helen, or buy it?" she asked.

Anna felt her headache and her spirits flutter and lift. In the middle afternoon, which was sooner than the late afternoon, sooner than you knew, really, the doctor would arrive, bringing all his training and reassurance. Before dinner, Claire would take her to the market, where she would linger among the array and plan a dinner for Chrissy, something special that she would love, and more interesting meals for Ike, with a lot of fruit. This day, she thought, would surely deflate to normal size and as quickly give way to the future as all the other days of the recent past. Its length would turn out to be spurious, a product merely of point of view. Anna smiled and held up the spiced apples. "Are you still interested in these?"

"Oh, yes!" exclaimed Christine, her mouth full, taking the dish from Anna's hand.

"That was very good, I thought," said Helen.

"Don't forget the souffle. What do you think, Susanna?"

"Soon, soon. We have to wait for the perfect moment."

"Mmmm," said Christine.

"Remember those strudels Aunt Dolores made all that one spring, Claire? Apple, cherry, poppyseed, one right after the other. I can't believe we got tired of them."

"Aunt Dolores was such a one for taking a notion to do something and then running it into the ground."

"Some of her notions were great while they lasted, but remember the blood sausage? She thought sure that if she just persevered, we'd be sure to get to like it."

"Dolores loved all that stuff that Mama used to make."

"Chrissy, your grandfather finally wouldn't even come to the table if one of those sausages was there."

"The strudels were great, though."

"I never had the patience for rolling out that dough, that's for sure."

"I'll split it with you."

Anna leaned back with a satisfied sigh.

"I think it's ready now," said Susanna, and in a moment brought it to the table, steaming lemon steam, golden with just the finest crispness, and already sinking in the middle. Chairs scraped with anticipation, and Christine set clean plates and forks on the table. Claire disappeared and came back. "Daddy respectfully inquires whether there's a morsel of ice cream to be had in the establishment."

"Take him a little of this."

"He wants to know if he's missed any arguments, political discussions, or gossip about himself."

"I hate to go back to work this afternoon, but I have to get started on my taxes."

"Don't mention that, please!"

"He seems better."

"I think he is, Mother, I really think he is."

"I think that anything that happens in the middle of the night worries you more than if the same thing happened during the day?"

"Oh, I'm sure that's true, Mother. But really, if you're ever worried, even the slightest bit, you should call one of us."

"Mother—" But even as the word *nurse* rose into the eyes of everyone at the table, and Anna again wondered why she hadn't just let Mrs. Cox look at Ike one time, Claire closed her mouth. The souffle was not entirely eaten and there were still cookies on the plate. "Coffee?" suggested Helen.

Four

ॐ

*T*hey were still at the table when Anna came down from helping Ike to the bathroom. She could see by Christine's lowered, sullen gaze that the subject of Todd had been broached. Helen's hand was in her purse, absently seeking a cigarette as always after meals or in moments of strain. Claire was clearing dishes off the table, and Susanna was pretending to look for something in her shoe, shaking it and reaching inside it, peering and obviously performing. Everyone was trying to think of something to say. Anna said, "Someone could go up and sit with Daddy."

"I will, Grandmother." But Helen's gaze, and then Claire's, pinned Christine in her seat. There was no more food Anna could offer to bring back the sense of simple celebration, and now that everyone was fortified, every point of view seemed that much clearer, clamored that much more for presentation.

"Well, I can't find anything," said Susanna. "It must be a knot in a thread or something. Chrissy, I didn't mean to silence the conversation. I just don't think

206

you know what you're throwing away."

"I think I do." Feeling Claire's presence, Christine was careful to sound courteous.

"It's your decision, of course—"

"Does your aunt Susanna know you're pregnant, Christine?" Claire spoke casually, pretending not to be dramatic. Helen took her hand out of her purse and shifted in her chair, having wanted a cigarette for so many years that she didn't even know she wanted it any longer.

"Since I haven't told anyone," replied Christine in a light voice, "I'm surprised anyone knows." She smiled too broadly. Nelson, whose eyes had been on her face, stood up wagging his tail. "Lie down!" Her whisper was furious.

"Mother," declared Helen, "I made you some tea." Anna took this as instructions to sit down. Did she have to trim her voice and her demeanor as Christine did? It was clear that Helen had mentioned something to Claire and that Claire had been stiffening Helen's spine. The tack being taken was too Prussian for Helen but just right for Claire. Anna blew on her tea, though it was already cold.

"I think that changes things," offered Susanna, and when no one spoke, she went on, rather tentatively, "After the baby comes you'll see things differently. You'll have a good reason to make up with Todd—"

"I'm not mad at Todd! That's the point! I'm not doing this out of anger!" She sounded extremely angry.

Claire grimaced politely. "Tell us again why you're

doing it, then."

"I can't think! I—"

"Take your time, we have all afternoon."

"That's not what I mean, I . . . Anyway, someone should go upstairs and be with Grandfather. And I don't think he should have to hear us arguing down here."

"If he came down, I think he'd be quite surprised and upset with what he would find."

"I know that, but—"

"If you're ashamed to say what you want to do, then maybe you shouldn't do it."

"Aunt Claire, I—"

"Why don't you go up and tell him what's on your mind, and see what he has to say about it? I don't think he would mince any words."

"You can love someone without sharing all his opinions."

With one familial motion, everyone, Anna too, fell back in her chair. Obviously, they could not go on about this. They were tired, and anxious about Ike and the doctor (Anna looked at the clock on the sideboard), ready to say things that ought not to be said. It was something they should talk about when spring was well advanced, when the sun shone on sixty-degree days and was reflected by the glitter of daffodils and yellow tulips. When they could sit in the yard and have half their words and all their anger carried off by the breeze.

Claire said, "It's simply wrong."

"What is?" challenged Christine.

"What you're planning."

"What am I planning?"

Claire shifted in her chair but managed to sound scornful. "An abortion, of course!"

"And how did you learn that? I never even told anyone I was pregnant, and now you've got me having an abortion!"

"Tell me straight out that's not what you're planning to do! Straight out! Look me right in the eye!"

"Stop fighting!" exclaimed Anna. There was a pause. Into it she uttered, "You loved dolls. You loved playing house."

She wished immediately that she hadn't said it. She'd been lucky, in a way, to live with Christine's childhood, to give her lunch when she walked home from school, to make doll clothes for her, to teach her to plant potatoes, to bake her pink-and-white birthday cakes, the sort that turned any adult's stomach but delighted Christine. Christine had been the child of her maturity, the subject of deeper contemplation and the beneficiary of greater leisure than her own children. Watching Christine's childhood so long after hers had impressed upon Anna the mystery of time. From day to day when Christine was two, she thought, Will this be her first memory, waking in the sun on Mama's grape basket quilt? Or this, falling out of the high chair (Anna had turned her back for hardly a second), or this, being shown how to roll down a grassy hill by a neighbor child? Usually, when she changed Christine's diapers, there would be the businesslike matters of rubber pants and pins between the lips, but occasionally she would see Christine lying there on her back, calmly waiting and looking up at her, and she would wonder about the dawn of thought, wonder how Christine could return her gaze with the steadiness of Anna's own and not remember it and care about it as much as Anna did. For years Anna spent so much quiet time with Christine that they came to seem the motionless center pulling Ike home from his job, holding Helen and Sam in orbit, seducing Claire into hope and Susanna, who married at twenty, into care.

Christine said, "Grandmother, I thought you understood."

Claire was exasperated. "In my day, there wasn't anything to understand! You're going to have a baby; a baby needs a father. Todd is its father. It seems downright simple to me."

"Someone should check on Ike." But they could not tear themselves away. The stack of plates continued to sit in the center of the table. "That souffle dish ought to soak," said Helen, but no one moved or, it seemed, even intended to move.

Christine exclaimed, "You don't understand!" And Helen said, "No, we don't! Explain it to us! Your husband is a good provider who loves you and does his best for you. You have a job and money of your own. No, I, for one, don't understand!"

"*I hate being married. I want to be alone!* Is that impossible to see?"

Helen pursed her lips and crossed her arms over her chest. Whereas Christine brought this out like a

210

bazooka, Helen dismissed it like a pop-gun. "No one likes being alone, really," she said. "It seems pleasant to think about when you are safely married and out of danger, but if you really were alone, you'd soon see—"

"Why don't you believe me?" Christine was almost crying again. "Can't you hear me?"

Helen waved her hand. "You're just being dramatic," but in spite of herself she fell silent, impressed with the vehemence of Christine's behavior. Anna didn't know what to do. She felt trapped in her chair, unable to speak. Finally Helen rose up out of her own chair and leaned across the table toward Christine. "Do you really want to know about being alone, young lady? I'll tell you, because I know all about it." She was not shouting, but her voice carried a threat of unthinkable retaliation if Christine failed to pay attention. "Do you want to know how long it's been since I slept with anyone, or even touched anyone, and had him touch me back? Nothing special, just something simple, like a hand on the back of the neck, or between my shoulder blades? Living alone is never having that, never! We don't talk much about that around this house, I'm sorry to say. Don't squirm in your chair, Claire! You can pretend you don't know what I'm talking about, now that you're fifty—"

"Forty-nine!"

"I won't have this sort of talk in my—"

"No, Mother, you don't want to, but I'm going to tell the truth for once. Being alone isn't simply having to dig your own car out in the winter and doing your own taxes and eating by yourself night after night! It's never being cared for or thought of or looked at, really looked at, or bumped against, or touched, or held, or—" But though no one interrupted her, she could not say the word, not in this house, not with Anna at the table, especially not with Ike upstairs, though her voice was low and intense, not audible through any floors or walls. She compensated for not being able to say the word by looking straight at Christine and saying, "You're a dope!"

All Christine could say was, "You don't understand. You just don't understand!" It was true, Anna thought, they didn't understand at all. Helen picked up the plates and marched into the kitchen. Unsorted images crowded Anna's mind: Todd in his wedding suit, mannerly and ebullient, wishing more than anything to be a married man; Christine alone, self-contained, neat, full of improving projects (how had they never seen the implications of that lifelong competence?); an unimaginable baby, mostly blankets; Ike at his best, leaning into the group of children, making them shout with laughter, promoting talk and activity and effort like no other father she had ever known; Ike at his worst, breaking things he could not afford to replace, grinding his teeth and shouting, raising his fist; herself at her best, alone, looking, smelling, hearing, all her thoughts concentrated on the quality of light or air; herself at her worst, falling away from Ike's needs like the waters of Tantalus. No single image pressed judgment upon her. No conclusions could be drawn, about Christine or Ike or marriage or birth. But she loved babies. She'd always loved babies.

She said, "I'm going to sit with Daddy a little."

Ike said, "Now get Christine and the boy to bring the television up here, because I don't want to miss Lawrence Welk tonight."

"Lawrence Welk is the day after tomorrow."

"What's today?"

"Thursday."

Ike looked around the room, and in a moment said, "Goddammit, Mother, where's my calendar from the shop? They always send me that calendar!"

"I put it up in the kitchen. You told me to put it up in the kitchen this year."

"Well, now I want it in here. I never know when it is. Why hasn't that boy come up to say hello?"

"You mean Todd, Daddy?"

"Is that his name?"

"Chrissy's husband stayed in Chicago, Daddy. He had to work."

"Does he work on the weekends?"

"It's not the weekend, Daddy. It's Thursday. I just told you that."

Ike had put in his dentures and now stretched his lips around them and clacked them absently together. Anna thought fondly of the doctor, soon to arrive, and Ike smiled triumphantly. "What are they all having lunch here for, then? Why isn't Susanna at work? Why isn't Christine at work?"

"Chrissy's taking some of her vacation, Daddy, and Susanna took the afternoon off. It really is Thursday."

"And what's going on down there? It sounds like

some kind of fight."

"Nothing."

"Tell me."

"It's just Helen and Claire."

After a moment, Ike said, "What's on the television tonight, then?"

"You don't like anything."

"What?"

"I don't know. Nothing you ever watch."

"Well, *what!*"

"Do you want me to go get the listings?"

"You could!"

"Ike, it's Thursday. You *hate* Thursday nights."

"*I just want to know what's on!*" After croaking this out, he fell back, panting. Anna didn't know if they had any television listings in the house. Usually Ike was so set in his viewing routine that she gave the listings only a cursory glance before throwing them out with the Sunday paper. His face was blotchy, very red, almost purple, and very white, almost chalky. She said, her voice trembling a little, "Daddy, are your hands swollen any, or your feet?"

He shook his head.

"Will you let me see?"

He shook his head again, then said quietly, "Why can't I have anything I ask for the first time?"

Anna heaved herself out of the clothing-strewn armchair and went to the top of the stairs. Voices from the dining room continued to rise and fall. She did not allow herself to disentangle the words, but as she descended the stairs thought of anything—whether she had thrown away the Sunday paper, when her seeds from Gurney's might arrive, whether she really should start any tomato plants this year, didn't the curtains in the front window need washing, how she hated to starch them, with all their ruffles—anything rather than responsibility and unhappiness and longing.

Christine was crying again. Anna averted her gaze. There was no Sunday paper in the newspaper pile, no television listings. Claire must have thrown them out with her usual efficiency. Rather than confront Ike's anger, or worse, hurt feelings, she plumped down in the rocking chair with a large sigh.

Claire said, "This has nothing to do with being oppressed as a woman! God forbid! This has to do with decision and responsibility!" Anna stood up again, and got to the stairs before she heard Helen's voice, "Mother?" and Christine's, "Grandmother!" She pretended to be out of earshot.

Only pretended. Halfway up the stairs she paused when the voices went back to each other, and she heard Christine give a huge catching sigh. There was one long moment of silence when she could imagine everyone frowning, looking around, reconnoitering. She stood very still, as if she were long gone. Her three daughters spoke almost at once. Claire exclaimed, "How can anyone not want her own baby?" Helen said, "A woman's got to have companionship!" And Susanna, in a sympathetic but unbelieving voice, kept trying to sort things out. "But you say that you still love him."

Christine exhaled sharply, exasperated. "I do. I love him when he's fixing the car, or trying to play that guitar he has, when he's not paying attention to me, when he isn't even aware that I'm in the room. I love him! I just hate our life together. I hate being married!"

"But it'll be dif—"

Anna shut out the rest of the sentence. Who could say what would happen? No one ever had.

Ike had forgotten about the TV listings and was thumbing through his book, always the same book, *Winesburg, Ohio*. He would open it anywhere and rummage around himself or, sometimes, ask her to read it to him. Whenever she did, he would interrupt her repeatedly, saying, "That's not a good part. Skip down a ways to where they stop talking." Then she would go to the indicated paragraphs and read them with care; Ike would lean back against the wall and inhale deeply. He had never given her a chance to read a whole story, much less the book from end to end, and she never borrowed it. She did not know whether he enjoyed it because he loved the memories it invoked of his rustic boyhood, or because he hated them. At any rate, he read nothing else anymore, not even the other Sherwood Anderson books Christine had found for him. These past few months he was as reluctant to move to a new book as he would be to move to a new house.

Anna sat beside his bed as he looked at the familiar words and searched for the most familiar. So Christine was like her in this way as well: she, too, loved her husband's inattention the most. Not that Ike had ever fixed the car. But he had been a great spectacle of play, with his high, rolling baseball swing, his long arms and big strides at second base; later on he got to be a ferocious tennis player, with no finesse but daunting power, and always in formal, dazzling whites (she bleached them herself). If there was nothing competitive, he swam and dove, or ran around the block, or took his golf clubs outside and practiced cocking the wrist or taming the elbow or addressing, the ball. She'd always liked to look out the window and see his eyes down and his gaze inward, his very corporeality remarkable.

"Mother, what are you smiling about?"

"I thought you were reading your book."

"Nah." He looked at her pointedly and rolled his eyes toward the bathroom. She sighed and stood up.

Susanna said, "Is Daddy asleep again?"

Anna nodded, but the others did not look up. Helen lifted her coffee cup, discovered that it was empty, and set it down again. It rattled, just twice, against the saucer. Helen coughed. They had argued themselves into a kind of surface indifference, indifference adopted as a strategy, until some outrageous statement might be uttered and they could leap to it again. In Anna's experience, conflicts were rarely dropped before the last word had been said, the last extreme position taken. Although apparently indifferent, no one stood up or even moved. Everyone waited for the next round.

And then a strange thing happened, something Anna might have expected but didn't. Helen turned to Christine, trying not to speak greedily. "Chrissy," she said, "bring the baby home to my house. There's plenty of room. The attic would be splendid for you, like your own apartment. We could have that bathroom fixed up, and you could use the little anteroom for the baby and the big room for yourself." She put her arms seriously, practically, on the table, but her voice squeaked with desire. Claire's head swiveled a hundred and eighty degrees, but she was too shocked, and perhaps betrayed, to say anything. "If you wanted to work, I'd be glad to babysit." Helen? Anna couldn't imagine it. Christine's eyebrows lifted.

It was Anna who said, "Helen, the ceilings in your attic are only five feet high."

"Not in the middle." She licked her lips. "Not in the middle, only around the sides."

Claire shrugged and Anna was the one who found herself growing angry. "I doubt that living with her mother is Christine's idea of independence," she snapped. "If I were her and I'd made up my mind to do what she wants to do, I'd move to New York or California, not to your attic, or even to your neighborhood. She can't spend her life going home to Mother!" Her hands were on her hips and she could feel her chin lift and her jaws clap shut. Here was something else that came from nowhere, a speech impossible in the mouth of a mother whose three used, consulted, depended-upon daughters lived within two miles of their mother's house. Except that

218

for the instant of speaking, she had not thought of them, only looked at their faces. Mama was who she'd thought of, and the way moving out of Mama's house into her own had felt like crawling out of a canvas pup tent into an alpine morning, but of course she couldn't explain. And everyone stood up. Christine began gathering placemats, careful of crumbs, sniffling. Susanna fingernailed a bit of the crusty souffle, and Helen sighed. Fully intending to proceed into the kitchen, weightily, tiredly, her heels aching and her calves tight, Anna sat down again, in Ike's armchair, the only armchair at the dining room table. They could have eaten all afternoon. They should have eaten all afternoon bringing course after course out on trays, one dish at a time, greenly garnished or lightly sauced or decorated with a ladle. They should have awaited the doctor surrounded by food like battlements, should have received him at the table like fresh reinforcements, heavy artillery to turn the tide away from death and anger and judgment and choice. Never once could they not be themselves, it seemed. Never once could their histories and habits fail to catch up with them. The table emptied at last, was brushed off and wiped with a sponge. Anna did not lift her eyes from it. In the kitchen, dishes rang, the refrigerator door sucked open, whispered closed. Christine blew her nose two or three times. Helen circled Anna, departed, returned, and circled again. Finally, she declared, "I don't think you understand how this thing is affecting us, Mother."

"But you must let Christine—"

"Not Christine. Daddy."

Anna looked up. "What about him?"

Helen peered at her for a few seconds, then shrugged. Anna's gaze traveled from Helen to the begonias in the window. They had new flesh-colored flowers. Helen sat on the edge of the table, bending it a little. She was looking into the living room, through the living room window at the Paullys' house. She said, "For the first moment, Sam's death, and Alfred's too, was like the beginning of a trip. In a way almost interesting, a change. As soon as it felt like a trip, then each day that I got through felt like an achievement, as if I had a direction. It was odd how for a few days that sense buoyed me up and gave me lots of energy. In the midst of it all, I felt intensely brave, each time, intensely full of purpose. Each time, and I made the mistake twice, I let that sense of its being a trip sort of take me over for a while. I let myself think there was going to be an end, that the little counter would move across the scale of days and then stop, and it would be all right, the same, good again. And each time I realized one morning that surmounting one day didn't lead me anywhere, at least not closer to Sam or Alfred again. It wasn't like a trip at all. It was final, forever. I would die myself and not see either one ever."

"Your father is not dying."

"Why are we gathered here? I think it's some kind of instinct."

"Everyone's not here. Todd isn't here."

"Do you think he would be after what she's said?"

"They were here together for Christmas. And the

twins, too. We live here. Chrissy came home for her own reasons."

"I can't help thinking—"

"Don't think it!"

"Mother." Helen slipped off the table and squatted with middle-aged difficulty next to Anna's chair. Her face ducked down and then up, like a shovel, scooping Anna's eyes into her own. She was not whispering, but her voice was low. Insensibly, Anna leaned toward it. "I think, Mother, that we aren't here for Daddy, not even Claire. We're really here for you. We're gathered around you. Yes! Like we've always been. That's why Chrissy is here but not Jimmy and Jeremy. I mean, you don't really like Jimmy and Jeremy, and never have. I often think you don't like men, actually, not even Daddy." She looked away toward the kitchen, but Claire did not appear. "I've never known how you did it, Mother, how you made yourself seem so right all the time, and so good; how it was that in the same room with you, Daddy seemed somehow wrong, always, even when we loved him best, and wanted to defend him and be with him more than anyone else in the world." She cleared her throat and jerked, almost losing her balance. "Here I am, the missionary to China, the foreign correspondent, the explorer-anthropologist, right here, with my mother—"

"Surely you can't blame that on me, I never stopped you—"

"And Claire, too. If anyone could have made herself the center of a family by sheer force of will, you'd have thought Claire was the one. But no."

She stood up with a crackle of joints that made Anna wince. "You have to see, Mother. You have to see in a way that you've never seen before. You can't keep Daddy simply because you want to. He can't be in the orbit anymore. Really not. *Really.* You've never let any one of us not need you, but now Daddy is going to escape."

"Maybe my failure is only that you can't take the blame for your own failures."

"No, Mother."

The others, having finished the dishes, seemed to sweep through, sweeping Helen away. There was talk of at last getting some work done, at last the sun breaking through. Nelson was let out, with admonitions about staying nearby. There was nothing for Anna to think. Inside her, top to toe, heart to fingers, a figure like the cartoon in the electric company ads sizzled and hissed.

"Now Mother," said Susanna, in her usual tone of voice—defeated? full of dislike?—"I'm just going over to the office for a few minutes. I want to pick up my tax forms, anyway, and see what came in the mail. I might have to show one house, but surely not more than one. Helen has to wait for the washing machine repair man, but he promised early afternoon, and she'll be back by three. Christine will be here, okay? She's got her own car and everything." She dropped her voice to a whisper. "Now don't worry about Daddy. I think he's fine. Claire is always ready to panic."

"He said today was Seth's hundredth birthday. I'm afraid he thinks he can let go now, or something."

"Don't worry! Things don't happen that way, and you know it."

"Besides, I just now realized it's Seth's ninety-ninth birthday. I'm sure it is. I'll find that old album." Still, however, she could not stand up. A narrowing glitter had fallen over things, and the knobby headache of the night before, the week before, the months before materialized at her temples and the bridge of her nose, spreading.

"Christine will find it. You make Christine do things for you, Mother. She can sit with Daddy when he wakes up and she can answer the phone and everything." Susanna was so close to her by this time that Anna could smell her cosmetic smells and the lemon juice she liked to rinse her hair with. It was all she could do not to lean away. Helen was wrong. Anna had not intended this nest of daughters. It was she who hated their leaving, who had knocked around the house so resentfully after Susanna's elopement, slammed down the phone angrily when one of his male friends declined a tennis date, refused pettishly to go swimming without the girls, and tried impatiently to teach her golf. Not she, not she. She, like Christine, swam through solitude like a seal, didn't she? Susanna's inquiring posture demanded acquiescence with all these arrangements. Yes. Helen would be coming back. Susanna would be going somewhere. Who would be staying? Oh, yes. Chrissy. To answer the phone. Anna nodded. Before Susanna left, she wanted to ask if today had to be the day for fingering her whole life, for deciding good and evil. Susanna said, "You'll be fine, Mother," and put her hand on Anna's shoulder prefatory to moving away.

I have worked hard and been happy, thought Anna. With my hands I have made something every day. Wasn't that good? Did she have to repent because happiness came easily to her, because in the midst of anything, however perilous, a color, a shape, a harmony, or a fragrance was enough, because activity itself was enough? Helen had her back to her, and she was looking once again in her purse. No doubt for the car keys. Helen would say, There was a bowl of happiness in this family, and you drank it all. Anna looked away before Helen could turn around.

She got up for good-byes, even went hospitably to the door, but then flopped down again, without having spoken. She did not know.

When Chrissy, after a huge preliminary sigh, opened her mouth, she did not mention Helen. She said, "You know what I really want to do, Grandmother?"

"What's that?"

"I want to spend the end of the world traveling around watching everything disintegrate."

"What?"

"I wouldn't even need that much money. I'd take Nelson, and we'd hitchhike around the country, maybe taking notes and pictures. We'd record the end of everything."

"I—"

"Grandmother." Christine leaned forward, intent.

"Everything they say about Todd and my being pregnant is predicated on the notion that things will go on as they are. But they can't, you know. They really can't. Since we got married, I've all the time been catching myself thinking, Well, if it happens, we've got the garden, and all these canned goods, and we don't live all that near Chicago, and the wind blows west to east. I think if I had a baby I'd be crazy, wanting to reinforce the concrete walls of the basement, or hoard water containers and cyanide pills. Whenever I think of having a baby, I think about pictures in old *Life* magazines about the war, these women walking out of Warsaw with babies in their arms, just completely powerless with love and fear. I don't want to be like that."

"Honey—"

"But, see, if I stopped now, threw myself into the life of a refugee, in a way, right now, I'd avoid that. I'd learn things, too. When I think about what I would learn, it takes my breath away."

The discussion was so outrageous that Anna was unable to make a reply when Christine looked up at her, anxious for one. She had hoped to gently probe, somehow, after clues to Helen's real opinion of her, to elicit the truth from Christine without igniting love and concern that would make for tact. She had imagined sneaking away with some perfect knowledge of herself from Helen's perspective, and possibly Claire's and Susanna's. Now, however, she had nothing to say. She could only pick up her knitting in amazement at the idea of Christine, shawled and fleeing, her banjo, her stereo, her blender, her wedding silver, everything wrapped in Indian bedspreads on a handcart in the shadow of the Prudential Building.

"If I were a man, no one would object. If I did have this baby, I'd tell her not to mistake love for adventure, believe me." She spoke grumpily.

"Well, it seems to me that a person thinks about the end of the world—"

"I do. All the time."

"Because all of this seems like the end of the world, but—"

"It is, though! Don't you read the newspaper? I mean it isn't just Vietnam, though we've done every-thing we could to make the country a wasteland! South of the Sahara, in Africa, people are dying of famine by the thousands. And the jet stream is moving! Did you know that? This whole area right here is going to be a desert, because when the jet stream moves, it makes all the weather patterns change. And there's pesticides everywhere! There was this guy in school with me who was really thin, like a hundred and twenty pounds. He started having these symptoms—weakness, trembling, feeling sick to his stomach. They thought it was too much fried food, and then maybe some other things. It was all one fall, about two years ago. Anyway, everything cleared up in January. Well, that spring I was reading *Silent Spring* for a course, and Rachel Carson was describing the symptoms of insecticide poisoning in birds, and they were just the same as Kent's. So I asked the girl who was living with this guy what he'd been eating in the fall, and she said he'd eaten a lot of apples from a neighboring orchard, only from that orchard. Well, it was well known that that grower used tons of DDT and always had. Anyway, this guy, this guy we knew and saw all the time, he got poisoned just from eating apples! It's all ending! People have been thinking that they could do anything and have anything. Anyway, it's coming. All the psychics say so. Nineteen eighty-one or two. What do you tell a ten-year-old kid when the end is near? 'That's life?' " Christine threw herself back against the sofa and snatched up a magazine. Anna's mouth fluttered open, ready with reassurances, but how could she reassure someone who had asked about the A-bomb at six, had begged for a fallout shelter at ten, had declared herself a Catholic during the Cuban missile crisis so she could be sure of going to heaven, and for all those years had hidden in the kitchen with her fingers in her ears while the news was on? Finally, Anna offered, "I thought you grew out of all that stuff."

"I put it out of my mind for a while, but everything got worse anyway."

"What does Todd think?"

"Half the time he thinks I'm neurotic and half the time he thinks that our love shows we're fated to survive."

Now this, Anna thought as she knitted stitches off the cabling hook, then put the hook between her lips, was interesting. Even in the most perilous cold war days, the habit of going on had been strong enough to bar any imaginings of "the end." On the other hand, the possibility of failing to survive had stalked her life, and Ike's even more. She said, "Did I ever tell you about that time on the ranch when I was really sure we'd had it?"

Christine shook her head.

"I was real young. We hadn't been there long, because your mother wasn't born yet. We'd spent a lot of money on some special feed, and then Abel had gotten in a poker game, and then, to top it off, I had actually lost a couple of dollars out of my pocket in town. After living with Mama and Papa, I wasn't used to thinking that a couple of dollars could really make that much difference, but a day or so later, when we all got together, it turned out that none of us had any money, just enough for either horsefeed or a part for a piece of broken machinery—I can't remember what it was, now—or some food. Well, Daddy and Abel were just as mad as Tucker at each other, and being hungry made them madder. So your grandfather got so mad that he ran out to the barn and jumped on the horse— there was only one then—and rode off into town. Abel wouldn't talk to me, and I was half afraid that he might beat me up, because he had just an ungovernable temper. I went to our room and wedged a chest against the door. Abel kept coming to the door and shouting at me to make him some biscuits, since we did have a little flour and some bacon grease. The more he shouted, the scareder I got; then I heard a loud crashing noise, and I just assumed that he had destroyed something, anything, the whole kitchen wouldn't have surprised me. So I got into bed and pulled the covers over my head and put my fingers in

228

my ears. Ike had the horse and the five or six dollars we all had between us, and he didn't come back by dark, or by morning the next day either. My stomach hurt from being hungry, and from having to go to the bathroom, but as hungry as I was, I figured Abel was hungrier, and therefore madder, and if he had wanted to beat me up the day before, he would kill me today. I began to think that your grandfather had just left us, and for some reason, I wasn't surprised. And then, sometime in the afternoon, there came a scratching noise. At first I thought it was Abel trying to lure me out of my room, but then I realized it was coming from the window. Well, it was your grandfather, grinning and singing, in a new shirt! I opened the window and let him in, and let me tell you, he could barely make it. I was all set to be mad, but then he made me look out the window, and there were all these parcels arranged there on the ground, and I saw that he'd bought food and even salt meat. And when I opened my mouth to say something, he held out his hand and in it was a diamond ring! I was so surprised that I'm afraid I didn't even say much, maybe *oh*, or something, not enough to please your grandfather, but that's a separate story. Well, he'd gotten into a poker game and won four hundred dollars! And, of course, being your grandfather, he'd bought a diamond ring instead of calves or chickens or machinery. I went right out to the kitchen and made a huge dinner, with a pie each for the two of them. Must have been peach because it was early summer."

"What was the loud crash?"

"Well, Abel had gotten so mad that he kicked the door to his room off its hinges."

"My Lord!"

"Your uncle Abel was something, you know."

"Sounds like Grandfather was, too."

"They had a pair of tempers between them, I'll say that."

"What happened to the ring?"

"We pawned it sometime. Probably the year after we left the ranch."

"You pawned it? You really did, after that romantic story?"

"Well, if it's diamond rings or rent and food, there's not much choice."

Christine shook her head, Anna noted, with disbelief. She could not imagine life without plenty but could imagine cataclysm, chaos, finality. Anna shook her own head.

"Whatever happened to the ranch, anyway?"

"We had to sell it."

"Were you sorry?"

"Yes and no."

"Whenever you talk about it, it sounds so beautiful."

Anna didn't know what to say. Had it been "beautiful"? Or had she, like Ike, touched things up? For a moment, she tried to remember with absolute care and fidelity something about the ranch. In silence, not speaking, not telling a tale, she could not. She said, "Sometimes the mountains were nice." When Christine twisted her mouth, a little disappointed, Anna said, "When I went up into the mountains as a child, it was very beautiful. We'd ride the train up the line to Kane, and then my father would get a horse and wagon and we'd bump up an old trail to a cabin my parents had. It wasn't way up high, but there were peaks all around. That was pretty." Christine still looked disappointed. Anna sighed. In a moment she said, "Your grandfather wasn't a farmer, and your great-uncle Abel wasn't much of one either. Everybody thought there was money to be made by the fistful when they went out there during the first war, but they soon found out that it takes more than a fondness for horseback riding to raise cattle."

"What happened?"

"Everything."

"Well, what?"

"Well, let's see. They got on all right the first year or so. They homesteaded some land, and then their mother gave them some money to buy it outright. She frankly didn't want Abel back in Iowa. He'd been into some kind of trouble, though I never got to know exactly what. But anyway, it was worth it to her to make sure nothing discouraged them, like a big mortgage payment, so they got this ranch and some cattle, and they did pretty well by themselves until the summer Daddy and I got married. There was a terrible drought that summer, no grass anywhere, and no hay or feed either, at least not till the fall. Ike's mother sent us a little, and my mother did, too, and then there was that poker game. We had rain the next year, and the next, so we hung on. Daddy liked to think of himself as a rancher, you know, and he sort of liked that life. He hated the work, but he liked being outdoors, and he liked the hunting and fishing and gambling and drinking. It was my home, so I liked it, too. We had friends all down the east side of the Big Horn mountains and family in the Big Horn Basin. But Daddy didn't pay enough attention. He wanted to play baseball and go into town. He was never convinced that he couldn't be a gentleman and a rancher at the same time. I don't know, though. We had neighbors who killed themselves working, but beef prices just went down anyway, and it seemed like everybody sold out or got sold up. And then Ike and Abel couldn't get along for a minute, and if an argument wouldn't settle it, they'd have a fight. I couldn't stand that. And your mother came along first thing and then Claire. The year we had Susanna, I think we all realized it wasn't going to last, and even when cattle prices went up, it seemed like nothing was going to keep us there. Iowa, Iowa, Iowa was all I heard about. So we sold the cattle and the horses and the chickens, and some people who thought maybe prices were going to stay up bought the ranch, and we left. At least we owned what we had, so we didn't sneak away because we were in debt like some folks had to. It was happening all around us, even with the dude ranches, so Daddy talked very sensibly about it and was hopeful about Iowa. I don't know. I don't know whether it was selling the ranch there or getting a job here, but after that he always kind of thought he was a failure, more so as time went on, in fact. Aside from the fact that what we'd sold for there couldn't buy anything here, farming here had nothing to do with horses and the range and the wild West. Daddy couldn't feature himself behind a plow."

"Hmm." Christine's forehead wrinkled, as if to keep her eyelids up, and she yawned widely. Anna resumed her knitting. In a moment the magazine fell from Christine's hand with a riffle of pages, causing Anna to look up. Christine had fallen asleep, her head cocked over the back of the couch, her mouth wide open. As Anna watched, her legs uncrossed, and her left foot hit the coffee table. She started, grunted, did not awaken. Anna sighed deeply, a sigh of fatigue, not chagrin. She smiled. Talk of vast destruction and of the ranch had lifted her spirits. Helen seemed small and querulous now, not huge and judgmental.

It was good to be free of talk. No, she had not wanted this nest of daughters. She yawned. Sleep would be out of the question, of course, since Christine had preempted her (and Nelson, too. As she glanced at him, he flopped over onto his side and stretched his nose under the couch). She closed her eyes, but it was risky. Her body felt too much like liquid, draining away from her. From here, it was true, she wouldn't be able to hear Ike at all, especially if she fell into the absolute unconsciousness that was likely. Opening her eyes, she quickened her knitting stitches. In the quiet, perhaps because of all the talk of the ranch, Dolores occurred to her, Dolores shelling peas. The popping sound of peas falling into a pot had always made Anna smile. A whole bowl, a mounded bowl of brilliant green peas seemed like plenty itself, the first plenty of the year. Dolores must have shelled hundreds of thousand of peas, and Anna, unlike Mama, hardly canned at all. One didn't often think of Dolores. She was mentioned, as relatives are always mentioned, and Anna sometimes told the story of the man in Basin who was made to kneel down and kiss the flag during the first war, after he had spoken critically of President Wilson, and how that very night, Mama had told Dolores that her name was no longer the German Lore but the vaguely Spanish, and certainly American, Dolores. Even so, Dolores herself was almost never imagined, recalled, visualized. For one thing, she never said boo, and not out of shyness, merely out of disinclination. If you questioned her, she answered forthrightly, but if you forgot to question her (and with Ike wanting this and that and the girls having to be tended to, who had time for inquiries) she volunteered nothing. Just to get the details of Mama's death out of her had taken six months or so. She'd been only twenty-five when she came to live with Anna, and Anna had planned all sorts of changes for her—suitors, marriage, children to take her out of herself—but Dolores had had nothing to say to either of her admirers, and when they became discouraged, she'd had nothing to say about that either. She seemed content to live with Anna as she had with Mama, silent, helpful, wordlessly enthusiastic over new cooking projects every so often. Yes, the strudels and the blood sausage, also puff pastry and homemade noodles, and one year pickles of all kinds of fruit.

At thirty-six, she had gone out West to visit friends

unseen for ten years, had caught cold on the train, and contracted pneumonia. She died in the home of her best schoolfriend. It was summer, hot (almost a hundred every day), and so she'd been buried right there, in the Baptist cemetery, because the friend was Baptist. Anna hadn't even been able to get there for the funeral. At ten she was sent away for Dolores' birth, at forty-six she missed Dolores' death. Her sister's silent life had grazed Anna's noisy one as lightly as the wing of a bird. About her there was only one family anecdote.

It was funny to Anna that she, the least enthusiastic anecdote collector in the family, had gathered this one, and gathered it at twelve when stories meant nothing to her. She had told it to Dolores once, as a curiosity, and then told it again, once, after Dolores died. She thought of it fairly often, though. Any toddler could remind her of the time Mama had ordered her to take the lacy little two-year-old in her ribbons and buttoned shoes down the street to the Lindsay twins, where she was to play for the afternoon and Anna Gertrude was to sew. Anna had worn shoes with heels and fancy-work stockings, a satin sash and gloves. It didn't matter to Mama that the street was ankle deep in dust, that tumbleweed flew against the picket fence. Mama thought in terms of "an afternoon visit." She would have been forty-five by then, and if anyone thought about a "babyhood" for Dolores, it was not Mama. Anna still remembered the difficulties of fixing Dolores on her hip, of managing her sewing, and having the front door, as she opened it, jerk out of her hand and slam against the wall, then pull like a sail when she had to put down the child and the sewing and struggle to close it. Dolores had cried at the grit in her face; they had leaned on the wind, ribbons snapping like banners, all the way to the Lindsays. Anna expected the child to be cranky when they got there, to have to spend the afternoon wiping tears and talking about sharing, but when they came into the room where the twins were, Dolores had thrown up her hands and exclaimed, "Here I am at last!"

As much as Anna knew, from parenthood and grandparenthood, that no infant exploit necessitated any particular development, she had sometimes wondered how the child who so heartily welcomed herself had gotten to be the adult who seemed to welcome nothing, whose joys, whatever they were, were as quiet as her dissatisfactions. Mama? Anna herself? Mama and Anna together, with their ten years start, their locked gaze, their incessant jockeying for position? Had Dolores ever announced herself at home? Anna couldn't remember. In spite of the one incident, she couldn't remember much of Dolores at all, only Papa and Mama, with their gaze on her, Anna, like beams of light.

Christine, slumped and twisted so that she was mostly lying on the couch, brought her feet up, one at a time, and writhed into a comfortable position. She let out a groan, and Anna got up, removed the blue afghan from under her feet and threw it over her. Nelson stretched, and Anna realized that it was the ten years of Dolores, silent always, that Mrs. Cox had reminded her of, that freighted the whole nurse idea for her. Ten years without knowing what judgments were being made but feeling them tick past like a clock. Dolores would have known if Helen were right; Dolores would have observed and considered and observed again, day after day, would have caught looks that Anna turned away from, agreed perhaps to keep secrets that a parent should know. Dolores would have been a huge ship of knowledge in their midst. Anna shivered. For the moment it seemed insufficient to think kindly of Dolores now.

Enough! Anna jumped as well as she could out of her chair, determined to do something: look down the street for the doctor, listen at the bottom of the stairs for Ike, pick up the magazine Christine had dropped and smooth the pages, straighten the piano bench a millimeter, smooth down a corner of the rug beside the door. It was almost two-thirty. She gave the doctor an hour at the outside. At the outside. Before then she could put away the luncheon dishes, water the plants, even go out into the garden again (she had no business in the garden, exactly, but the garden had been so warm and airy this morning, so reminiscent of the mountains. Anna licked her lips. Ike could wake up, she better not go into the garden). Or check the mail. Ah. She would check the mail.

With the sun out, the hazy air glared like mid-summer. She put her hand into the box and grasped a folded something without looking. She hated to catch a glimpse of anything before she was ready, hated for her hopes of a letter or a new magazine to be dashed before she was ready. Long ago she had made it clear to the whole family that the mail was to stay in the box until she took it out, that no one was ever to say, "Nothing today, Mom," or even, "I left it on the table for you." Ike was this way with the paper, liked it only crisp and new, untorn, unmarked by crayons, uncreased. Ought she to hate these habits? Could signs of age have come upon them so long ago, when they were so young?

There was nothing today. A circular from Sears, nothing else. For the first time all day she actually felt the tickle and catch of imminent tears. She forestalled them with a brisk "Don't be sentimental!" and then shouted, "Yoo hoo! Hello, Mrs. Paully! Almost spring, I see!"

Esther Paully shouted back, nothing Anna could hear, and Anna called, "Hope you're feeling well today!" They always called back and forth like this, never heard each other, knew what was going on (Esther had sprained her back on the ice some three weeks ago) through the other neighbors, who were willing to cross the street. Esther called and smiled and waved. A good neighbor. Anna went back into the house. Nelson was waiting at the door, but she shooed him back and told him to lie down. He looked at her quizzically before going into the kitchen.

Christine turned her face to the crack of the couch. She was sleeping hard, a lover of naps. Anna never took a nap without waking in despair, a crown of perspiration around her head and her dress and stockings twisted. What she really wanted was not a nap, but to have one of those June days with the work sliding under her fingers as smoothly as a satin ribbon.

Beyond the pleasure of hot bath or a good meal, beyond the pleasure of church with the windows open in May, beyond even the pleasure of a good mystery story late at night, was the pleasure of a lot of work on a nice day: troweling holes for the pepper plants, weeding, drawing mulch over warm soil, snipping off old flower heads, raking up prunings and grass cuttings, hosing down the steps and scrubbing the porch, throwing away old bottles and magazines, kneading some sweet rolls, half to send to Christine, half for the freezer, letting one long intended task drift into another, such as sorting old clothes, that might have been so long intended as to be almost forgotten, then resting with some knitting or crochet, not idling, never idling, going outside and in, letting doors swing, pausing in the sunlight with your hands on your hips, as if there were too much to do, but really only sniffing the air for that first aroma of heat on turf. The very best days accumulated that way, each completed task announcing itself discreetly: a small bag of old clothes by the door; caramelly, cooling buns; every shoe paired at last and slotted in the shoe bag on the closet door; then after dinner when you sat on the porch spotting cardinals and orioles and woodpeckers, the rays of the sun would grow so long that they seemed to lacquer the leafy trees without penetrating them. The odd thing about such days, something that did not exactly make them less perfect, only more mysterious, was the way her heart would begin to pound toward dusk, as if night were agitating, even frightening, as if twenty-five thousand nights, or thereabouts, hadn't come and gone since the day she was born.

Anna sighed. She had never gotten used to Ike's retirement. He still only entered her daydreams at about five o'clock in the afternoon. Her fantasy self, she saw with interest since her morning conversation with Christine, was always alone. Oh, to have some work now! Nothing that she merely ought to do but something huge and complex that she had to do, that forced itself upon her, that put her out, allowed her a little annoyance, and no time, no time at all.

Nelson came to the dining room doorway and whined. "Hush!" She looked up, irritated, and her eye fell on the picture of Ike and all his brothers and sisters that hung above the piano. Fell, actually, on Seth, already thirty-four then, already a millionaire, possibly, though Anna didn't know the history of his fortune. Probably he had found his own rise very exciting; there were family stories (legends to Ike) about his tinkering career in Ames, about his post-college trip to Germany, where he fiddled with refrigerator systems for railroad cars, about his excited return, his clever purveying of these systems to a number of local railroads, about the small something be patented to improve the system, about the big contract, at twenty-seven, with the Illinois Central, that gave him the house not far from the Hubble Mansion and the farmstead in West Des Moines. Anna had seen him a mere handful of times, found him a pleasant man who shared the family interest in sports and was not allowed, in family baseball games, to use his own bat, which had a crook and practically assured a home run

ribly in time. Time, of course, was the enemy. Nelson yipped and twisted his head out of her grasp. The worst, would happen, but what the worst was, her fear itself would not let her imagine. It would not let her do anything, merely filled her with a kind of arctic, freezing light. The one thought she was allowed to have was that such paralyzing fear was actually her proper condition, perhaps her underlying, actual condition. And then she grew terrified of the fear itself.

Almost immediately, three things happened at once: the telephone clamored, Daddy shouted, "Anna! Mother!" in a querulous, angry voice, and Nelson went to the door with an imploring whine. Automatically she went after him and let him out.

Her voice sounded normal on the phone. She said, "What?"

"Mrs. Robison, I said I've been held up on this end, but I should be there around six."

"You have to come now."

"Is Mr. Robison worse? Is he complaining of any pain or shortness of breath?"

"No."

"Itching, nausea, any other kind of discomfort?"

"No."

"I can surely get away before six—"

"Now? Just for five minutes? A minute? Please!"

"You have nothing to worry about, really. I'm sure two hours won't make any difference. I'm terribly tied up. We have a little boy—"

"I'll see you then." Anna hung up. She had nothing more to say.

Ike's face was red and he was gritting his teeth angrily. She cut him short. "How do you feel, Daddy?" she barked. "Is there any pain? Shortness of breath? Itching? Other—" She fell silent, dreading that Ike would hear doctor's jargon in her words and knew to whom she had been talking.

Ike was too annoyed for subtlety, though. The muscles of his jaw were positively knotted. "Now, Anna," he declared testily, "I called you six times! Where is everybody? One moment it's chaos around here and the next it's like a tomb! All day, all night, I've got to shout for you over and over!"

"I can't be at your beck—"

He shifted himself angrily around, made a fist. The fist, only the fist, made his hand look swollen. "What's so important to do—"

"The phone was ringing! The dog wanted out!"

"This one time! But another time you're in the garden or the bathtub with the water running or some damn thing!"

"Well, do you want a nurse? That's what the girls want! They want to move your bed downstairs and have a nurse in the house all the time!"

"Mother, goddammit!"

"Is that what you want, some stranger?"

"Now we don't need any nurse! You tell them—"

"A nurse would be at your beck and call every single minute, Daddy. All night long."

"I won't have a stranger. You just need to pay more attention, that's all. That's the only problem. Now, you pay more attention and everything will be all right."

"But what if I can't pay more attention? What if I'm sick to death of running up and down the stairs and dropping whatever I'm doing every time you roll over in bed?"

"That's your job right now, to take care of me! I'm ashamed of having to tell you!"

"When did you ever take care of me? The only time I was ever sick, that time with the pleurisy, Helen was eight years old and you had her doing everything, even cooking!"

"That was different—"

"Not different!" Anna flopped down in the clothing-strewn armchair. Of course it had been different. Everything had been different. Ike, for example, had been lithe and muscular and teasing. "I don't want to fight with you, Daddy."

"Since when?" Ike chuckled. In a moment Anna looked at him and smiled. "Would you like something to eat, Daddy?"

"What am I, a baby? Every time I wake up, you women want to shove something in my mouth, and then whenever I've eaten, you ask me if I feel sleepy!"

His hands did look swollen, both of them. The thin bones had disappeared, and the filmy skin was terribly pale between the liver spots. Anna inhaled sharply but made it into a cough.

"Who was on the phone?"

"What?"

"Who was on the damned phone?"

"Uh, Susanna."

"You're not telling me the truth."

"Yes, I am. She had to show another house and can't come till dinner."

"Are they all going to be here for dinner?"

"I'm sure they are, since Christine's here."

"We need some peace and quiet."

"Now a minute ago you were complaining about how no one's here to answer you, and now you're worried about peace and quiet." She paused, then asked, "Have you taken all your medicine today?"

Ike nodded.

"Sure?"

"Don't second-guess me!"

"Well, look at your hands!"

He held them up, turned them over, thrust them under the covers. "Been lying down all day, that's all."

"Do you want to get up?"

"Why do you think I called you?"

"I mean up. And go downstairs."

"Maybe in a while."

When he brought his feet out from under the covers, they were swollen too. She saw him look hard at them before he reached out to her and stood up. As she arranged his arm over her shoulder, her heart began rattling furiously. Only the practical difficulties of moving carefully to the bathroom kept the fear at bay. And then, in the doorway, Ike shuddered and shied violently, almost making her stumble. She felt every muscle, from his fingers on her upper arm to his hip against her waist, grow rigid. She dared not ask what was wrong, dared not utter anything for fear of panic in her voice. She stopped, pretended to rearrange him, pretended to be annoyed. He said, with a kind of trembling joviality, "Saw that damn cat again."

"Must be something in the way the tiles are. Just an optical illusion. I used to wake up every night when we first moved here and think I saw a rabbit in the window. Remember that? It was those curtains I made, remember?"

Ike nodded. In the center of the bathroom, when she made her customary moves to disengage herself and leave him alone, his arm squeezed around her, almost like a hug, and the side of his body pressed through her clothing. Unconsciously she squeezed back, and then looked up at his face, startled. With a tiny flick of the head and lifting of the eyebrows, he motioned toward the toilet. She led him right to it, and he pushed his pajamas down with one hand, then facing her, a hand on either of her shoulders, he looked her in the eye and lowered himself onto the stool. She looked determinedly at the wall above his head, considered resolutely the notion she'd had, after that squeeze, that she might embrace him and be embraced. He did not motion her away, and so she stood carefully at his knees until he replaced his hands upon her shoulders and levered himself upright again. In the guise of aid, she put her arms around his back. For the first time in her life, they overlapped. She helped him back to his bed.

Although to all appearances she was calmly sitting in the chair beside Ike's bed with the cabling hook in her mouth and her knitting in her hands, Ike alternately gazing out the window and at the newspaper she had brought him, in reality she was dangling from a rope at the peak of a high dome, below her a vast floor of fear, bone hard and bleak as a desert. Still, however, she felt the great calm of doom, the lengthening of moments, the intensification of colors and sound, the welling up of pure physical pleasure. Though she would plummet to that floor, for now she was dangling. Ike was calm too. Not angry or impatient, not fidgety or complaining. He looked up, he looked down. He took deep breaths that were almost sighs. Twice he picked up his pencil and filled in a few words of the crossword puzzle.

And so, in 1927, when Helen was seven, Claire was six, and Susanna one and a half, they had come back in the new car, a 1920 Model T, purchased from a friend of Mama's when cattle prices rose the year before, perhaps for the last time, perhaps for the first. A Model T with a canvas roof. To Iowa. They started, not from the ranch, but from Patrick's store in Sheridan with their purchases: the last two paper parasols Patrick had (one pink, one blue—one each for the older girls), a red-and-green metal horse with wheels and a string for Susanna, a *Ladies' Home Journal* for Anna, and a carton of cigarettes for Ike, plus three inner tubes, an assortment of fan belts, a big spouted bucket, and some motor oil for the car. In her purse was secreted a large bag of horehound drops, for impossible moments in the back seat, and at her feet were jugs of drinking water. It was May. She had bread and jerked beef, fried chicken and sugar cookies, hard-boiled eggs and dried apples, carrots she had wintered over, and potatoes for roasting, full of sprouts, for emergencies. Ike and Abel had parted without shaking hands, and she had heard from neighbors that Abel would be heading for Oregon, or maybe Washington State. They had made enough from the sale of the horses, cattle, chickens, and the larger pieces of their furniture to get back to Iowa, where, though they had not spoken of it, they would ask for help from Seth or Ben until Ike could find a job. Anna had never been to Iowa, never lifted her eyes without seeing sage, rock, mountains, snow. Iowa, Ike said, was green all summer. You had to cut everything back— shrubs, grass, fruit trees—or it got jungly. Topsoil twelve feet thick in places, not so much as a pebble in it; you just put the seed in the ground, or even on the ground (he knew this lady down the street from his mother who came outside in February and just threw her spinach seeds on the snow; two months later, salad!), and up it came.

She bustled around, settling Helen and Claire with some dolls and books in the back seat, putting the cans of evaporated milk within easy reach for Susanna, arranging their coats in case it got cold, plumping up pillows, and all the time she watched the cloud shadows over the smooth eastern slope of the Big Horns behind her. On the other side, the side of her childhood, the mountains rose black and steep, full of the heart-stopping declivities and hairpin turns that she'd loved and never feared, but here, deceptively gentle, grass and wildflowers spread far up the gradient, an endless meadow. Helen and Claire thought only of their parasols. Ike could practically see Iowa ("Huge oaks. Maples a hundred feet tall.") already, but Anna had to watch those peaks, watch the huge sky and the dazzling, flat-bottomed clouds floating in the sunlight. A little later, they drove south, then east. It took a week.

Anna had never been with Ike for so many hours on end. There was, of course, the business of the trip, which was to seem leisurely, as if on vacation, not in retreat. There were cousins, both Ike's and Anna's, that were not to be avoided, in spite of the questions they would ask and the commiserations they would perpetrate. Even Cousin Jean Fountain, whose husband had moved to Casper, who would meet them in Gillette to really see them off, inspired a fight. They drove around, could not find her, drove around some more, with Daddy cursing her indefinite plans, kicking the tires, and yelling at Helen and Claire to decide once and for all who got the blue parasol and who the pink. As if by magic, the moment they decided to stop and eat anyway, there she was, on the step of the hotel where she hadn't been ten minutes before, with presents to stop the crying of the girls, gossip for Anna, and that air of jut-chinned sassiness that always shamed Ike out of his temper. She had ordered dinner for them. All they had to do was shut up the car, shake out their dresses, and come inside. It was like being with Mama and Papa again, when they traveled to Yellowstone and stayed in Old Faithful Lodge. Hotels in the Midwest weren't the same, didn't have the combination of buffalo heads and linen, rifle racks and chandeliers. They spent real money. With Cousin Jean in tow, Ike did not complain, but they camped the next two nights in Sturgis and Hot Springs. Anna loved the Black Hills, and Ike, though he complained at every scenic detour and every plea to stop and have a look around, was almost calm by the end of the day.

In Winner they had to stay at the hotel. It was raining, for one thing, and everyone needed some kind of bath. In Winner some kind of bath was what they got. At the supper table they ate what they recognized, to be polite, then assuaged their hunger on Anna's remaining cookies, apples, beef jerky, and horehound drops. Iowa was where they were going. Anna kept reminding herself that even the poor in Iowa had gardens, apple trees, raspberry canes, but she cried anyway, because the country was so flat and windy, the hotel so dirty, and their fund of money so irreversibly small.

In Sioux City they stayed with Ike's cousins. Anna barely saw them. They arrived in time to go to bed, got up and left immediately, with promises to come back for a longer visit. Now she couldn't even remember their names. They would be dead. The visit had never been made. In Fort Dodge were Naomi, her husband Harold, and their daughter, Hephzibah, a girl the same age as Helen but tiny and porcelain. She showed Helen and Claire all her toys and clothes but did not allow them to touch anything. Naomi, glassily sisterish, quizzed her about Abel and "all that money"

251

Ike's mother had invested in the ranch. To Ike himself she said, "These days, money doesn't just drop into your hand like some peach!" Harold alluded a lot to immigrants from southern Europe. For dinner they ate smoked salmon, and Harold spoke to the serving girl in Norwegian. After breakfast the next day, Hephzibah launched herself off the porch swing into the corner of a shutter, cutting open her head and bleeding all over Helen and Claire. Anna left with a feeling of remorse, as if she had wished for the accident.

With the driving and the camping and the visiting and the sightseeing, not to mention the three flat tires, the change of oil, Susanna's throwing up in Ike's lap, the continuous squabbling over the parasols and then the shreds of the parasols (Helen never did decide which color she wanted and never ceased trying to manipulate Claire out of whatever color she had), the loss of the spouted bucket, the bad roads, the slender means, the rain, the mud, the wind, and the sun, what time was there for talk, or even thought? Nevertheless, what Anna remembered best from her first long trip was the silent, jouncing passage of miles, the sense of meditative purpose she got from looking where she was going, the way travel made idle thought seem like an occupation. For any number of reasons, known and unknown, Ike was not in a mood to talk or even be civil much of the time, but in spite of that, Anna remembered something else.

She sat back in the armchair and followed his gaze out the window. There was a bluejay perched on the leafless tree. She remembered watching Ike drive, the attitude of his hands on the wheel, the vigilance of his neck and chin, the movement beneath the skin of his arms, shoulders, biceps, forearms when, hand over hand, he turned the wheel. She remembered how she watched him covertly for what seemed like, but could not have been, hours on end, alternately admiring him and feeling sorry for the failure of his project. She noted the timbre of his voice, the thickness of his hair, anything, everything. Sitting a foot from him for those seven days was like sitting inside a dome of energy. She grew fascinated with the untanned skin inside his elbows, so rosy and pearly at the same time, as if his athlete's heart pumped hot blood right to the interface of body and air. By the end of the trip she was madly in love for the first time in her life.

Of course there had been no sexual relations, with the children in the same room or the same tent. And perhaps Ike had been too distressed to think of that, anyway. She had remained quiet, reserved, while seven years of exasperation, acceptance, companionship, dismissal, routine, and accommodation had simply evaporated. She blushed when she met his mother, thinking of him as a newborn, and she panted when he touched her. Looking back, Anna could not honestly say that she believed in such things as turning points, watersheds, lost chances. But she had known no actions for such a feeling to result in. At any rate, in this unexpected torrent of admiration, regret for having left the mountains was swept away, at least for a time. Anna dropped her work and gave a huge sigh.

She could remember that feeling, but after all she was too old now to sense it. Had it justified everything to follow, as she thought it would at the time?

Ike coughed wheezingly, from the chest, then said, "I feel funny again."

"What do you mean?"

"I don't know."

Downstairs Christine's voice called, "Nelson? Grandmother? Grandmother!"

Anna exclaimed, "Oh my goodness!"

"What's the matter, Mother?"

"I let Nelson out! Ages ago!" She jumped up and went to the top of the stairs, calling.

"Grandmother? What time is it? Are you all right? Where's Nelson?"

"Oh, Chrissy! I let him out and then I forgot all about it! Will he know to come back?"

"I don't know, I—"

"I'm sorry, honey! Your grandfather called, and the phone rang; I just—"

"I'll go out and look for him. It's okay, Grandmother. He might be right around the house. Anyway, he knows about cars and stuff."

Anna hadn't even thought about that possibility. "But it must have been an hour ago!"

"I'll go look. We won't worry until we can't find him, all right?"

"All right."

Ike was shifting around angrily in his bed. "Now what's the matter?" he demanded.

"The dog! I let out the dog!"

"What dog?"

"Nelson! Chrissy's dog." She paused and then said, "Ike? Are you all right?"

"No, I'm not all right."

No, he was not all right, that was obvious. His color was blotchy, his breathing uneven, his hands perhaps more swollen. When he saw her looking at them, he put them behind his back.

"What's the matter?"

"I told you! I feel funny!"

"But how? What exactly feels funny?"

"I don't *know!* Everything! It's like I'm scared, except not in my mind!"

"Now listen, Daddy. Listen to me." She sat down on his bed and put her hands on him, one on his arm and one on his chest. "You've got to lie still. On your side, like that. There. Now take deep breaths." She was afraid to touch his chest, afraid she'd feel his heart unmoored, dancing. She muttered the question she could not bear to proclaim, "Is it like before?"

Either he read her lips or read her mind because he said, "No. No, there isn't any pain."

"Good. Please don't be angry or scared. Just think of something. Think of a song or something."

"Dammit, mother—"

"Be quiet, please, please just breathe. I'll talk, okay? And then, when everything's calmed down a little, I'll go call the doctor, okay?"

Ike nodded. She opened her mouth, but there was no subject, at least nothing suitable. Her arms holding him on his side were rigid with exertion, and she had to make herself relax them. She said, "Do you want to sit up more? I'll fix the pillows. Maybe it'll be more comfortable to sit up."

Ike shook his head, and immediately she could think of nothing except the time the doctor had said, "Heart patients are better off sitting than lying down." And now she was letting him lie down! She said, "Yes, you'd better sit up."

"Unh-hunh. Don't want to. Can't."

"Yes, you can, just—"

"Anna!"

"Okay, Daddy, I'm sorry. You just do what's most comfortable. Okay? Okay." Still she could think of nothing to bring up that would be calming, neutral, sure not to touch off anger or fear or, worse, longing. Pressing to her tongue, clamoring to be given utterance, were a multitude of memories and of questions she had always meant to ask. Ike's eyes closed, his breath came laboriously but evenly. His pajama top gapped a little over his heart. At least there was no fluttering of the fabric. Where were Helen and Claire and Susanna and Christine now?

"Aren't you going to talk?"

"I keep forgetting to."

"What do you remember?"

"Everything else."

"Me too."

"Ike—"

"I think it's a bad sign."

"No, it isn't, I—"

"There's so much light. It's more vivid than it ever

really was, like the bottom of one of those pools up in the Big Horns, when you could see every pebble and stick and grain of sand. It's like that. That's what I think is a bad sign."

"But it's like that for me too and I'm not even sick, so—"

"I didn't like the mountains much."

"I know."

"Not enough folks around."

It came thoughtless to her voice, not something she would have brought up, no matter where her thoughts had been turning for the last day or so. "Daddy, after we were in bed together, and it was over, were you mad at me? I always felt you were mad at me because you didn't say anything."

He seemed less surprised than she expected. He said, "No."

"I think you'll be okay. This isn't like before, is it?"

He shook his head, but hopelessly, she thought, as if it's not being like before was another bad sign.

"I'm going to call the doctor, then an ambulance."

He shook his head again.

"Yes! It'll be much better!"

"I don't want to go to the hospital again."

"Now you're making me mad! They've got equipment there and people who know what to do!"

He breathed, said nothing.

"Do you want to—" But she stopped herself. Her fear of the very word was frantic.

Still Ike did not speak.

Anna sat down beside him on the bed. Suddenly she

was more curious than afraid. Once, when she was alone in the mountains back of the ranch, a rock under her left foot had given way and plummeted down a little ravine, twenty-five feet, nothing, but enough to kill her, as she realized even while shifting her weight, dropping to the right. Another time, in the car, someone had crossed into their lane. Only Ike's reflexive turn onto the shoulder saved them, and even so, the other car, out of control, fishtailed, spun, and skimmed the air off Ike's door. She had seen a tornado, been followed in the street, stumbled in front of an oncoming bus. Each time, the light of her own mind seemed marvelously bright, seemed to slam hugely into the event, the long-awaited event, and now here she was. Ike too. A hammer had fallen to the floor beside him when workmen were making repairs in the rafters at the printshop. Abel had tried to push him out of a hayloft window when they were kids. Diving once, he had seen the board with his open eyes millimeters from his face. The high board. He had had a heart attack, gone into surgery. Here he was. She stood up, arranged his covers. "Can I make you more comfortable, Daddy?"

He shook his head. He said, "Talk."

Anna cleared her throat. She began, "I saw Esther Paully today. She seems better. Remember I told you about her falling on the ice up the street by Harmon's. Remember? It's a sin the way that boy of theirs gives the snow a lick and a promise all the time and never really clears the walk. You've got to be a tightrope walker . . ." She paused and took a deep breath. What had they talked about in fifty-two years? "Christine—" Now, there was a tightrope. "I think I'll make a couple of sweaters for the twins. It's late in the season, but Helen saw a darling pattern, and I could finish two for their birthday. It's funny. You don't think we loved them less than Christine, do you? They were so rambunctious, but we always thought they were as cute as can be, don't you think? You had them out there throwing balls and batting . . . they got into stuff all the time . . . It is natural to get mad, don't you think? Claire never thought . . ."

Ike groaned, tightened his lips. He seemed uncomfortable but also angry, and in the midst of everything, a gloriously familiar annoyance overtook her. "I never get mad," she had often said to him. "It's you that always makes me mad!" Now she was mad! With resentful luxury, she let her gaze drift over his angular and anxious form, let herself think that he was about to burst out, impatient, full of vexation and complaint. She had been floundering, frightened, but now she was irritated. She almost smiled. "Daddy!" she said, "sit up! I'll help you. The doctor says that's much better, and it'll relieve your discomfort! There's no sense in being more uncomfortable than you have to be. I mean it! And I'm going to call the doctor and get you an ambulance, I don't care what you say. I'm not going to stand by and watch you d—, get sick again, really sick, when I know you could be helped."

He looked her directly in the eye. She squirmed slightly. "Well yes," she went on, "I suppose you could die, but only if you want to! Now, just because you think it's Seth's hundredth birthday today and a hundred is a nice round number doesn't mean you can give up. Seth isn't a hundred, he's only ninety-nine, and anyway, even if he were, that's not your family. Always, the whole time we've been married, whenever you've said, 'My family,' you've meant *them*. That's always made me just as mad as Tucker! We're your family! And today isn't anyone's birthday, and if it were, there wouldn't be any round numbers. You're only seventy-seven. That's not very old when you come to think of it. People are always living into their nineties and dancing and driving to Mexico with groups on the bus. Or taking up musical instrument repair or something." She took a deep breath and twisted her faltering anger tighter. "Besides! We need you! You're the only man we've got. How can you just give up? How can you? I can't stand it! Without you around, Helen and Claire and Susanna will just eat me alive. Don't you turn away from me!" But he did anyway, his face white and shocked from the bitterness of her tone, or from the profundity of his "funny feeling." For once no pugnacity answered hers. "Daddy!" But it didn't come out insistent, it came out imploring. "You don't have to give in. Not going to the hospital is just a way of giving in. It's going to be a lovely spring. When I was outside in the garden this morning, the soil was already thawed, even warm almost. I could get out there and plant spinach tomorrow and have it come up, I'll bet. I was thinking about the brambles, too. Christine could get back there with gloves and prune it all down in an afternoon. I'm sure she wouldn't mind a bit. And Margaret Lacina's friend, that gym teacher from the school, offered to do our dormant spraying when she does Margaret's. It'll be time for that soon. We could have a wonderful garden this year, Ike, lots of flowers and fruit. You know how you used to say that some year we were going to have rain every other day between six and seven and then sunshine all day long?" She stopped. It was too much to promise that this would be the year. "Christine will be glad to dig for me. She can do a few rows before she goes back Sunday. We could have Early Alaskas by the end of May, and good Buttercrunch. I don't even have to buy spinach seed, there's all that Bloomsdale from last year." Her voice tapered of itself into silence.

Ike said, "What I like is that oakleaf stuff," and she could have leaped all over that, promising row upon row of the pale green lettuce, hand dug, hand planted, hand thinned, cultivated daily, mulched with yellow straw, new straw like a percale sheet, nothing moldy or odorous, straw you could walk on in your bare feet, except that his voice was so full of effort that she had a sudden horrified vision of herself heaping things on him.

She sat down at once, afraid of looking down, of leaning enormously over him. She bit her lower lip, and said, "That might come up right away, Daddy, let me call the hospital!" Ike shook his head. He was hollow at the temples. When had she gotten so much bigger than he? Was there a moment that passed unnoticed, when she could have ceased feeling overtopped, surrounded,

261

invaded, muscled here and there, when the balance changed and she could have stepped back, sat down, eased away? Had her self-defense, out of habit, gone on too long? She had always felt breathless in his family, as if he and Abel and all the big-shouldered brothers and sisters were using up the air, and now she found herself holding her breath, watching his lips and nostrils, afraid of stealing something from them. She shook her head briskly to clear it. It failed to clear. She said, "Why not?" but not so he could hear.

Did she really promote herself at his expense? Of course Helen had always preferred Ike, everyone knew that, but setting aside such bias, had she been one of those wives and mothers who oozed into the cracks of a man's thoughtlessness and preened ever so discreetly, who let herself be seen coping, who gave up the last word when his last word was blatantly foolish, who fortified an impregnable position with looks and silence? She could remember the satisfaction of being right, but also the horror of being continually encroached upon by a handsome man, a youngest son, an athlete, a person not of limitless self-confidence but of limitless self-sympathy, who didn't know how not to be the center of his own attention. Which was true: victimized or victimizing? Would Ike know? She dared not ask.

He seemed to be breathing more easily. Voluntarily he shifted over onto his back, and then pushed himself up against a pillow by the bookcase. It was a great effort but also somewhat of a relief. His breathing eased further, his face cleared. She said, trying not to demand anything, "Do you feel a little better?" It was on the tip of her tongue to say that she had called the doctor already, that he would be here in an hour, but she dared not. When he got there she would pretend that he had come of his own accord. Ike pushed the newspapers irritably off the bed, and Anna did not allow herself to pick them up, so vivid was the thought of herself stiff with self-righteousness, grunting a little for his benefit, in the way she had picked up after him all these weeks and years.

Oh, but it was too bad that he of all people should die! No one had inherited the playfulness of his wit, the dimple in his chin, his generosity; in each daughter and grandchild, he was mitigated, twisted, faded. She said, "And Daddy, Christine's going to have a baby in the fall!" She said it like a promise and he heard it like a fact.

He smiled but nodded, as if that was her department, and she stood up, suddenly more fearful. "At least it doesn't hurt, does it, Daddy? That's a good sign. It would hurt, I think."

"It hurts."

Anna bit her lower lip and looked out the window. The bluejay, oddly, was still there in spite of the violence in the room. When she looked back at Ike, his eyes were closed and his body had loosened a little. That was that. She stood still and did not say anything.

After a time, a deathly silent time, the phone rang. Anna turned gigantically, like an elephant turning, and left the room. It was Christine. She said, "I still can't find Nelson, Grandma. Has he come back?"

"No, honey, I don't think so."

"Well, don't worry. I ran into Aunt Claire and we're going to look with the car for a little while. Are you all right? How's Grandfather?"

"Nothing to worry about."

"Okay."

"Nothing to worry about at all."

"Do you want one of us to come there?"

"No."

"Grandmother—" But Christine thought better of herself, and Anna was able to put down the phone. In a moment—funny the properties of a mere moment—she was sitting in Ike's old chair. If she closed her eyes, she got that bowl sensation again, except that now it was not merely Ike in his bed, the walls, the books, the window, the half-open closet that curved around her, but everything else as well—the fanning streets with their ranks of homes, the spreading cornfields that rolled into hills in the east, flattened in the west, came to ponds and rivers and lakes, turned to deciduous glades, evergreen forests, wheat, acres of nodding sunflowers, rough pasture, and rose, far far away, to that dazzling rim of mountains. In her backyard in Basin, as a very little girl, she would sometimes get this same sensation, of being the pinpoint focus of a tremendous space. She would tumble in her mind the words *Big Horn Basin* over and over until they were meaningless, or until one or the other of them popped out of the phrase. She would think of Mama's washing basin, think of her tiny self, living, sitting up, lying down, at the bottom of the basin and the sides rising up just like the mountains on every side.

She was very tired. It was better to open her eyes and sit, exactly in that place, a few feet from the closet door that could not be closed, a few inches from the wallpaper she really could not stand, exactly in that time, at the end of one life and the beginning of another. She held her eyes open until they watered, staring at Ike's body propped neatly among the pillows. The irreducible, practical fact of him was oddly reassuring. Something had to be done with him, and thus, something would be done with her. And not only would she be taken care of, she would be forced by circumstances to walk and talk and bathe and cook and sew and dress and have opinions. The occasion for these activities would call them out of her automatically. Her eyes watered, Ike blurred, but that didn't make him less clearly there.

Then her eyes closed. Sleep was the most tempting thing, but she was afraid of dreams and afraid of being caught by her vigilant daughters. Asleep! Daddy dead only a few minutes! Not cold yet! Not stiff! What can she have been thinking of, babble babble. The right sort of person would try to get them on the phone, wait for them at the door, run screaming out of the house. And could you sleep in the same room with death and not dream of it? She placed her palms one at a time on the arms of the chair and tried to stand up, but her wrists and calves drooped like putty. Her thighs would not lift, her hips stuck fast to the seat of the chair. Of the past thirty-six hours she had slept almost none, but how could she sleep now? The doctor would need to know, and a funeral home, the coroner? Some county department of health? Everyone! She was the bearer of news! Bearing it properly was a matter of pride, of respect to her husband and her life with him. She willed herself to the phone but managed only a half dream about dialing in which she could see her own fingers going round and round and even hear Helen say, "Hello." When she woke up she realized that she was still in the chair, still had all of those steps to take, those numbers to dial. It was impossible that she should not do this! Impossible that her head should drift back against the chair, her mouth drop open! Was she dying too? It was something like the fatigue after eight or nine hours of labor, except that there would be no baby to take matters upon itself, to bend her to its own will. The darkness of sleep closed in on her like despair, and even as she relaxed her spirit sank in remorse. Her last thought before total somnolence was that, having failed Ike so consistently for fifty-two years, it was only to be expected that she would fail him in the end.

It was a sleep of absolute fatigue, the sleep of a stone. At first she did not dream, merely felt the presence of the room, the event of death, her own regret. Then, for a while, she felt nothing. The dream burst upon her like sudden daylight. She had on a brown bathing suit and she was treading water. Ike was nearby, and seeing his shoulders just beneath the surface of the water reminded her of her own neck and shoulders, her whole body drifting downward in the blue. The day was bright and beautiful, as only a day on earth could be. For once she was a no less powerful swimmer than Ike, but the strength in her limbs felt like grace. It seemed she could tread water for eons, reveling in the sun on her face and the water circulating around her ankles and elbows and waist. Ike was right there, but the glory of her own pleasure was so consuming that she didn't have much attention to spare him. And then the whales came. At first she was afraid and glanced over at Ike in alarm, but they came too quickly for her to speak. They were so enormous that Anna didn't know where one ended and the other began or how many there were. They seemed to lift the sea on their backs and she was afraid that one would swim beneath her. As soon as she had the thought, one did. She rose and rose. Water streamed off her shoulders and breasts and legs, then off the glistening dark hide of the beast, which she felt come up under the backs of her thighs and then her calves, lifting her still higher. Then it plunged downward, leaving her bobbing in the surf. Another came and lifted her again, and another. It was the most exhilarating feeling she had ever had, the mix of water and sunlight and speed and the sense of being cared for by the whales. She awoke in a whirl of delight.

Even though she instantly realized where she was, what had happened, what was still to come, the dream would not let her go. The feeling of having been tossed by the whales seemed to tingle in her limbs, and the joy of discovering that the whales meant her no harm pleased her at the same time she knew they were the whales of her own mind. She shifted position to evade an imminent throb of pain, and realized that for the first time in years, she had just dreamed of herself as slender again, and strong, forgetful of her body, as in fact young! That of course was the miracle of the dream, that the nerves of this body had buzzed with youth in spite of themselves, that she had not simply remembered what it was like to be young, but that somehow she had been young.

She sighed and sat up. Not happy, exactly, but still astonished by her dream, by the rise of the whale's back through the shining veil of water, the smoothness of it against the backs of her legs. Hair was falling in her face. She reached and twisted it up again, then straightened her dress. No one had come home, no one had found her sleeping. When Christine came in, or Helen, or the doctor, she could go to the top of the stairs and call whoever it was up. She or he would know by Anna's manner, by the tone of her voice, and no one would be taken by surprise. That was the gift she would give them—the moment of foreknowledge in which the best self could be recollected. What she was afraid of was the coming night, a multitude of rooms cavernous around her, perforated with doors and windows, but her fear was a distant one. Anyway, perhaps Claire would come over from her house, where she was alone every night, and stay for a few days. Or Susanna. Or even Helen. It was true. Each of her daughters checked windows and doors and burners and faucets every night, turning out the lights and leaving a trail of dark rooms behind her. Each one habitually did what Anna was about to do for the first time in her life. How did they learn? Would they show her? She thought with a start that now she was a "widow." She would watch them. She would learn. Maybe, after all these years, Christine could teach her to drive a car.

She went to Ike and arranged the coverlet over him, pulling it up to his rib cage and over his hands. For now she was a little squeamish about touching him or moving parts of his body, but she did not mind looking at him. His death was remarkably complete. In the summer, maybe she would go out west. March would come first, of course, and April and May, every day without Ike, every day full of second thoughts and broken habits with nothing to replace them. She could feel the beginnings of grief already, always a physical sensation, always the same, the throat and neck and back stiff and outraged, as if a sheet of metal had been hammered into your tissues and now hampered your movements. It was perfectly familiar, the one act you practiced all your life and never improved at. It would be a cold spring no matter what the temperature. She would look around and ask herself what love was and if she had ever loved Ike, and her answer would be different every day. Perhaps they had never been suited, but yes, she loved him right now.

She met them at the door and really, the news, or a prelude to the news, was on her lips, but they were talking excitedly, especially Helen and Claire. Yes, they had found Nelson, here he was, all the way across the tracks and up by the school where some children were playing ball, and the funny thing was, he kind of hid when he saw Christine, just like a naughty child! Christine made herself smile, and Anna tried again, she really did, but the news would not come out amid all this flurry and cold, the fragrance of damp wool and the stomping of feet.

"I'll make coffee." Helen grinned and her hand, as she passed through the room, lighted fondly on Nelson and scratched his ear. From this, Anna thought that Christine had changed her mind, and when she then looked at her granddaughter, she saw confirmation in Christine's drawn face. No one mentioned anything though; the decision was apparently too new for Helen and Claire to begin with exhortations and suggestions. That was well enough, for once they began with something so unimportant as, "You know, there are scads of clothes and toys in the attic, a little out of style, maybe, but serviceable enough," it would never end: what kind of vitamins are you on? you'll surely need a bassinet; I gained fifty pounds with the twins, and they were right up under my heart so I could hardly breathe; make Todd do it, four dozen diapers is not too many; some mothers just let them cry, but I never did mine; don't baby yourself, don't be afraid to baby yourself. Claire said, "How's Daddy?"

Without saying anything, Anna let it be known that he was quiet even though, with Helen carrying coffee in from the kitchen and everyone else flopped into their usual seats, she could have made her announcement. She did not. She thought about how she would get on the bus in June, or maybe July, and ride out to Denver, then up, through Fort Collins and Laramie and Casper and Sheridan, then over the Big Horns to Yellowstone where she would walk around Old Faithful and stay in the Lodge. She would see lupine and wild iris and Indian paintbrush, miles of sage and dark pine forest. She would come back through the Black Hills and the Badlands. Her daughters would ooh and ah and worry and advise her, but she would go alone, refuse to take their delegate with her, refuse to call when she got there, refuse to put herself in the care of a tour guide or a bus driver.

They were tired. It was the end of the day. All around her they drank their coffee and sighed, letting the conversation fail. Anna took a deep breath and closed her eyes, promising that when she opened them, she would tell, but she didn't. Helen said, "Mother, Christine—"

Anna said, "I thought maybe." She saw in her daughters' faces relief that the family would go on, and for a moment she was strangely afraid of it: Christine unhappy, Ike dead, herself an apprentice at the widow business. Relentless. She thought of the day she married Ike, in Mama's bedroom, dressed to the chin in white crêpe de chine that Mama, in her usual fashion, had produced out of the fabric cupboard as soon as Anna informed her of the marriage. It was a beautiful dress, and there were hat and shoes and stockings and gloves to go with it. In fact, Anna was stitch perfect and ready to go when Marna noticed a smudge on her cheek. Even as Mama said it, "Ach, there's a smudge on your cheek!" Anna could see it grow in her mother's eyes until there was nothing but smudge. "Don't move!" she ordered, and at once was approaching with a washcloth, large and wet, spread over her hand. For the first time in her life, Anna turned away, and then, to sustain it, she turned all the way around and walked out of the door. She didn't even look back to see what Mama was thinking. In the parlor she recollected that she was about to get married.

Claire said, "Is that Daddy?" and in the listening silence that followed, Anna spoke.

Center Point Publishing
Brooks Road • PO Box 1
Thorndike ME 04986-0001 USA

(207) 568-3717

US & Canada:
1 800 929-9108